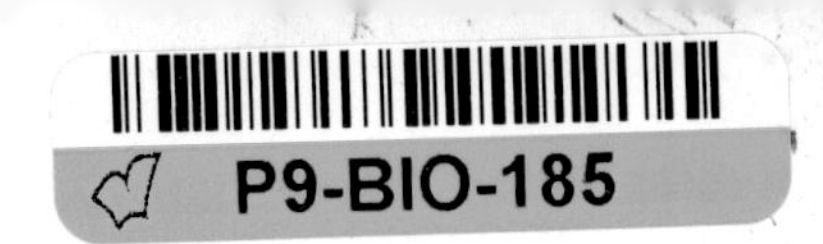

EST. 1894
BOOMTOWN

On behalf of the business owners and community organizations the Welcome Wagon cheerfully welcomes you to Boomtown.

BOOMTOWN COMMUNITY ORGANIZATIONS

Boomtown Town Hall
Boomtown Library
Boomtown Museum
Boomtown Power Plant
Boomtown Fire Station
The Boomtown School
Boomtown Train Station & Telegraph
Boomtown Chamber of Commerce
VFW Hall Local #1214
FFA, Future Farmers of America
First Presbyterian Church
St. Bernard's Lutheran Church
Boomtown Church
Boomtown Cemetery
Lavatube Landfill
Public Pool - Chang Park
Farmer's Market - Farmer's Park
Boomtown Arts League
The "Lions" Club
Boomtown Historical Society
Men's & Women's Rotary Club

CHAMBER OF COMMERCE MEMBERS

Chang's Famous Fireworks Factory
Chang's Black Powder Plant
Bank of Boomtown
Boomtown Grain & Feed
Rexall Drug Store - Post Office
Fannie's Fleece & Feathers
Guenther's Gun Corral
Mabel's Diner
Walt's Barber Shop
Gertrude's Beauty Parlor
Wayne's Warehouses
Boomtown Curiosity Shop
Gus's Gas-N-Go, Towing & Repair
Greyhound Bus Station
Mitterand's Boarding House
Dr. Emil Goldberg, M.D.
Candice Oldham, Midwife, R.N.
Dr. Xu, D.D.S.
Dr. Don Haydinger, D.V.M.
Brown & Son Red Bird General Store
Martin's Mercantile
Boomtown Music
Boomtown Hobby Center
Boomtown Books
Rocket Ridge Gold Mining Co.
Soisson Winery
Tebs's Salvage Yard & Thrift Store
Carpenter King, Fine Furniture & Upholstery
Straightline Lumber Mill
Black Smith & Tack Shop
Sneed's Feed & Grain Store
Dover Hardware
Reynold's Rope
Bun's Bakery
Nuthouse Restaurant
Kellogg's Clothiers, Men's Fine Clothing & Tailoring
Women's Fashions, Hats and Handbags
Big Bang Explosives
Arturo Caruso, Plumber/Electrician
Far East Apothecary, Tea and Herbs
Top's Soda Shop & Candy Store
Rosenbaum's Jewelry and Timepieces
Maxwell's Machine Shop
Vasco Bardelli, General Contractor
Boomtown Garbage Service & Recycle

BOOMTOWN

(REVISED EDITION)

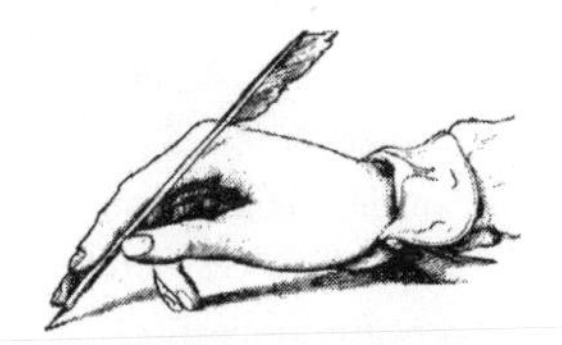

Written and Illustrated by

Nowen N. Particular

THOMAS NELSON
Since 1798

NASHVILLE DALLAS MEXICO CITY RIO DE JANEIRO

Published in Nashville, Tennessee, by Thomas Nelson. Thomas Nelson is a trademark of Thomas Nelson, Inc.

Page design by Mandi Cofer.

Thomas Nelson, Inc., titles may be purchased in bulk for educational, business, fund-raising, or sales promotional use. For information, please e-mail SpecialMarkets@ThomasNelson.com.

ISBN 987-1-4003-1553-6 (revised edition)

Library of Congress Cataloging-in-Publication Data

Particular, Nowen N.
Boomtown / Nowen N. Particular.
p. cm.
ISBN 978-1-4003-1345-7
Summary: On the day of their arrival in Boomtown, Washington, Reverend Button and his family make a grand entrance into town by accidentally blowing up the firecracker factory, and as they settle into the community their escapades continue.
[1. Family life—Washington (State)—Fiction. 2. Adventure and adventurers—Fiction. 3. Washington (State)—Fiction. 4. Humorous stories.] I. Title.
PZ7.P25625Bo 2008
[Fic]—dc22

2008019439

mfr: R. R. Donnelley / Crawfordsville, IN / March 2010—PPO #102863

For my dad, "Sparky,"
who burned down a chicken barn,
worked in a match factory,
and set a paint room on fire.
(Those are the ones we know about;
I'm sure there're a bunch more.)
You ignited an entire family
of crazy inventors.
Thank you.

LAKE CAONA
ROCKET RIDGE
CAONA CREEK
LEFT FOOT ISLA
OKANOGAN
CHANG PAR
LOOKOUT FALLS
CANYON CREEK
WEST CHANG
SHORT FUSE
CAVE-IN
LAVA
LONG FUSE
SLIPPERY SLOPE
DYNAMITE DRIVE
G
F
POPGUN POND
TNT TRAIL
BOOM BOULEVAR
BLASTING CAP AVENUE
IFILAMI BRIDGE

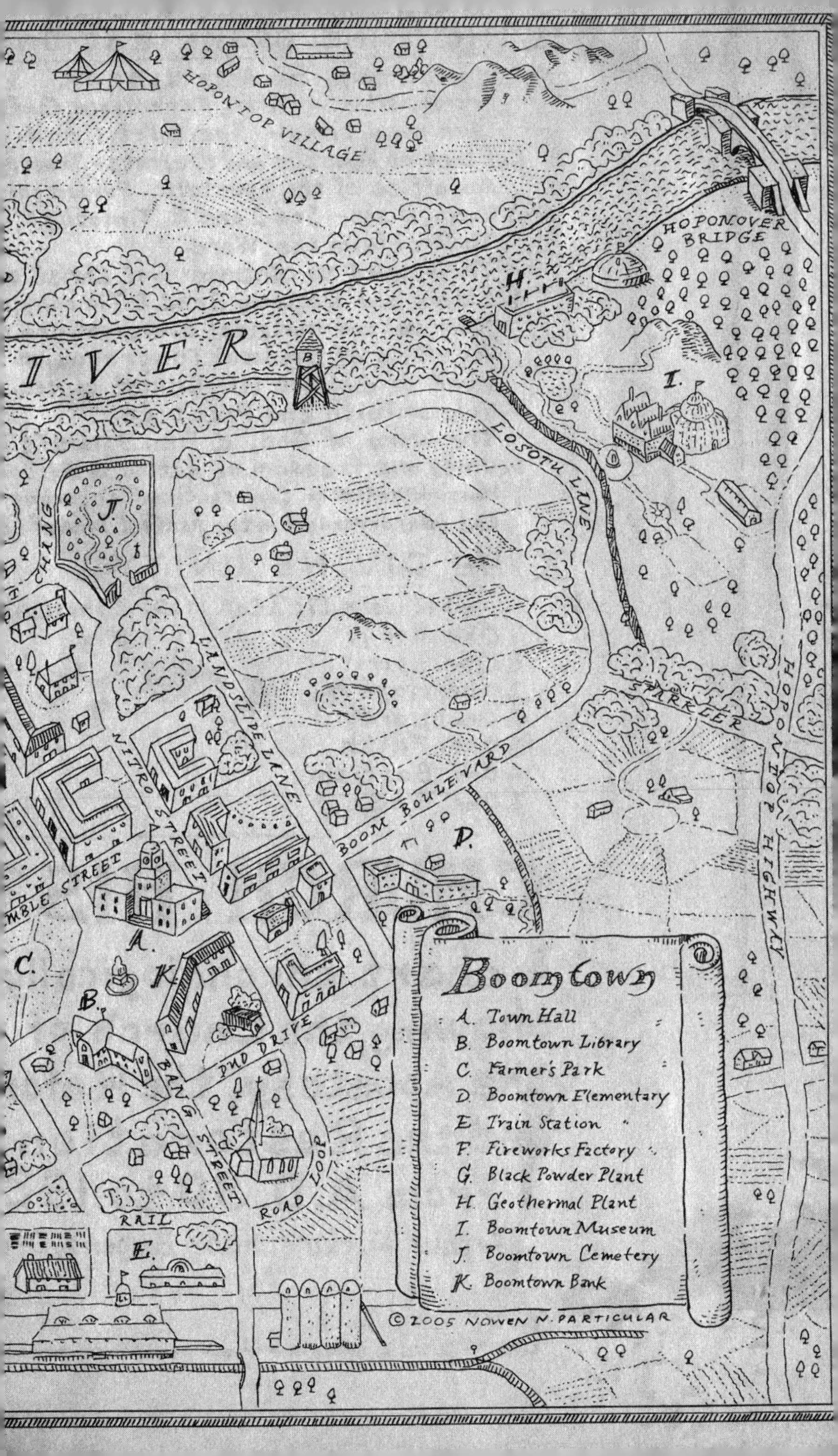
HOPONTOP VILLAGE
IVER
HOPONOVER BRIDGE
H.
I.
J.
LOSOTU LANE
LANDSLIDE LANE
NITRO STREET
BOOM BOULEVARD
SPARKLER
HOPONTOP HIGHWAY
D.
MBLE STREET
A.
C.
K
B.
PUD DRIVE
BANG STREET
ROAD LOOP
RAIL
E.
Boomtown
A. Town Hall
B. Boomtown Library
C. Farmer's Park
D. Boomtown Elementary
E. Train Station
F. Fireworks Factory
G. Black Powder Plant
H. Geothermal Plant
I. Boomtown Museum
J. Boomtown Cemetery
K. Boomtown Bank
©2005 NOWEN N. PARTICULAR

Contents

Contents

Acknowledgments

If this book is worth reading, it's because better books have already been written by better authors, books like *The Lion, the Witch and the Wardrobe*, *The 21 Balloons*, and *Charlie and the Chocolate Factory*. My hat's off to C. S. Lewis, William Pené Dubois, Roald Dahl, J. R. R. Tolkien, Lloyd Alexander, Madeleine L'Engle, Dr. Seuss, and so many other favorites. As a boy, these authors introduced me to the great adventure of reading. As a writer, they have shown me how to find Boomtown.

I couldn't have written this book without the constant support of my wife, Jamie, and my four children, Brandy, Christian, Faith, and Brittany. They patiently endured the long process of writing and editing, especially my youngest, who read each chapter as it was finished and laughed in all the right places (thanks, Bert!). My father, Bob, is the inspiration for most of the crazy inventions you'll find in Boomtown (we'll never forget the purple car he built out of spare parts—the red fur interior was a nice touch). Also thanks to my mom, Betty, who taught me to love life in general and books in particular. I'm grateful to my brother and sister and extended family for their encouragement and humor.

I need to thank those who previewed and edited the early drafts of the book with brutal honesty and keen insight. A special thanks goes to Faith Howard and Rachelle Longé McGhee for technical expertise and guidance. Thank you also to my friends, namely Seth Crofton, Julie McIntire, Shane Taylor, and especially Darin and Janell Jordan and their children, Tommy J. and Julie, and Chad and

Lisa Larrabee and their children, Davis, Annabeth, and Mitch—they have been cheerleaders since the very beginning. You have been voted honorary citizens of Boomtown. Congratulations!

Sam Barnhart, the music minister from Common Ground Church, introduced me to Jennifer Gingerich at Thomas Nelson Publishing. She was responsible for getting the original hardback version of *Boomtown* published. MacKenzie Howard has been the driving force behind getting this brand-new paperback edition on the shelves. They prove what the people of Boomtown have always believed: *nowen ever succeeds on his own*.

A final nod goes to all the teachers over the years who never quit on me even though I gave them a thousand reasons to justify it. You are the unsung heroes of any book that has ever been written. Keep on teaching! You're changing the world one noisy kid in the back row at a time. We'd be nothing without you.

INTRODUCTION

If you are a kid like me, you will *not* read this introduction. Introductions are written for grown-ups who are impressed by that sort of thing. Kids, on the other hand, want to skip past the "boring parts" and jump ahead to where the dragon is attacking the castle or the brilliant detective uncovers the clue that finally solves the case. We don't want to read long paragraphs that explain why a particular book is going to be "good for you." That's like having your mom make you eat lima beans before you can have dessert. Yuck! It may be good for you, but it isn't any fun.

If you had skipped past this introduction, then you'd already be reading about Boomtown—where every single day is like the Fourth of July. It's a kid's paradise, that's what I'm telling you—loud, unpredictable, and slightly dangerous, like a firecracker with a short fuse.

Boomtown wasn't exactly what my dad was expecting. In August of 1949, Dad decided to move our family there from California. He wanted rolling hills, picket fences, and snow on Christmas. That's what he wanted, and *that's exactly what he got*—plus a few hundred other surprises and an exploding omelet for breakfast.

He found one more thing he wasn't expecting—we both did—a lesson in what it means to live in a place where people make room for each other. It doesn't matter if you are rich or poor, famous or infamous, or what color your skin happens to be. The people of Boomtown love their neighbors, work together, forgive mistakes, and try to fix whatever gets broken—and if it can't be fixed, they strap a rocket to it and blow it to smithereens.

So that's it. That's my introduction, if you bothered to read the whole thing, although I can't imagine why you did. I've already lit the fuse. This book could go off at any second! *Kaboom!* What are you waiting for? Hurry up and turn the page and find out what happened the day we moved to Boomtown. You aren't going to believe your ears!

CHAPTER 1

Fireworks Factory

I almost killed my dad today. Well, not me, it was mostly my sister. Well, not exactly her. It was a rocket. A big rocket. A big, crazy, out of control, exploding rocket that almost took him to the moon. Well, maybe not to the *moon* . . . but it would have taken him to the hospital if the truck driver hadn't knocked him down. You should have seen it! Sparks flying everywhere, smoke, screaming, people running, and my dad . . . he almost blew up *twice*. He almost sent *me* to the moon. It was, like . . .

Hmm. Maybe I should tell this story from the beginning.

It all started early Friday morning on the last day of our move from California to Washington. We had stayed overnight at the Travelodge in Wenatchee. It had a big pool and donuts for breakfast. We had cocoa and waited until the driver with the moving truck showed up. His name was Lars. He was an ex-football player and as big as a house. When he laughed it sounded like a clogged vacuum cleaner. He was always snapping his gum, and he could blow bubbles as big as my head. I liked him a lot.

From the hotel we followed in the shadow cast by his giant, bright orange truck as it made its way up Highway 97 toward our new home in Boomtown. We were driving in our old, stinky station wagon, the one with the hot plastic seats and the window that wouldn't roll down, but the three of us kids hardly noticed because there was so much new stuff to look at.

Sitting next to the sticky window was Ruth, my older sister. She's almost eighteen and about to finish high school so she can be pretty bossy sometimes. My younger sister was sitting on the other side. Her name is Sarah and she's only nine—and a whole lot of trouble. I'll get to that in a minute.

And then, of course, there's me. My name is Jonny, and I am eleven, handsome, brilliant, and soon to be a famous astronaut. Or maybe a baseball star or a cowboy; I haven't decided yet. I was named after Prince Jonathan, from the Old Testament. He was what you'd call a hero's hero. He was famous for taking on a whole army single-handedly. I used to ask Dad to read me the story over and over again when I was younger. I hoped I'd be a hero one day too.

As the middle kid, I was stuck in the middle of the seat where I couldn't see as well as my spoiled sisters. I had to sit up extra straight to see over Ruth's big head when I wanted to look out the window on her side.

"Look, Mom, apple trees!"

"Look over there—pears and peaches and raspberries."

"Look at all the cows and horses and sheep. And what are those?" Sarah asked.

My mom answered, "Those are llamas, dear."

"Really? A herd of llamas? Can I have one?"

"Of course not. They're only for looking at."

"Can I have a cow instead?"

"No, dear, you can't have a cow."

"What about a sheep? They aren't very big. I could keep it in my room."

My dad interrupted the negotiations. "Be serious, Sarah, what would you do if you had a *sheep* for a pet?"

"They make wool, don't they? I could cut off the wool and Mom could make yarn out of it. She could knit sweaters. That's what people do in small towns. They have sheep and they make sweaters."

"Your mother doesn't know how to knit."

"She could learn."

"Maybe she will, but you still can't have a sheep. They're very messy."

"That's okay," Sarah insisted. "So am I. You'd hardly notice."

"No!"

The judge had spoken. Jury dismissed. Case closed. Dad could be like that.

We kept driving until we passed through a small town called Ainogold. "There Ain't No Gold in Ainogold." That's what the sign said. We stopped for some Cokes at the general store, and the owner explained how the town got its name.

"A hundred years ago, during the Yukon Gold Rush, this prospector named Coyote Jones showed up out of nowhere to stake his claim. Spent all he had buying equipment and gunpowder right from this very store! Then he went up into the hills for a year and a half. Came back down without even a nugget. He weren't the only one. More'n two hundred other miners had the same bad luck. Coyote said, 'There just ain't no gold!' That's what they've been calling this place ever since."

After Sarah and I finished our burping contest (she won), we got back in the car and kept driving north. We went past canyon streams, pine forests, and wheat fields.

My mom kept saying how beautiful it was. "Wide open spaces. Bright blue sky. Puffy white clouds as far as the eye can see. It's like paradise. I can tell we're going to like it here."

Mom's name is Janice. She was from crowded San Francisco, and Dad was originally from New York. The only place you could see animals in New York was at the zoo—or in the subways during rush hour. And all us kids had been born in Los Angeles, California—home to a lot of asphalt and fences. So it was great to see the huge river and tall, rocky cliffs through the sticky window, and the rolling fields and farmhouses through the other one. Hills to climb and creeks to swim in and cows to chase! And then, before we knew it, our map showed Boomtown only eight miles farther up the road.

Dad made the announcement, "Only a few more minutes and we'll be there!"

We turned right onto Blasting Cap Avenue, and we cheered when the tires bumped across the Ifilami Bridge and over the Okanogan River. The first thing I saw was a brightly painted sign that said Welcome to Boomtown! Underneath that were the words Home of Chang's Famous Fireworks Factory. There was also a round logo with a picture of an Asian man painted in the center. I figured that had to be Chang.

"Dad!" I shouted. "Did you see that sign? They've got a *fireworks factory*! You never said anything about a fireworks factory!"

"I didn't say anything about it because I didn't *know* anything about it. The search committee from the church never mentioned it. Strange how they'd leave something like that out . . . I wonder what else they didn't tell me?"

"But where is it? I want to see it!"

"I don't know, Jon. Let's get settled in our new house first. We'll have time for fireworks later."

Actually, we didn't have to wait at all. We turned left onto Dynamite Drive, and the first thing we saw was Chang's Black Powder Plant, with trails of smoke snaking up from its twin cones. They looked like two smoldering witches' hats. From inside the station wagon, we could smell the sharp odor of sulfur. It smelled like a million matches all burning at the same time.

On the opposite side of the road was the fireworks factory. That's what really got my attention. It was five stories tall and built completely out of red brick. There had to be a hundred windows along each side, and on the roof were four towering smokestacks that had the name of the company painted in black. The stacked-up letters spelled out Chang's Famous Fireworks Factory, big enough that you could see them for miles. Black wrought-iron stairs climbed the outer walls like spider webs, and we could see dozens of workers moving up and down, like ants in an ant farm, carrying supplies and equipment. There were railcars parked alongside the building, and workers were loading them with stacks and stacks of boxes. I wondered what would happen if someone tripped and set one of them off. *Pow!* That would be something to see!

Dad was so busy staring at the building that he almost slammed into the back of the moving truck when it lurched to a sudden halt. We couldn't see why the truck had stopped, so Dad opened his door to go investigate. The rest of us started to get out too, but Dad motioned for us to stay put.

"You can stay in the car. I'm just going to ask Lars what's going on."

"*Stay in the car*, Mr. Button?" my mom answered. She always called him "Mr. Button" when she wanted something. "You want me to keep three kids trapped in a hot station wagon while you go running around a fireworks factory?"

"I'm not going *into* the factory, Janice. I just want to find out why Lars stopped the truck."

"We want to find out too!" Sarah said for both of us.

"And me," added Ruth.

Dad shrugged his shoulders, climbed out of the car, and walked around to the front of the moving truck. We all jumped out and followed him. Lars was snapping his gum and talking to four Chinese men in white lab coats. One of the men was holding a clipboard and gesturing to this pointy metal thing that was anchored in the center of a wide, shallow pond in front of the factory.

"Excuse me. Is there a problem?" Dad asked.

The Chinese gentleman answered politely, "No, sir. But as you can see, we were about to conduct a test. Pardon us, but if you need to get beyond this point, you will have to go back to Blasting Cap Avenue and drive around through the town. Sorry about the inconvenience."

I pushed through my family and stood next to Lars. "What are you doing? What kind of test?" I asked.

In the center of the road was a small console on a metal stand. Sprouting from the console was a nest of black and red wires connected to a black box on the ground. From there the wires ran across the ground to the pond where they disappeared under the water. I guessed they were connected to the small boat that was anchored in the water—I could see the heavy ropes. Inside the boat was a silver tube lying on its side, about the size of a water heater, with a metal bell at one end and a cone on the other.

The Chinese man smiled, and instead of answering my question right away, he held out his hand. "My name is Han-wu Weng," he said. "And who are you?"

"My name is Jonathan, but people call me Jonny. This is my big sister, Ruth, and my little sister, Sarah. You can call her 'Sorry' though."

"Sorry?" Mr. Weng asked.

"Yeah, because she's always saying, 'I'm sorry.' Like the time she broke open a pen to find out where the ink came from. We had to replace our sofa and the carpet."

Sarah laughed and said, "I'm Sorry!"

Ruth added, "Then there was the time she tried to wash the cat—except she couldn't find the soap, so she used Vaseline instead."

"Vaseline?" exclaimed Mr. Weng.

"Yes, *Vaseline*, a whole jumbo-sized jar of it! By the time she finished, the cat was so slippery it took us a week to catch it. Then it took another month to wash out the Vaseline. Ever try to wash a wet, oily cat? It's pretty hard."

"I'm Sorry!" Sarah giggled.

"Oh, sure, you're *Sorry*," my mom continued. "Like the time you wanted to see what would happen if you put marshmallows in the clothes dryer."

"Then there was the time when she glued her shoes on because they kept falling off," I added, "and that time she flushed one of my soldiers down the toilet because she said he was caught in a 'whirlpool.'"

"I'm Sorry! I'm Sorry! *I'm Sorry!*" Sarah said, taking a bow.

Mr. Weng and his team laughed along with us. "I guess we shouldn't turn our backs on you or maybe *we'll* be sorry—you think so?"

Sarah narrowed her eyes and warned them, "I'm trouble, that's for sure!"

It was funny at the time, but just a few minutes later, she proved it all over again.

CHAPTER 2

Kablooie!

I shook Mr. Weng's hand, and then Dad took over and finished the introductions. "This is our driver, Lars, from the moving company. This is my wife, Janice, and our three children, whom you've just met. And I'm Arthur Button. *Pastor* Arthur Button. Maybe you've heard—I'm the new pastor of Boomtown Church."

Mr. Weng returned his smile. "Pastor Button! Of course! We heard you were coming. It's an honor to be the first to welcome you to Boomtown."

He introduced the others who were standing with him, each of whom bowed respectfully as their names were called. "These are three of the members of my team, Lu-shan Wu, Tong Chen, and Wei Jiang. We all work together in the research building over there." He pointed across the pond at a smaller outbuilding near the driveway entrance.

Mr. Weng turned back to me. "You were wondering what we're testing this morning. Do you like gadgets? Machines? Rockets? That sort of thing?"

"Sure! I *love* all that stuff! My favorite thing in the whole world is my Erector Set. I make cars and Ferris wheels and trains and weird machines. I like the motors and all the gears. And rockets! I've always wanted a rocket, but my dad won't let me have one."

I glanced at Dad, and he nodded vigorously in agreement. No dice.

"Is that what you got out there on the boat? A rocket?" I asked.

"Exactly so. Except it's not a boat, not precisely. Why don't you come with me so we can get a better look at it?"

We followed Mr. Weng across the road and down a small slope where we could stand next to the water. "This is Popgun Pond, and the small stream you see over there is the canal we dug leading from the river. It supplies water for the factory and for the fire hydrants—in case of emergency." We could see brightly painted red fire hydrants scattered all over the factory yard. "We try our best to avoid using those. Safety First, that's our motto!"

He pointed at the boat with the rocket mounted inside. "The boat-shaped object you see out there is actually one of our testing platforms. Whenever we want to test something new—and potentially dangerous—we put it on one of those boats, float it out into the middle of the pond, and anchor it down with ropes and weights. This morning we're testing a new rocket motor, something with a little more *kick* than anything we've tried in the past."

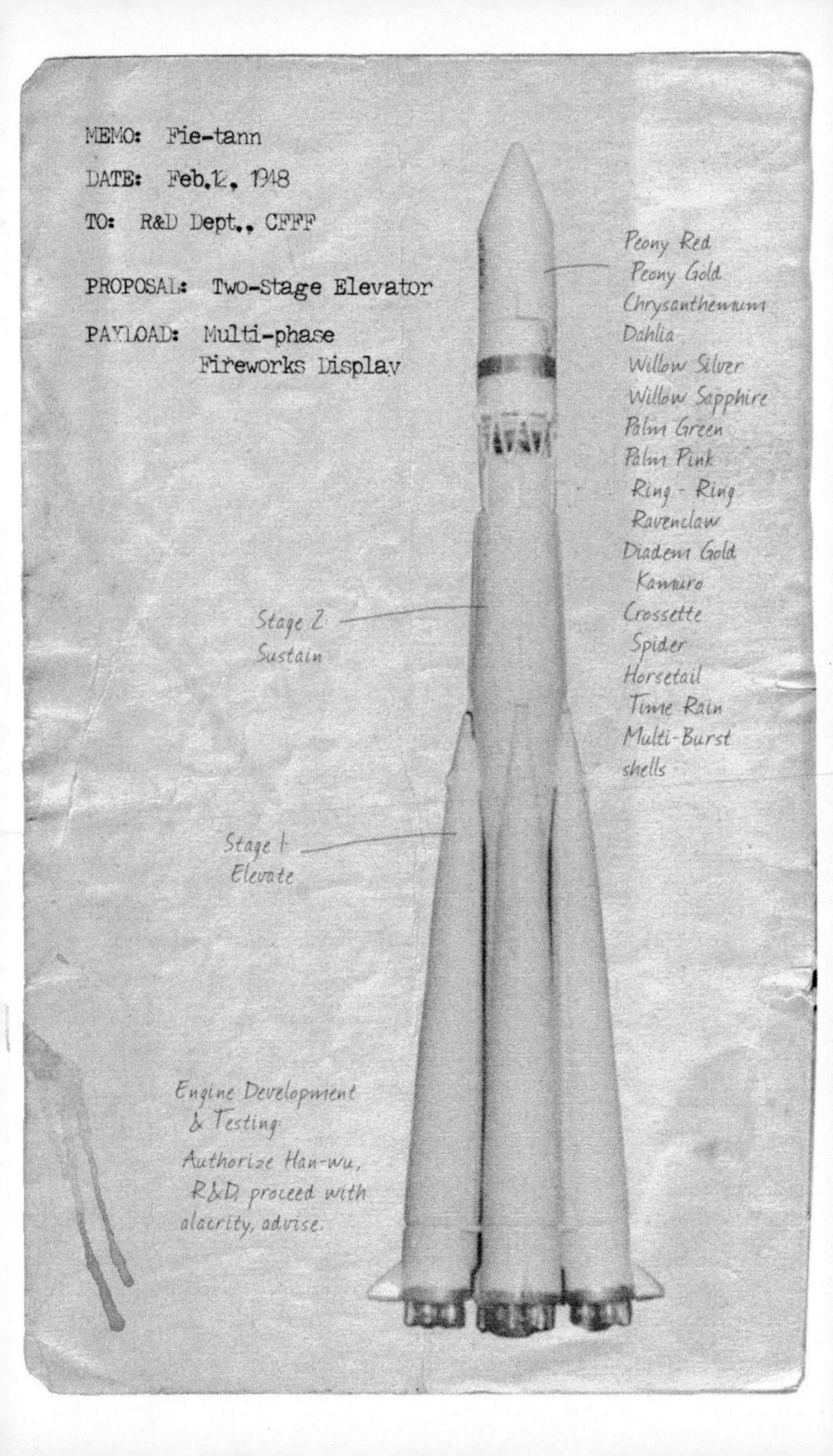
MEMO: Fie-tann

DATE: Feb.12, 1948

TO: R&D Dept., CFFF

PROPOSAL: Two-Stage Elevator

PAYLOAD: Multi-phase
Fireworks Display

Engine Development
& Testing:
Authorize Han-wu,
R&D proceed with
alacrity, advise.

My dad looked worried. "A rocket motor? Exactly what are you planning to shoot off with that thing?"

"Fie-tann Hsu, the current manager of the fireworks factory, has dreamed about this rocket for quite a while now. We've always had to build all our fireworks displays on the ground and then shoot the rockets up into the air. But then he came up with this idea to lift the whole fireworks display off the ground. *Whoosh!*"

"Huh?"

"Just think about it. Instead of shooting all the rockets from down *here*, we lift them up and launch them from up *there*." He chuckled happily. "All we need is a rocket engine powerful enough. If this works, we can build four of them and mount them to a huge payload—get our fireworks display airborne. Nobody's ever done it before. *Kapow!* It'll be fantastic!"

I liked Mr. Weng. He thought just like a kid. But Dad wasn't so convinced.

"Are you *serious*?"

"Why not? We'll be able to ship an entire fireworks display in a single container—anywhere in the world. Just imagine it. This big crate shows up. You set it on one end. Bust open the crate. Light the fuse. Launch the rockets. Once it's airborne it goes off automatically—a complete fireworks show all in one box."

"But what if something goes wrong?" Dad asked. "What if the rockets blast off in some crazy direction? What if the whole thing just blows up on the ground? People could get hurt. You could knock down a building!"

"That's what testing is for." Mr. Weng smiled, dismissing the concerns with a wave of his hand. "We shoot off a test rocket and look for any problems. And besides that, it's a lot of *fun*!"

I was amazed by everything Mr. Weng was saying and wanted to get a closer look, so Sarah and I slipped away and ran up to the road to examine the launch controls.

"Look at this," I said, pointing at the black box on the ground. "I think that's the battery. These wires run up to the panel here and hook into the switches. Hmm. One of the wires is loose. I better fix that."

I bent over and connected the black wire that was hanging loose on the ground. That ought to do it.

I stood up again and held my finger close to the panel. "You see that red switch, the one with the yellow square around it? That's probably the trigger button. When you flip the switch, the battery power runs through the wires and goes out to the rocket boat. That's how I *think* it works, anyway."

Sarah leaned forward to look at where I was pointing. "And then what?"

"Then the electricity sets off an ignition pack, and that lights the rocket fuel, and then it blasts off! I read all about it in a copy of *Popular Science*."

Sarah stood on her tiptoes and reached across the controls. "You mean *this* switch right here?" she asked.

"Don't touch that! Sarah! Watch out!" I tried to grab her, but it was too late.

There was a buzz and then a pop, and then flame and smoke started pouring out of the rocket motor. The sudden roar of the engine was deafening. We both covered our ears with our hands. Mom and Dad and everyone else cringed in surprise, and then Dad looked over in our direction—that's when he *knew*. You could see it in his eyes. Oops.

Workers from the fireworks factory heard the noise, and within seconds fire crews came running out of the buildings carrying coils of hoses and wrenches so they could hook up to the fire hydrants and turn on the water. The noise got louder and louder as men and women scattered in every direction shouting and waving their arms. At first I didn't know why everyone was panicking. I thought the rocket was *supposed* to go off. Not by Sarah—*that* wasn't supposed to happen—but it was a planned launch, wasn't it? That's when I saw what everyone else had already seen. The ropes and the anchors weren't strong enough. The boat wasn't supposed to move. But it was heading across the pond and picking up speed.

"Run!" shouted Mr. Weng. "Run for your lives!"

I could barely hear what he said over the blast of the rocket boat that had turned into a rocket missile. The ropes finally ripped loose and the rocket broke free. It tore through the water, hit the edge of the pond, and launched into the air. The weight of the boat caused it to spin in circles. It spun toward the fireworks factory where it chased a group of workers across the asphalt. Then it flipped around and headed back the way it had come, straight to where Sarah and I stood on the road.

"Ahh!" she screamed. "It's out to get me! It's going to make me pay for all my crimes!"

It would have flattened us if it hadn't spun sideways and headed for the moving truck instead. It bounced off the hood, made three fast turns, flipped around, skipped off the roof of our station wagon, and blasted down the driveway, straight to where my mom and sister were standing.

"Get down!" shrieked my mom, throwing her body on top of Ruth. They fell in a tangled heap near my dad's feet, where he tripped over them and gaped in terror as the rocket looped left and then right, bouncing off a tree, through some nearby bushes, scraping along the ground, skipping down the driveway, and making a beeline for his head. He stumbled to his feet and froze.

With only seconds to spare, Lars, former pro football linebacker and truck driver, took Dad down in a running tackle that would have knocked the shine off a flagpole. He scooped him up like a rag doll and drove him backward head over heels into the pond. Like a ton of bricks landing on a soft pretzel. *Splash!* Lars had saved my dad's life!

Since they were tangled up in the water, they missed seeing the rocket's final moment of impact. The rocket smashed into the research building in a shower of shattering glass and flying furniture. The ground shook from the explosion when the rocket detonated, igniting all the flammable materials stored in the lab. By the time Lars got my dad back on his feet, the building had been turned into a raging inferno, surrounded by teams of firefighters from the factory as they tried to extinguish the flames.

The fire was decorated by bursts of silver and gold and red and green sparks as all the chemicals and compounds ignited with the blaze. We could hear the whistling of Piccolo Petes and the pepper blasts of firecrackers. There were flashes of sparklers and Roman candles as they exploded from the heat. There were the rockets' red glare and bombs bursting in air. In fact, if it weren't for the total destruction of the building, you might say it was pretty. But it *wasn't* pretty. Not for me and Sarah, anyway.

While all this was going on, she and I had slipped behind the moving van and were watching the disaster from our hiding place. Mom and Lars helped Dad out of the pond while Ruth ran to our car to fetch some towels. My dad stood there dripping and shivering, looking as though he'd been hit by a freight train. Mr. Weng ran around making sure that no one was hurt in the accident. Workers dashed back and forth fighting to get the blaze under control. There were hoses and bucket brigades everywhere we looked.

"So," I whispered to Sarah, whose eyes were as big as dinner plates, "which continent should we run away to?"

"Africa," she whimpered. "Maybe Australia. We could live with the kangaroos."

"Not far enough away."

"What about Antarctica?"

We both looked up and saw my dad standing over us. He had a damp towel wrapped around his shoulders. His shirt was pasted to his chest, drenched by the water and coated in mud. His hair had stringy pieces of grass sticking out of it. There was a new bruise forming on his left cheek. But none of that compared to his eyes. They were both on fire, worse than the factory building that continued to burn in the background. I couldn't think of anything to say. But Sarah started to cry.

"I'm *sorry*?" she sniffed.

"You're *sorry*?" our dad exploded. "Of *course* you're sorry! You're *always* sorry. What were you *thinking*? What are we going to *do*? This isn't a cat covered in Vaseline! This is a *disaster*!"

He stood with his hands shaking and his mouth hanging open while the sound of the firefight continued. We didn't know what he was going to say. We'd seen him upset before. Lots of times, really. We gave him plenty of practice, especially Sarah. But he hardly ever yelled. He usually sat us down quietly and tried to teach us a lesson. But this was different. This was huge.

We both held our breath and waited, while Dad stood there

dripping and burning. But then we saw the glint of anger fade. It flickered out at the sound of the building collapsing in the distance. His shoulders and face fell along with it. The ground shook as the roof and walls caved in, raising a cloud of ash and smoke, until all that was left was a pile of smoldering rubble. We could see it as we crouched behind the tires of the truck.

He finally leaned over and took each of our hands and stood us to our feet. We followed as he stumbled around the corner and out onto the grass. I tried to imagine what he was thinking. Our first day in Boomtown. The new pastor in town. His kids blew up the fireworks factory. The end of his career. He'd have to look for a new job as a washing machine salesman or maybe an elevator operator. Someplace where no one had ever heard of the Buttons.

Instead, we were greeted by an amazing sight. Not a bunch of angry factory workers or the police waiting to arrest us. We weren't chased by FBI agents or a mob of townsfolk carrying pitchforks and torches. Nope. We saw Mr. Weng passing out packages of graham crackers and Hershey bars. We saw groups of people standing around the burning embers with sticks in their hands roasting marshmallows. We saw Mom and Ruth helping Lars put together one of the sticky, gooey sandwiches. He was happily licking marshmallow and chocolate off his fingers.

"You've *got* to be kidding," my dad murmured in disbelief. "They're making s'mores! You see that? *S'mores!* What's *with* this crazy place? Rockets? Exploding fireworks factories? Roasting marshmallows? What have I gotten myself into?"

And *that* was only the first day!

A4 News | The Stickville Times | SATURDAY, AUGUST 20, 1949

Fireworks Factory in Flames

Research Bldg. at Chang's Burns to the Ground

Workers at Chang's Famous Fireworks Factory attempt to douse the blaze allegedly sparked by Jonathan and Sarah Button (age 13 and 10 respectively).

BOOMTOWN — Early Friday morning the Reverend Arthur Button and family arrived in Boomtown and interrupted a scheduled rocket test, leading to the destruction of Chang's Famous Fireworks Factory research building.

Witnesses place Jonathan (13) and Sarah Button (10) near the controls when the rocket was accidently launched, resulting in a catastrophic conflagration involving the entire research ...ts.

Employees from the factory, organized by Han-wu, senior researcher, and Fie-tann, factory manager, limited the blaze to the single building.

Han-wu said, "I don't recall the last time we've enjoyed this much excitement. We had a lot of fireworks stored in the lab. It was a spectacular show! I only wish more people could have seen it."

Damage was estimated to be in the tens of thousands of dollars. No injuries were reported.

CHAPTER 3

Big Bang Boom Box

We were celebrities!

News about the explosion at the fireworks factory spread quickly. By the time we finally pulled up in front of our rental house, we were swamped by a chattering mob of neighbors who couldn't wait to ask about all the thrilling details.

One man slapped my dad on his sore back and spoke in a very loud voice, "My name is Matthieu LaPierre, and this is my wife, Pauline. We're your neighbors, five doors down on the right. I just had to come on over and shake your hand!"

"You did?"

"Sure, sure! I had to say howdy to the man who burned down part of the fireworks factory on his very first day! How about *that*!"

"It was an accident. Really, we didn't do it on purpose."

"'Course you didn't, I know that. But we don't care. What matters is that you did it! Wow! What a story! I wish I'da been there to do it myself!"

"You do?"

"Absolutely. I've never been lucky enough to burn anything down. My only real claim to fame is our twelve children."

"Twelve?"

"Yep, with lucky thirteen on the way. That'll make a baker's dozen!"

"That's . . . um . . . a lot of mouths to feed."

"Is it? Hadn't noticed. I got my farm—and with all the extra hands, we do pretty well."

"You have a farm? Where? Is it down the street?"

"Nah!" he bellowed gleefully. "That's just the house. The farm is out on Hopontop Highway, southeast of here."

"Oh, I see. So what do you grow out there on your farm?"

"All sorts of things—radishes, potatoes, apples, corn, beets, the usual stuff. And I got me the pettin' zoo, of course."

"Petting zoo?"

"Sure, people stop by and pay a little to pet the animals. Got me a cobra, a yak, a coupla' skunks, and a porcupine—I wouldn't pet that if I were you—two buffalo, five kangaroos, a gorilla, three ostriches. Oh, and an alligator. Just got me that one. Shipped it in all the way from Florida."

"An alligator? In a petting zoo?"

"Well, he's not really for *petting*. I got him because of the rats. I got a huge rat problem in my barns."

"Why didn't you get a cat?"

"A cat! The alligator would eat a cat if it ever got the chance."

"I meant, why didn't you get a cat *instead* of an alligator?"

"Oh, that would be boring. Everybody's got a cat. Cats are everywhere. But I'm the only one who's got an alligator."

Mr. LaPierre wasn't the last person who surprised us that afternoon. Mr. Weng and Mr. Hsu stopped by at the house after the fire was under control to make sure everybody was okay.

"I don't know what to say," my dad stammered. "I am *so* sorry. Jonny and Sarah shouldn't have gone anywhere near that control panel. I don't know what they were thinking. And now your lab is burned to the ground. I'll try to pay for it somehow—if you'll give me a chance."

"*Pay* for it?" Mr. Hsu chuckled. "Why would we make you *pay* for it? It wasn't your fault. The ropes broke. The rocket was too powerful. It would have happened with or without you. All in a day's work, that's what I say. Don't worry about it."

"But what about the damage? I feel responsible for that."

"Nonsense," replied Mr. Weng. "If *I* had been the one to flip the switch, then *I* would have been the one responsible. That's really the only thing I'm upset about. Now I won't get to brag about it to my friends."

"*Brag* about it?"

"Sure! There's nothing we love more than a good show here in Boomtown. This was one of the best ever! We'll be talking about it for years, thanks to you."

It wasn't any use. No matter how hard Dad tried to apologize, they just wouldn't accept it. They were too excited about the fireworks show—and they were especially pleased about how powerfully the rocket had performed—never mind that it destroyed part of their factory.

Mr. Hsu said, "We'll just have to cut back on some of the rocket propellant and get some thicker rope. Then we'll fire it up again! You're invited to come and watch, of course. Guests of honor. But I get to flip the switch this time."

After satisfying the curiosity of all the neighbors, we finally were able to make it to the front porch. Next would come all the hard work of moving our furniture into the house and up the stairs, and there were all those boxes and chairs and tables and books to lug inside. Dad wasn't feeling very well after being tackled by Lars, but we were surrounded by an army of volunteers, all of them insisting on helping the new minister and his family of firebugs to move in. But first we wanted to get a look at our new house.

Sarah was jumping up and down on the porch and singing, "Let us in! Let us in!" while Dad and Lars and a few of the neighbors laid out the plan for unloading. Lars had changed into a clean pair of overalls, which is a good thing, because he had been covered in mud, and my mom is never too happy about mud. She dug through our suitcases and found a fresh pair of jeans and shirt for Dad.

As soon as the door was unlocked, we ran all over the house—out the back, around the side, back inside, up the stairs—and we began to fight for bedroom territory.

"Sarah and I will take this room at the end of the hallway," Ruth announced.

I agreed, "You can have it! This one's mine!"

My room was tiny with just enough space for a bed and a dresser. There were two small cupboards along the wall for storage. The peak of roof pinched tight over my head, and there was a single window at the end. But it was fantastic because just outside the window hung the thick branches of a walnut tree that stood towering in the backyard. I didn't waste any time climbing out the window—to the sheer terror of my mom and the pure delight of Sarah, who insisted on climbing out there with me.

"We can build a tree house out here! A tree *castle*! Look how thick the branches are. It's like a tree *road*! Look how easy it is to climb down!"

Whoever had lived there before us had already nailed steps to the tree trunk to make it even easier. And there was a tire swing. And a hole in the trunk where you could hide stuff. And if you climbed up to the top you could see the fireworks factory in the distance with a finger curl of smoke from the smoke stacks. The only thing missing was a moat and a dragon.

After Mom chased us down out of the tree, Sarah ran to release our cat, Effeneff, from his carrier. This was the same cat she had "greased" a few years before. It stretched its long gray body, shook out its fur, licked each of its paws carefully, then scampered across the lawn and began to patrol along the front steps and porch, looking for mice and shrews. Sarah had given the cat its name; she insisted he was descended from the great lions of Egypt.

"He's Fierce *and* Friendly," Sarah had said.

We soon shortened that to "F and F" and the name stuck. After only a minute or two, Effeneff pounced and captured a shrew and went to find a shady spot where he could play with it in private.

Mom said, "That's a good sign. If a cat likes a house, then it's probably a good place for people too."

The house really was perfect. The church secretary had found this three-bedroom house for us that was walking distance from the church. The backyard was big and had a picket fence around it. There was a large window in the family room, a small kitchen, one bathroom, and three bedrooms upstairs. There was an extra room downstairs where Dad could put a desk and his books for a study. He was plenty happy about that.

With help from all of our neighbors, the job of unloading got finished pretty fast, leaving the more difficult job of unpacking and putting everything in its place. As the sun crawled higher in the sky, Edna Kreuger, the widow lady who lived next door, brought us a monster lunch of ham and cheese on wheat bread, homemade potato salad, bright red apples, and a delicious blackberry pie with vanilla ice cream. The lettuce, potatoes, apples, and berries had been grown in her very own garden, she proudly declared.

"There's lots more where that came from!" she said. "You'll never go hungry with Gramma Edna next door!"

She turned out to be a member of Boomtown Church where Dad would be preaching that Sunday. She was pink and airy like a balloon and floated from place to place making everyone happy. All she needed was a string. Sarah fell in love with her immediately, and we adopted her into the family. We've called her Gramma ever since.

At three o'clock, the mailman marched up our sidewalk carrying his blue canvas mailbag. His name was Ed Gamelli. He had a black handlebar mustache that was waxed and curvy, with two curly cues on the ends that looked like a couple of question marks. The crease in his black pants was so sharp you could peal an apple with it. He snapped to attention, gave us a smart salute, and added our names to his route list.

Then at four o'clock we met Mrs. Robin Byrd, hostess of the Boomtown Welcome Wagon and lead soprano at St. Bernard's Lutheran Church. I thought the name was funny because she kind of looked like a bird, with feathery hair and a sharp beak for a nose, and she had trouble standing still; she kind of fluttered her arms and hopped up and down whenever she talked. She also had a birdie voice, very chirpy and tweety. I could just imagine her singing in the choir, like a proud bird that had just caught herself a worm.

Mrs. Byrd presented us with a straw basket decorated with green and yellow ribbons and filled to the top with apples, pears, peaches, and several jars of homemade marionberry jam. Then she handed us an envelope filled with all sorts of things: a welcome letter from the Wagoneers, a note of greeting from the mayor, and coupons from local businesses.

She chirped, "There's a coupon in there for a free Family Gutbuster Sundae from Top's Soda Shop. A free hairdo for Janice when she visits Gertrude's Beauty Parlor for the first time. There are special offers from the Boomtown Bookstore, the Hobby Center, Bun's Bakery, Martin's Mercantile, the Red Bird General Store, and of course, Big Bang Explosives. And speaking of that . . ."

Behind her she had a large gold-colored box, trimmed in red

and green, with the Chang's Fireworks logo painted on the side. It was about the size of a small steamer trunk with wheels at the four corners and a handle for pulling it along. On the lid and on each of the four panels, in bright red letters, were printed the words "BIG BANG BOOM BOX."

She presented it to us with a wink. "Every family who moves to Boomtown receives the deluxe one-hundred-and-fifty-pound box of Chang's Famous Fireworks as a welcome gift from the factory. You've got sparklers, firecrackers, smoke bombs, Roman candles, fountains, spinners, flaming whistles, aerial repeaters, rockets, and mortars. There's enough firepower in there to relocate your house if you're not careful!"

I couldn't believe it. "This is for *us*? All of it? For *free*?"

Dad put his hand on my shoulder. "Hang on a minute there, buster, before you start lighting any matches. We've had enough fireworks for one day, don't you think? Probably enough for a lifetime."

"Ah, c'mon, Dad. Just look at it. A hundred and fifty *pounds*!"

Mrs. Byrd cooed, "Now, Reverend, don't look so worried. On every fourth Friday, from May through September, everyone gathers down by the river in Chang Park and shoots off fireworks. We'll be down there tonight. It'll be a great way to celebrate your first day in Boomtown—and having a Big Bang Boom Box and some new friends to fire it off makes it that much better. But don't fret. It's all carefully supervised and a real blast, if you know what I mean. My husband will be there—and so will the fire chief with his truck."

"And an ambulance? And maybe a few stretchers? You heard what happened at the fireworks factory?"

She twittered, "Sure, I heard about it. You really know how to make an entrance!"

"I almost made an exit! I'm not looking for a repeat performance, not tonight anyway. It's totally out of the question. My back is starting to hurt all over again just thinking about it."

"Dad!" I complained.

Sarah joined in, "It's not fair!"

Even Ruth was pouting.

Good old Mom came to the rescue. "Listen here, Mr. Button. We're new to this town and you know what they say: 'When in Rome, do as the Romans do.' We should join in. We'll meet more of the neighbors and let the kids have their fun. It'll be fun for us too. *Please*, Mr. Button? Please say yes."

"That's right, Reverend," Mrs. Byrd sang. "It's a great way for the kids to make friends. Just think about it—after this morning Jonny and Sarah are famous! The park will be swarming with kids from the town. The whole Welcome Wagon committee will be there. Please say you'll come."

I could tell Dad was cracking. He looked at Mom and frowned. Then he looked into the shining eyes of his two youngest children. Then he looked at Ruth, who kissed him on the cheek and told him how special he was. He really didn't have any other choice.

"Okay," he decided. "We'll go, but only on *two* conditions."

Once we finished cheering, he told us what they were.

"Number one, we aren't going anywhere until we've finished moving in. That goes for *all* of you—especially you, Sarah—all your things put away, your room cleaned, your bed made."

"Aye, aye, Captain Father, sir! I will! I promise!"

"And number two, you will *not* under *any* circumstances push *any* buttons or flip *any* switches without complete and total adult supervision, and *not* until I am hiding behind a rock—is that understood?"

"Thanks, Dad!" I agreed, grabbing Sarah's hand. "I'll watch her like a hawk. You can count on me."

"All right. Then it's settled. First the hard work. And then the fireworks."

CHAPTER 4

Captain Marvel

We never worked so hard to get our chores finished. By the time it started to get dark, all the furniture was in position, all the boxes were unpacked, all the beds were set up, and we still had time before the fireworks show to eat another big meal. We were that hungry! Gramma Edna and her sewing ladies insisted on feeding us until it felt like I'd swallowed a hippo. But I still made room for chocolate cake.

By eight o'clock Dad was so tired and sore that he tried to get out of going to the park, but we wouldn't leave him alone.

"C'mon, kids, I have to get some sleep. Tomorrow is Saturday. I have to get ready for my first Sunday. I'm going to stay home. Ruth and your mother can take you."

"But you *gotta* come, Dad! Have you even *looked* inside the box?"

I had. It was splendiferous! The Big Bang Boom Box was split into two sections. The lid contained all the loose fireworks: strings of firecrackers, Roman candles, sparklers, fountains, bottle rockets, and that sort of thing. There were smoke bombs and squirmy snakes and smoke worms and spinning flowers and buzzing fire bees—I'd seen things like that before. But then there was a whole lot of stuff I'd never even *heard* of.

In one package there was this tiny army of cardboard soldiers that, when you lit the fuse, were supposed to go marching across the ground until the fuse reached their heads. Then they would shoot up and parachutes would pop out, like flying paratroopers. I wanted to do that one first.

Then there were two dozen of something called Fire Frogs. The package said to light the fuse and watch them jump all over the place, flip upside down, and spit fire and smoke, until they finally croaked in a blast of green flame and sparks. That sounded pretty great.

But that was nothing compared to the grand finale. The main box contained a whole fireworks display, complete with launcher tubes and a timed fuse mechanism. The instructions said all you had to do was set the box a safe distance away from spectators, light the extra-long fuse, duck for cover, and watch as the thing blew up. There would be pink, blue, and green rockets, gold and silver showers, loud explosions, balls of fire, shooting and crackling and whistling fireworks for almost ten solid minutes. And I was the one who was going to light it!

When we got to the park, there were already hundreds of people there waiting for us. We recognized a lot of the folks who had helped us move in, and we saw the ladies from the Welcome Wagon, Mr. LaPierre with his twelve kids, Mr. Gamelli and his family, and tons of others. Mom and Dad got a chance to meet some of the members from Boomtown Church, and Ruth was swarmed by a few of the high school girls who invited her to try out for the cheerleading squad.

But Sarah and I were that night's main attraction. There had to be a line of forty kids who wanted to shake our hands. They wanted to meet the two people who had blown up a factory building with a rocket.

At the front of the line was a kid about my same age, except he was a few inches taller and had a face full of freckles. He wore a patched Dodger's baseball cap, his dark hair sticking out in all directions from underneath it. When he smiled I saw he was missing two teeth. He also had on one of those green army shirts, the one with all the extra pockets; I could see a slingshot and a harmonica and a ball of string poking out.

He shook my hand and then pounded my back like it was a dirty rug. "Howdy! The name's Busy. What's yours?"

"Jonathan. But people call me Jonny—or sometimes Jon for short. Is that your real name?"

"What, Busy? Nah, that's just what people call me."

"Why?"

"My real name is Bartholomew Zed Gunderson—that's a mouthful, ain't it? My initials are B. Z., so my pals started calling me Busy. Get it?"

"Sure, that sorta makes sense."

"My dad's nickname, now *that's* a story. People call him Lazy. Lazy Gunderson, that's him! Exactly the opposite of mine."

"Why do they call him that?"

"'Cause he flattened our house with a tractor."

"He did?"

"Sure enough!" Busy grinned proudly, hitching his thumbs in his pants. "Flattened the house! Flat as a pancake!"

"You're pulling my leg."

"Nope. It's true! He was out in the cornfield one afternoon plowing with his tractor. It was hot, and he fell asleep with his foot jammed right there on the pedal. Just kept on going."

"What happened then?" Sarah interrupted, getting caught up in the story.

"Who's this?" Busy asked.

"That's my little sister. She's Sorry."

"Sorry 'bout what?"

"Sorry about everything, usually. Hang on a few minutes. She'll come up with something."

Sarah punched me in the shoulder. "I'm not *that* little. I'm nine years old. Big enough to keep up with any of you ol' farmer kids."

"You think so?" Busy replied, sizing her up. "Well, I'm the leader of my gang, and I say we don't allow any girls in it. We'll take Jonny. 'Course we want him, after he blew up the fireworks factory and all. He's my new captain; that's what I say."

"I am?"

"Sure enough. I need a guy who knows his way around rockets and stuff. We're gonna call you Captain Marvel, after the super hero."

Sarah cut in, "That's not fair! I am the one who burned down the fireworks factory!"

Busy thought about it for a moment before he answered, "That's true. I heard you were the one who threw the switch. I'll have to talk to the other guys about it, but I won't make any promises. We don't want to catch no girl germs."

Some of my favorite Captain Marvel stuff. – *Jonny*

Sarah crossed her arms and pouted. "Don't bother, cootie-breath. I'll start my *own* gang! You'll see." She stomped off into the night looking for any girls she could recruit.

"She's a real firecracker," Busy decided. "She always goin' off like that?"

"Yeah, pretty much every five seconds. Forget her. I want to hear about your dad."

"Right." Busy continued his story, rubbing his hands together. "So my dad, he falls asleep on the tractor with his foot jammed on the pedal and the engine still in gear. The tractor starts to turn in this big circle, you see, right through the rows of corn, right across the field, right through the fence!"

"He didn't wake up?"

"Nah, he can sleep through anything. Besides, it was after lunch and it was pretty hot that day. So he kept on snoring, even when the tractor drove through the barn. The doors were wide open—he went in one side and out the other!"

"Boy, I wish I was there to see that!"

"Same here. I was in school so I missed the whole thing. But my mom was there, outside in the yard hanging the laundry. He plowed right through her clean sheets—right over the top of her laundry basket! She started screaming and chasing him across the yard, but he didn't wake up till he was halfway through the living room—'course by then it was too late."

"You're joshin' me!"

"Nope. There he went—right across the porch, through the front door, across the living room, smack-dab into the kitchen, and right out the back!"

"What'd he do when he woke up?"

"About the time he was smashing through the kitchen, he opened his eyes and saw what was going on, but before he could get the tractor out of gear, he was in the backyard. There was nothing he could do—there was already a big ol' gaping hole right through the middle of our house! Just as my mom ran around to make sure he was okay, the house tipped over and fell down flat as a penny on a railroad track! *Whomp!* Just like that!"

"Wow!"

"Yep. Ever since people 'round here call him Lazy. Lazy Gunderson, that's my dad!"

I was impressed. "You're so lucky. Your dad is famous."

"What about *your* dad? He was almost killed by a rocket!" Busy countered. "What could be better'n that?"

"Yeah, you're right. That *is* pretty neat."

Busy introduced me to all the other guys. There was Frankie and Tony Mitterand, they were twins; their mom and dad owned Mitterand's Boarding House. There was Bobby Odegaard; his dad owned the Gas-N-Go. And Rocky, his dad was the town junk man.

All of them were going into the same grade I was, sixth grade at the Boomtown School. They took a quick vote and accepted me into the gang unanimously and made me an honorary captain. They showed me the secret handshake and told me the secret password and promised they would show me their hideout the first chance they got. From then on whenever they went fishing or camping or tree climbing or exploring or whatever else, I got to be a part of it—Captain Marvel and his five superhero friends. We were inseparable.

We spent that whole first night getting to know each other, and by the time I fired off the Boom Box, we were friends for life. I'd never had a group of friends like that in California. It's a good thing I had them in Boomtown. If it wasn't for them, things might have turned out differently in the days ahead.

What we didn't know was that events were already being set in motion that would change the town forever. That night in the park, none of us saw the man hiding in the bushes, watching us play. He almost fainted when he laid eyes on the Big Bang Boom Box—when he saw the picture of Chang for the first time—like looking in a mirror, he told us later. He had slipped into town unnoticed, that very same night. He followed the noise and ended up in the park. None of us knew there was a mysterious visitor in town or what he was doing there, not me, not the guys, not anybody else in town.

But we would find out soon enough.

CHAPTER 5

Walter the Butcher

The next morning was Saturday, and after being up so late and working so hard the day before, we were all pretty tired. I didn't get out of bed until almost ten o'clock. I woke up to the sound of birds building a nest just outside my window. I watched them for a while and decided the momma bird looked a lot like Mrs. Byrd. Same color feathers and everything.

By the time I tumbled downstairs, Mom was busy in the kitchen putting away the last of our dishes. Sarah was spilling her cereal and feeding Cheerios to the cat. Ruth was out on the front porch with two of her new girl friends. And Dad was in his little office studying his sermon notes for the next day.

Gramma Edna popped in with some freshly baked muffins. We gathered around the table while she talked about where to find things in Boomtown. Mom wanted to visit some of the shops, especially Gertrude's Beauty Parlor, and Dad insisted on getting a haircut—and I had to get one too. Rats!

"Tomorrow is our first Sunday. We're all going to try our hardest to make a good first impression—even if it kills you. That goes *triple* for you, Miss Sorry Pants. I will have a fresh haircut and put on my best preaching suit and my favorite tie. *You're* going to wear a suit and tie as well," he informed me. "Make sure you wear your white shirt—and *keep* it white—at least until after the service."

Double rats! Ties always made my neck itch.

Grandma Edna told us where to go for a haircut. "For the gentlemen, there's Walt's on Bang Street and for you, Janice, and the girls there's Gertrude's Beauty Parlor on Boom Boulevard. We aren't the biggest town in the world, so those are your only choices."

She got up to leave and then stopped at the screen door; she had a strange look on her face. "Oh, and one more thing. Arthur. Jonny. Take my advice. Whatever you do—*don't upset Walter!*" The screen door slammed shut, and she was gone.

"Wonder what she meant by that?" my dad muttered, counting the buttons on his sweater. He was always doing that when he got nervous. Count the buttons. Make sure they're all still there. I think Boomtown was making him jumpy.

We spent the next hour straightening up, getting dressed, and taking turns in the single bathroom. The girls always took too long. There were things to see! Following Gramma Edna's directions, we strolled down our street and went by Mr. LaPierre's house. We stopped to talk to eight or nine of his children who were out playing in the yard.

"Where you goin'?"

"Into town."

"Watcha gonna do?"

"Get haircuts."

"That's boring."

"Yeah, I know. Maybe we'll get ice cream."

"Really?"

"Yeah, we got a coupon for Top's Soda Shop."

"You gonna have the Family Gutbuster?"

"Yeah, I hope so. What's that?"

"It's an ice-cream sundae with twenty scoops of ice cream, any flavor you want, with bananas and pineapple and nuts and chocolate sauce and whipped cream. Alonzo—that's Mr. Top, the man who owns the soda shop—he puts it in this big silver bucket as big as your head and you eat it and eat it until your guts want to explode! We went there once. Me and my mom and dad and my brothers and sisters, and we tried to eat the whole thing, but we couldn't, and we got sick and couldn't eat anything else for a whole week!"

Sarah's eyes lit up like a pair of sparklers. She grabbed Dad's arm and started yanking on it like a church bell. "Can we go, Dad? Can we have a Gutbuster? I'll bet I can eat it all by myself. Can we?"

He rolled his eyes and groaned. "Twenty scoops of ice cream and our stomachs explode and we get sick for a week? Sounds like fun."

"You mean it?"

"We'll see."

We kept walking, past Chang Park where we had shot off the fireworks the night before. The road curved around Boomtown Church on the right where Dad would be preaching the next day, and then we turned right on Bang Street. Sarah had been begging my dad to get the Gutbuster the whole way into town.

I could tell she was wearing Dad down. He said, "Sarah, I've got to get my hair cut first. You and Ruth and your mother are heading to Gertrude's. Jonny and I might pop into the bookstore after that."

Mom said, "We could split up and meet back at the soda shop. It's eleven o'clock now. We could meet there at two thirty. That should give us enough time."

Dad shrugged in defeat and answered, "Bring a spoon—and a wheelbarrow to carry me home."

Bang Street was one of the busiest streets in town. We passed the offices of Dr. Goldberg, family physician, and Dr. Xu, the town dentist. We looked in the windows of the Red Bird General Store. We saw the music store, the bookstore, and a butcher shop on the opposite side. As we walked along, we were greeted by all kinds of folks who were out shopping on a Saturday—ladies in their hats, men in their best overalls, and children running in and out of Top's Soda Shop. The bell rang merrily every time the door opened

and closed. We stopped long enough to peek through the window and watch a family try to eat one of the Gutbusters. We were going to need a shovel.

"See you boys later," Mom said as she took the girls down the street and out of sight. That left Dad and me trying to find the barbershop.

"Excuse me," Dad asked a man sweeping the sidewalk in front of his store. The sign said Guenther's Gun Corral. I figured the man with the broom had to be Guenther. He was dressed head to toe in blotchy-colored fabric, one of those camouflaged hunter's suits. He had a lumpy hump on his back and a hood over his head. He looked like a camel.

"Hello, dere," he said in a thick Swedish accent. "Vat can I help you vith?"

"We're looking for the barbershop. We seem to have missed it."

"Yah, sure, you betcha. Right over dere. You see it, next to bookstore?"

"Where?"

"The sign over dere. The vun dat says Boocher? Vith the chicken leg and pork chop painted on der vindow? That's Valt's, for sure."

"But that's a *butcher* shop."

"Yah, you betcha. Valt iz de boocher—*und* the barber."

"That's where we get haircuts?"

"For sure, yah."

We turned to walk away, but I just had to ask, "What do you call your suit? I've never seen anything like it—with the hump and all."

"Oh, dis vun here? Dis is vat I call 'Camel-flage.' Great for hiding in the dry grass. It verks vonderful, yah?"

"Yah."

We waved good-bye to Mr. Guenther and crossed the street until we were standing underneath the wooden chicken leg and the pork chop. Peering through the window, we could see that it was the barbershop after all. Down one whole side was a white counter with a glass case and a weighing scale and meat hooks and refrigerators, but instead of beef and chicken, it was full of hair tonics and combs and scissors.

"Look, Dad, there's a poster showing how to butcher a cow right next to the prices for shaves and haircuts."

Near the door were some men reading magazines waiting for their turn in the barber chair. They looked up and nodded to us as we came in. There were two empty spots at the end. We slipped into our seats and took a closer look around the room. That's when we saw Walter for the very first time.

He had to be more than seven feet tall. His head almost touched the ceiling when he stood up straight. His arms were like tree branches, covered in a forest of hair and tattoos. Each of his legs was as big around as I was, and his shoulders were as wide as a bale of hay. His head was shaved and it was bumpy, like the bark of a walnut tree. His nose was like a lumpy potato, and he had tiny black eyes and a crooked mouth full of broken teeth that looked like splintered glass. His hands and fingers were as big as two bunches of bananas. In his left fist he clutched a black comb, and in his right fist he hacked away with a giant pair of scissors half as long as my arm. The poor man in the chair squirmed around like a nervous octopus as the monstrous scissors went *clip, clip, clip* right next to his ear.

Walter shouted, and the windows rattled. "Hold still, you little runt! One slip and you'll lose an ear! Then you'll look like me!"

Walter thought it was a pretty good joke so he started to laugh.

It sounded like a thousand marbles being sucked up by a vacuum cleaner. The man fainted in the chair.

"Looks like you lost another one, Walt!" called out one of the men.

The barber propped the man's head with a towel and quickly finished the haircut. He growled, "Easier that way. They don't squirm so much."

He whipped off the apron, lifted the unconscious man with one hand, and plopped him in the corner by the front door.

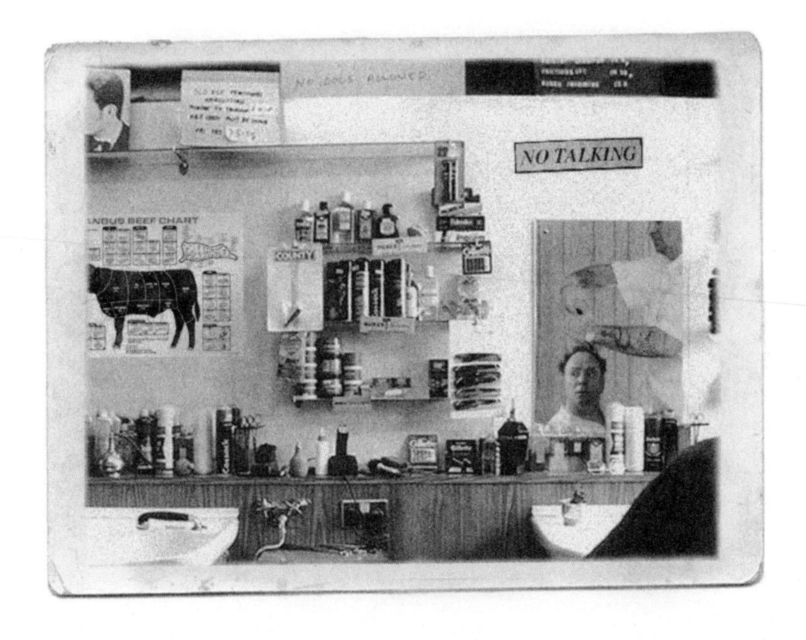

"Next! Who's next? I haven't got all day!" The men shivered like a basket of newborn puppies. He pointed a huge finger at one of them. "You! You're next. Get in the chair!"

His next victim stumbled across the room. I could hear him whispering a prayer as he went by. Ed Gamelli, our mailman, was sitting next to us. He nudged Dad and joked, "More people find religion at Walt's than they ever will in church, eh, Preacher?"

Dad whispered, "Where did you ever find a giant like him? A *butcher*? How did he ever get to be the barber?"

The mailman just smiled and answered, "Ol' Walt? He's not as bad as he looks—though his bite *is* worse than his bark, if you know what I mean."

And then, while we waited for our turn in the chair, he told us all about Walter the Butcher.

CHAPTER 6

Close Shave

"You see," the mailman explained, "Walter's ancestors, the Kravchukniaks, hail from old Russia. You can trace his lineage all the way back to the Siberian wasteland. His forefathers crossed the frozen tundra on foot and then crossed the Bering Sea by canoe. His great-great-grandfather, Vladik Kravchukniak, settled on Kodiak Island near Chiniak Bay, married a Shoonaq Eskimo, and joined a whole bunch of other Russians who were fishermen and fur trappers like him."

"He's part *Eskimo*?" my dad asked. "He doesn't look like an Eskimo."

"Oh, he's Eskimo, all right—and part Russian—and part Kodiak bear probably."

The mailman continued with his story. "Anyway, as I was

saying, among other attributes common to men of their size and strength, Walt's people have got a sturdy constitution. I heard about this one snowstorm in the dead of winter—forty degrees below zero and snow blowing sideways. Vladik and his son went out to get firewood, and they got lost in the blizzard. Three months go by and everybody figures they're frozen to death. After the spring thaw, they come marching back into camp like nothing ever happened."

Another man leaned over and chimed in, "I heard it was more like four months."

"Four? I heard it was five," said a third man.

The mailman huffed, "It was three."

The second man said, "And it was twenty below, not forty."

"Listen here, George, this is *my* story. Let me tell it my way."

"That's fine. You go ahead. Just get it right, that's all I'm saying."

I was getting impatient with their fussing. "S'cuse me, Mr. Gamelli, what happened? How did they make it through the blizzard?"

"Well, son, I was trying to tell you that before these old codgers butted in. Here's the way it was. They wander around in the pitch dark and the blinding snow for about three days until they fall into this cave, you see? They build a fire and dry out their clothes. The snow is forty feet deep, they got no idea of where they are, so they hunker down and ride out the winter in the cave. They survived by catching sea otters and eating seaweed and oysters."

"I heard it was beavers and pine cones."

"I heard it was moose meat and tree bark."

"Don't start that again!" Mr. Gamelli shouted.

"I'm just saying what I heard."

"What difference does it make?"

"It makes a *huge* difference. Ever eat a sea otter?"

"No, I haven't, not that it matters a hill of beans. *I'm* saying it was seaweed and oysters. That's what they ate until the weather cleared up. As soon as it did, they climbed out of the cave and headed for home. That's how it happened."

I wanted to hear more. "But how did he get here to Boomtown?"

"Good question, son. The Kravchukniaks decided to work their way down the coast of Alaska and find a more hospitable climate. They were looking for a place suitable for folks of their wild and giantish nature. They've been here ever since."

"So that's when he became a barber?"

"Nope. Not right away. Just look at him. Seven and a half feet tall, three hundred pounds of pure muscle, as ugly as a flowered couch, and as angry as a bee up your sleeve. Nah, he followed in his pappy's footsteps and took up logging. I figure Walt's spent his whole life cutting things up or cutting 'em down, one way or another. He likes sharp things."

I looked over at Walter as he used the giant scissors to snip away at the customer's hair. "I don't think I want a haircut . . ."

"Oh, don't you worry none." The mailman grinned. "He's been cutting my hair since I was your age. See? I still got both my ears and my nose. You just got to keep your mouth shut while he's working on you."

Mr. Gamelli leaned back in his seat and continued wistfully, "You shoulda seen Walt in his prime. He'd pick up an ax with a blade about as big as an encyclopedia and chop down a tree with a single swipe! Trees falling one after another like dominoes. I seen him clear an entire hillside in a single afternoon.

"But then we started running out of trees 'cause he cut so many of them down and the mill couldn't keep up with him. So he got himself a job working at the mill. He'd strip the bark off the logs with his bare teeth and dump the logs into the saw all by himself. After the wood was cut, he'd stack up the boards and haul them out to the yard for sorting, 'bout forty boards at a time. Didn't even break a sweat."

"Really?"

"Sure thing. But when the logs started to run out, the mill shut down and Walt was out of a job—again. That's when he decided to open the butcher shop."

The other fellow piped in, "You forgot about the bear."

"I didn't forget about the bear. I was about to say something about the bear until you stuck your big fat nose in. Who's telling this story, anyway?"

"You are. Just not very well."

The mailman sniffed at the interruption. "Walt was way up in the hills when all of a sudden a bear the size of an elephant fell down out of a tree right in front of him. It was hard to tell them apart; they were about the same weight and had almost the same amount of hair. They circled each other—round and round—until the bear took a swing at Walt's head."

I was perched on the edge of my seat. "What happened then?"

"It was pretty much an even match, that bear and ol' Walt. They wrestled day and night for a week until finally that bear up and died from sheer disappointment. Soon as it was dead, Walt took out his hunting knife and had the bearskin off in five minutes flat! He ended up with enough bear steaks to feed half of Boomtown. Walt figured it was a sign from heaven, so the next day he opened up a butcher shop right here in this very spot."

The mailman leaned back and crossed his arms over his chest, proud of the way he was telling his story. He dared the other men to correct any of the details.

I wasn't so sure about it, though. "You're saying the trees started running out, so Walt worked in the mill. And when the logs ran out, he opened the butcher shop. So why is he cutting hair?"

Mr. Gamelli smiled and twirled the end of his mustache. "That's the best part. After Walt had his butcher shop for a while, a new supermarket opened over in Stickville, only about ten miles away. First one in the whole county. Some of our folks started going over there. It wasn't a problem at first, but after a while, enough folks stopped coming into Walt's. That didn't make him a bit happy, no sir.

"After losing two careers already, Walt was madder'n that old bear. He ran the whole ten miles over to Stickville and burst into the store. He was still wearing his red-stained apron, and he had two butcher knives—one in each hand. He charged up and down the aisles until he cornered the owner back by the milk and eggs. By the time Walt got done yellin' at him, the milk was curdled, the eggs were boiled, and all the hair on that poor feller's head had fallen out.

"Walt figured it was another sign from heaven. He closed up the butcher shop and put in a barber chair. He's been cutting hair ever since."

"Wow! Isn't that something?" I gasped.

My dad had listened quietly to the mailman's tale, but now he had something to say. "That's a very interesting story—rather hard to believe, if you ask me—but here's what I'm wondering about."

"What's that, Preacher?"

"Walt's temper. The man's a hothead; he might even be dangerous."

"Dangerous? Walt? Nah, he'd never hurt a fly."

"He killed a bear!"

"Not on purpose. It was mostly the bear's fault."

"But why in the world would you let him cut your hair?! And with those huge scissors? I don't understand."

The men stared at my dad like he had two heads. "What are you talking about?"

"I mean, why keep getting haircuts from a man who's impossible to deal with? Why not get a haircut somewhere else?"

The mailman answered, "We can't turn our backs on Walter. He's one of us! He's part of the town—like the fireworks factory. You think we should get rid of the fireworks just because they're loud? Just because occasionally we accidentally blow something up? Is that what you think—get rid of anything that's difficult? We don't want to live without fireworks! Why would we want to live without Walt?"

Before Dad could answer, we suddenly had something more important to think about. The man in the barber chair was complaining about his haircut. He was pointing at the crooked line over his forehead. He didn't like the way it looked. Oh boy!

Everyone in the room stopped breathing. Walt's face turned white and then bright red. His beady eyes swelled up as big as two silver dollars. His hands began to shake. The tiger tattooed on his arm started pacing back and forth. The top button of his shirt popped off, hit the wall, and put a hole in it. His body began to shake like a train coming into the station. I think I saw steam coming out of his ears.

Mr. Gamelli jumped up and shouted, "It's quitin' time! Everybody out! Right now! *Walt's about to blow!*"

We all made a mad dash for the door. The man who had been in the barber chair pushed past us and ran down the street with his apron flapping from his neck like a flag in a storm. Dad and I dashed across the street and watched the rest of the men scatter left and right and duck behind telephone poles and mailboxes or run inside stores and slam the doors and pull down the shades. It only took another few seconds before we heard the explosion.

An ear-splitting bellow echoed down the street, followed by the unique sound of a two-hundred-and-fifty-pound barber chair flying through the roof of a butcher shop. I watched it sail up and up and up—at least forty feet in the air. It wasn't the sort of thing you see every day, a barber chair passing over the sun like an eclipse, the chrome handles of the arm rests glinting in the afternoon light, the soft brown leather seat and headrest casting a shadow onto the ground. It was mesmerizing, seeing that chair flying like a giant bird without wings. But now it was starting to come back down. And it had to land somewhere. It was going to land straight on top of us.

"Dad! Dad! *Look out!*"

He must not have heard me. Our ears were still ringing from Walter's scream. And he seemed to be locked in a trance—he couldn't take his eyes off the flying chair. So I did what I had to do. I really didn't have any choice. I stomped on his foot and gave him a push. He fell sideways, and I fell on top of him. That's when the chair hit the ground with a *thump*.

It buried itself two feet deep in the sidewalk—right in front of the Red Bird General Store. It landed in the exact spot where we had been standing only a second before. It was a close shave. If I hadn't pushed him, Dad wouldn't have needed a haircut. He would have needed an ambulance. When we stood up, Dad took one look at the barber chair and gave me a tight squeeze.

"Let's go get some ice cream," he groaned, wiping the dust off his pants. "You've earned it. As much as you want."

The Sunday edition of three different newspapers in neighboring towns reported hearing Walt's yell as far away as Stickville. Lazy Gunderson claimed that his prize cow was so upset that it stopped giving milk. All the dogs stopped barking for a week, and some people noticed that there weren't as many birds in Boomtown as before, but that may have just been a coincidence.

Gramma Edna, she just laughed at my dad and said, "I warned you. Whatever you do, *don't upset Walter!*"

RED BIRD
BROWN and SON
RED BIRD
S.&H. GREEN STAMPS
OLD TIME
VALUES!

CHAPTER 7

Beware the Curse!

It was the first Sunday Dad was going to preach at Boomtown Church, and he was acting a little crazy. It was the same morning our lawn mower turned up missing. I remember because I had mowed the front yard the day before, but it wasn't in the middle of the sidewalk where I'd left it. I asked Ruth if she had moved it. Nope. Not Sarah, of course. Not Dad either.

"That's just great," he grumbled. "First my jacket button goes missing and now the lawn mower."

That's how the morning had gone. We had all been running around taking showers and combing our hair and getting dressed while Dad was on his knees trying to find the missing button. Mom had helped Sarah change her dress for the third time—she had spilled milk on the first one and got grape jam on the second. I had gotten ready early and was standing around scratching my neck because of the tie.

"Jon, can you help me find my button? Maybe it's under the bed."

I crawled around until I finally found the button in Dad's shoe, but by then it was too late for Mom to sew it back on. We had to leave. He took one last look in the mirror and smoothed his hair and adjusted his brown vest and checked the crease in his pants and double-checked the polish on his shoes. Everything was just right except where his jacket popped open like a window shade. I could tell already—that was going to bother him all day.

It was a bright summer morning, and we walked down the street and arrived at the church about twenty minutes before the service was supposed to start. After all of Dad's worrying, we were still on time!

The church looked like one of those white churches you'd see on a postcard. It had a tall bell tower, and a large, cast-iron bell was ringing as we walked up. I wondered who was ringing it. And I wondered if Dad would let me climb up there and look after the service—not very likely. We pushed through the double doors and went inside. There were real stained-glass windows and old wooden pews with velvet cushions. An ancient-looking pipe organ and a loft were in the back. Busy told me that's where the kids always sat during worship services. There was a piano up front. The room smelled a little musty, like burnt oil and dusty candles. Mom said the building was more than seventy-five years old, so I guess that's why it smelled kind of funny, but I still thought it was pretty neat.

The first person we met was the "hall monitor," Gertrude Feeny, the owner of Gertrude's Beauty Parlor. She looked like she was in her fifties and was built like a football player—broad shoulders, short, muscled legs. She had gnarled fingers and a stern, puckered face that looked like she was sucking a lemon. She had met my mom and my sisters just yesterday at her beauty shop, but she acted like she'd never seen them before.

She barked as soon as she saw us and motioned for us to come back into the foyer. "Good morning! Take a bulletin. Are you visiting? Here. Put on this visitor's ribbon. Have you signed the guest book yet?"

Before we could answer, she was pinning a bright, silk ribbon on each of us with the word *Visitor* printed in large, black letters. She pushed bulletins and flyers into our hands. She shoved a pen at Dad, grabbed his arm, pulled him over to the guest book, and hovered like a hungry vulture. Dad was too startled to tell her that he was the new minister. He just signed the book and handed back the pen. She looked at his entry like she was checking for spelling and penmanship—I have seen that look on plenty of teachers' faces—and then waved permission for us to move along.

A woman standing nearby saw the whole thing. "Don't mind Gertrude," she apologized. "She's really quite harmless. She lost her husband a few years ago when he used dynamite to unclog their sewer pipe. Should have used a shovel, I suppose. After that . . . oh well, just do what she says and you'll be okay."

She smiled and continued, "You must be our new minister. I'm the church secretary, Ingrid Hofler. We're so glad to have you here."

My dad sighed in relief. "Of course, Ingrid. You were a great help in getting us to Boomtown. It's nice to finally meet you in person."

Mrs. Hofler took us into the sanctuary to meet some of the other members. Gramma Edna was there; Mr. Guenther from the Gun Corral, Ed Gamelli and his wife, and Matthieu and Pauline LaPierre. While we shook hands, Sarah caught sight of two LaPierre girls and ran off to play. We were introduced to the town sheriff, Burton Ernie, and his wife, Laverne. We met Vera DeFazio, the song leader for that morning, and Manfred Heinzmann, the presiding elder.

Mrs. Hofler pulled us off to the side. "We have a few more minutes before the service starts. Do you want to come and see where your office is?" Mom, Ruth, and I followed Dad down the hallway.

"The bathrooms are here. The storage closet and office supplies, right there. My office and your office are down here."

As we poked around, I noticed a line of photos hanging on the long wall of the hallway. They were all pictures of men, dressed in western suits and hats, holding Bibles and looking serious. Some of them had big mustaches; one had a pair of six shooters around his waist. The first ones were orangey-brown and faded. You could tell they were really old.

"Look at all the photos, Dad. They've got names and dates under each one of them. See?"

I counted them out loud as we moved down the hallway: Twenty. Twenty-one. Twenty-two. Twenty-three. Twenty-four. At the very end was an empty frame—number twenty-five. I wondered what that was for.

Mrs. Hofler smiled proudly. "These are all the ministers we've had over the years, ever since the beginning, starting more than seventy-five years ago."

My dad did the math in his head. "Ingrid," he stammered nervously, "you've had *twenty-four* pastors since the church was founded? Twenty-four? That's about one pastor for every three years."

She nodded cheerfully. "And you're the twenty-fifth!"

"No one mentioned anything about you having had that many pastors in the letters. Nobody said anything about it on the phone. I'd think it would be the sort of thing you might want to bring up when you interview your next minister!"

"Is that a lot?" she asked, scratching her head. "I guess I never really thought about it. Though, now that you mention it, it *does* sound like quite a few. First Presbyterian has had only three pastors since it started. St. Bernard's has had only four."

"What happened to all of them?" My dad shuddered. He pointed to the man in the picture just before the empty frame. "What about him? It says, 'Pastor Sergeant Gibson, In Loving Memory, 1947–1949.' In *loving memory*? What happened?"

"Oh, the dear man. I simply adored him. Tragic story."

"Tragic?"

"We were having several baptisms over at Canyon Creek just below Lookout Falls when all of a sudden the weather changed. Pastor Gibson insisted on finishing even though it started raining something fierce. 'It'll pass!' he said, bless his heart. He was *so* dedicated. Then we heard this roar coming from upstream. Everybody scattered and got out of the way, but poor Pastor Gibson—he didn't get out in time."

"Get out?"

"Out of the river. Flash flood. A real gully washer! Pretty rare around here. Washed him downstream, clean out of sight. Just like that!" she said sadly, snapping her fingers.

"A flash flood? You can't be serious. He was never found?"

"No. At least, we don't think so. There's been a rumor that he turned up in the next county and that he's been preaching at the Baptist church in Gorton, but it's never been confirmed."

"What about this one? Pastor George Stomopolis? He lasted only a year."

"It was just terrible. Train accident. It jumped the tracks just as he was coming home from performing a funeral. Ironic, when you think about it."

"And this one? Pastor Albert Vanderpool?"

"Sink hole."

"And him?"

"Lightning strike."

"And him?"

"Snake bite."

"And this one?"

"We're not exactly sure."

We worked our way back down the hallway until we reached Phineas Culpepper, "Beloved Founding Pastor," who had somehow survived a miraculous five years in the pulpit.

"And what about this guy? Five years. That's a world's record for this bunch."

Ingrid shook her head. "The saddest story of all. I wasn't here at the time, of course. He was pastor long before I was born. But a few of the older members like Werner Holz—he's ninety-four this year—he could tell you all about it.

"Pastor Culpepper was down south ministering to the railroad men as they put in a spur from the main line. He was always doing that, visiting the miners up in the hills or the farmers out on their farms or the railroaders down at the tracks. He was a true evangelist. On that particular day, just as he was finishing up a prayer meeting, he caught his foot on the handle of a pickax and fell into an open case of nitroglycerin. They say he almost reached heaven before he came back down. Such a shame too. Everybody loved Pastor Culpepper, or so they say."

By the time she finished, Dad's eyes were red and his head was pounding. His face was as white as a bowl of sour cream. He was breathing funny. He looked like he might faint.

"You okay, Dad?"

"Am I *okay*? Did you hear what she just said? Twenty-four pastors in seventy-five years, *all* of them died tragically or disappeared under mysterious circumstances—and I'm next!"

I really didn't see the problem. "It's like a curse! Wait till I tell the other guys! Busy isn't going to believe this!"

"But I don't want to be part of a curse! Not that I believe in that sort of thing—there isn't any such thing as a curse—but still. This is an awfully strange coincidence!" He faced Mrs. Hofler and cried, "What about these other men? Have any of them ever been killed by a rocket boat?"

"Not so far."

"Any been crushed by a flying barber chair?"

"Nope. You would have been the first."

"Ingrid, do me a favor, will you?"

"Sure. Anything. Just name it."

"Order me a suit of armor. Size medium. Extra-thick plates. And a bus ticket to New Zealand."

"Oh, Arthur!" The secretary laughed. "You're such a kidder."

But I don't think Dad was kidding.

Sunday Morning Miracle

Just then we heard the sound of the piano drifting down the hallway. My mom grabbed Dad's hand and gave it a squeeze of encouragement as we weaved our way back to the sanctuary and down to the front. As if Dad didn't have enough to worry about, Sarah came running up the aisle and shoved a white rat into his face. "Look, Dad! Isn't he cute? Can I have one?"

"Sarah! What *is* that thing? Get it out of my nose!"

"It's a gerbil, Dad. It's Katrina LaPierre's. She's got a whole mess of 'em. Can I have one?"

"What? No. Sarah, the service is about to start! Janice, can you do something about this? Ruth?"

Ruth took Sarah's hand. "I'll take care of it, Dad. C'mon, Sarah."

I followed Sarah and Ruth as we climbed the stairs up to the balcony, Sarah chattering all the way. "His name is Whiskers. See how long they are? Do you think Dad will let me have one? I wonder what it eats. I want a black one. Or maybe a white one like this. What do you think? I can make a nest in a shoebox. I got one in my closet. What do they eat? Do gerbils smell?"

After the piano overture, Vera DeFazio was supposed to give the announcements. I was dreading what would come next. For me, going to church was like my tie—it made me itch. I loved my dad, but the church we went to before . . . it was as dull as a busted pencil with quiet hymns played slowly on an ancient organ by a woman who was twice as old as the songs. Long prayers and even longer sermons listened to by silent people sitting on hard pews, standing up and sitting down on cue. That was how it had been.

My dad took care of the sick, visited the widows, and preached on Sundays. He did all the stuff he was supposed to do. He was good at it. People liked him a lot. They were sad when he left. But I was happy to leave. I couldn't say that to him, of course. How could I tell him? I was eleven years old. I had ants in my pants. I couldn't sit still. I wanted some fireworks!

So I was pretty thrilled that first Sunday at Boomtown Church. Not only did I have Busy and Rocky up in the rafters with me, I got to see Mrs. DeFazio jump up from her seat and run down the aisle smiling and waving like a cheerleader at a football game.

"Don't forget!" she shouted. "October is just around the corner. We're hosting a booth in Farmer's Park from the last week in September until Halloween. We'll be selling cakes and pies to raise money for our missionaries. And this coming weekend, the youth are having a campout on Left Foot Island. The theme is

Antarctic Adventure, so, kids, remember to wear your penguin costumes and your mukluks!"

Announcements were followed by fifteen minutes of the happiest singing I'd ever heard in church. The church secretary was also the pianist, and she banged away on the keys like she was pounding a loaf of bread dough. The members of the choir clapped their hands and stomped their feet in time with the music. Every now and then someone called out the name of a favorite hymn and we'd sing that too. It was fun! My tie never made my neck itch even once.

After the music, it was time for the offering meditation and then the Morning Prayer. One of the elders struggled to his feet. He had to be more than a hundred years old. He had more wrinkles than a peach pit. He introduced himself in a shaky voice as Manfred Heinzmann. Busy leaned over and told me that Mr. Heinzmann was born at the same time as the dinosaurs. There were cave paintings of his face. I tried to hide my laugh behind my fist.

Still, Mr. Heinzmann seemed like a very nice man. He thanked everyone for coming and talked about how excited they all were to welcome the new minister and his family. He prayed for my dad's protection and thanked God for saving my dad's life—twice already. Third time's a charm, he said and winked.

Then he introduced Dad to the congregation. "Friends! As you know, in the absence of our former minister—who may or may not have drowned, may he rest in peace or whatever the case might be—it is my pleasure to introduce his replacement, the honorable Arthur Button. We hope he will endure far longer than his beloved, yet unfortunate, predecessors."

After the clapping and cheering died down, he continued. "As most of you already know, our new minister has distinguished himself as the father of the two children who nearly burned down the entire fireworks factory. I see the young man, Jonathan, sitting up there in the balcony with his older sister, Ruth, and next to him, Sarah, I believe?"

"That's me!" she shouted. "I'm Sorry!"

"Yes," Mr. Heinzmann answered chuckling, "we know you are, but *we* aren't! We are thrilled to welcome you this morning! Welcome to Boomtown!"

This was followed by applause that lasted almost three solid minutes. I could tell Dad was embarrassed; he wasn't used to this sort of attention. He fiddled with the spot where his jacket kept popping open, and a nervous grin spread across his face. I think Boomtown was having a positive effect on him, if you ignored the exploding rocket boat, giant bear-wrestling lumberjack butcher, flying barber chair, and Big Bang Boom Box overflowing with fireworks. And maybe he could forget a hallway full of dead ministers and deal with the loud music, stomping, and applause if it meant he had a chance to do something good.

I watched him shuffle his feet, counting his buttons. Three on his vest. Only three on the jacket. He kept coming back to that missing button. It was bugging him. He counted them one more time, and then taking a deep breath, he raised his hands for silence. Everyone sat back and waited in anticipation.

Dad's sermon that morning was probably the best he'd ever preached. I'll be honest; I usually tried to listen to every word he said, but it was hard. I had the same problem in school, fidgeting all the time, making doodles on the sides of my math papers. But this time it was different. Dad was great. Really great. I think the taste of death in his mouth must have inspired him. It sure inspired all of us. Even Busy kept his mouth shut the entire time.

And that's when the miracle happened. At the loudest part of his sermon, when he stood up tall and waved his arms and pounded his fists . . . when all of us were hanging on the very edges of our seats, a loud squeak came from the very back of the room. First a squeak and then a squawk, followed by a holler and a hoot.

The noise seemed to be coming from an older woman who had been sitting near the back. I'd seen her walk in before the service started. She had shuffled across the floor using a walker for support. Her back was bent, and her legs were thin. I had heard her moan when she sat down and groan when she stood up. But now, all of a sudden, the pain seemed to be gone. She launched out of her seat like one of Chang's rockets. She spun around like a windmill in a tornado.

"Ahhhhhh!" she squealed, leaping over the pew. "Eeeeek!"

All eyes swung around to see what was happening.

"Ooooh," she squirmed. "Eeeee!" she squeaked. "Woooohoo!" she squawked.

Busy had whispered her story to me after she had come in. The woman's name was Mrs. Corine Beedle, and for some reason for the last ten years she had been unable to stand on her own without help. She had visited every doctor in town (there was only one) and every other doctor in the county (there were only three). They each told her exactly the same thing: She was perfectly fine. Nothing was wrong with her. It was all in her head. But she knew different.

"They're all *quacks*!" she would tell anyone who would listen. "Charlatans, counterfeits, con men, cheats, swindlers, phonies, humbugs, flimflam artists!"

No matter what anyone told her, she was absolutely convinced that she suffered from some sort of exotic tropical disease. She was dying from a mysterious ailment. She had been bitten by a strange bug. Her joints ached, her muscles hurt, her back was out, her feet were swollen, her eyesight was blurry—even her hair was sore.

"Something is *wrong* with me!" she persisted. "Something is terribly, dreadfully, incurably wrong!"

But now, for some unexplainable reason, she was on her feet, not holding on to anything. And she wasn't just standing; she was wiggling around. Well, she wasn't just wiggling around; she was turning, hopping, jerking, jumping, leaping, twisting, and twitching. She spun to the left. She spun to the right. She grabbed her legs and back and sides. She hooted and howled and yelped and yammered.

"It's a miracle!" someone shouted. "Mrs. Beedle has been cured!"

Everyone started talking and pointing all at once, but Mrs. Beedle was too busy to notice. She jumped around like popcorn in a pan of hot oil. She spun like a top on a table. She whistled like a teapot on a stove.

Manfred Heinzmann stared. Mrs. DeFazio sang. The Widow Feeny blocked the door. The LaPierres chased their laughing children. Everyone else just stood there wondering what it all meant until someone finally shouted, "I know what it is! I know what's happened! *She's got the Spirit!*"

Everyone gasped and fell silent, gaping in awe at the miracle happening in their very midst. Then they turned and looked at my dad, their new minister, the instrument of the Almighty, the one who had drawn Mrs. Beedle up out of the pit of despair and turned her into a shooting star. The only other sound besides Mrs. Beedle swinging from the chandelier was the laughter of my sister, somewhere between the pews. The giggles sounded like they were coming from downstairs.

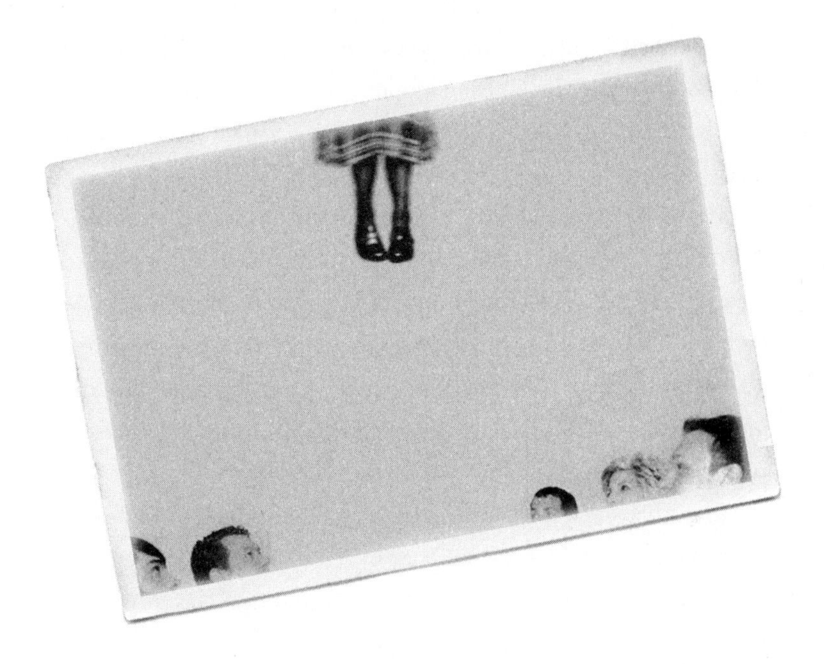

Where's Sarah? I thought. *Oh no. How did she get away*? I was supposed to keep an eye on her. What had she done *this* time?

Suddenly, her head popped up.

"Sarah!" my dad hissed from the pulpit. "This isn't funny! This is *serious*!"

Mom got up and went over to Sarah. "Honey, Mrs. Beedle has got the Spirit. That isn't something to laugh about."

Sarah tried to catch her breath. In between snorts and snickers, she finally managed to say, "Mrs. Beedle hasn't got the Spirit! She's got *whiskers*!"

Whiskers? Everybody had been listening to Sarah, but now they turned back around to look at Mrs. Beedle. I squinted my eyes to try to get a good view of Mrs. Beedle's face as she was flailing around. She had a dark shadow over her lip, but not enough to call it "whiskers." More like a tiny mustache. Not enough for a beard.

Sarah suddenly realized what everyone was thinking and this just made her laugh even louder. "Not whiskers on her *face*! Whiskers, Katrina's gerbil! He got away—and ran up Mrs. Beedle's dress!"

At that very second, Mrs. Beedle jumped down from the chandelier, and when she landed, Whiskers the gerbil finally popped loose. Turns out, Sarah had dropped him during the sermon. We were so busy listening we didn't notice her crawling down the stairs chasing after him. The poor frightened gerbil must have run around until he found a dark place to hide. Unfortunately, it happened to be under the folds of Mrs. Beedle's skirt.

Now that she was free from the furry little rodent, Mrs. Beedle made a hasty exit. She grabbed her purse and straight-armed her way past the Widow Feeny at the door. She left in such a hurry that she even forgot her walker.

"Wait!" Dad called after her. "We're so sorry! Don't leave!"

But she was gone, taking the Spirit with her. At least, that's how it must have felt to my dad. In the seventy-five years since Boomtown Church had started, twenty-four ministers had been crushed and burned and drowned and blown up. My dad had had his ministry come crashing down after only one day because of a *gerbil*. It was humiliating! I felt bad for poor old Dad.

But this was Boomtown, after all. I had to keep remembering that. We were quickly surrounded by a hundred people, all of them slapping Dad on the shoulders and congratulating him on the finest Sunday they'd ever witnessed. They shook my hand, gave my mom hugs, and kissed Ruth on the cheek. We were heroes all over again!

"Good job, preacher!"

"Excellent!"

"Outstanding!"

"Inspirational!"

"Whatcha gonna do next week?"

In the middle of it all was Sarah, grinning like a Cheshire cat, cuddling Whiskers like it was her new baby. She was the center of attention, on parade like she was queen of the Nile. All the other little girls wanted to stand next to her. Most of them wanted to *be* her.

"Wow!" they said. "You burned down a building *and* you healed an old lady. What else can you do?"

After the excitement died down, Dad stood at the door of the church sheepishly shaking everyone's hand as they left. Every last one of them said it was the best church service they'd ever attended, the greatest thing since the day they put fire into firecrackers. I agreed. It was the most fun I'd ever had in church.

When the sanctuary was nearly empty, a fellow stopped at the door and put out his hand. He told Dad it was the first time his family had ever visited.

"We haven't been to church in more than fifteen years. But when we heard that the new preacher in town had blown up the fireworks factory, we wanted to come by and check things out. If I'd known church was this exciting, I'da been here every Sunday. We're coming back—yes, we are—and we're tellin' our friends. See you next week!"

They went out the double doors, chatting happily as they went. Mom stood next to Dad, patting his hand. Standing next to him was Sarah, holding Whiskers up to her face, kissing his head and whispering in his tiny ear.

"You see that, Dad? It's just like you always say."

"What do I always say?"

"'The Lord works in mysterious ways.'"

Dad looked down at my sister, and it seemed like he was trying to be upset with her—I've seen that expression on his face before—but he couldn't seem to manage it. Instead, he burst into laughter and scooped her up in his arms.

"There's no mystery! You're my lucky penny, that's what you are. You always come up heads."

"Yep!" she agreed, beaming with pride. "And I'll *never* be Sorry about that!"

CHAPTER 9

The Stickville Slugs

Two weeks passed after that first Sunday without any more exciting episodes at the church, which was okay, I suppose. There was plenty else to keep me busy and interested. I was getting to know my new friends and exploring the town. The leaves started to change as September arrived. School would be starting soon, and in Boomtown that could mean anything! It also marked what the guys said was the single most important event in our little corner of the world—the start of football season.

In Boomtown, high school football was the number one obsession (other than fireworks). Everyone, including the mayor's three-legged dog, was fanatically, fantastically forever committed to the Stickville Slugs. Boomtown was too small to have its own high school, so all the kids went to Stickville High. Busy said that whenever the team played a game, huge caravans of fans would faithfully follow them wherever they went. You knew when it was game night because Boomtown turned into a ghost town.

Now that football season was fast approaching, there were huge green and brown signs hanging all over the place:

Go Slugs!

Slime Time!

Stick with the Slugs!

We May Be Slow, but That's Because We're Slugs!

My mom joined the local chapter of the Hug-a-Slug Booster Club. She went to regular meetings where they printed flyers with the team schedule so no one would miss a game and made all those signs. One night we all crowded around the radio and listened to an interview on the local radio station, KSLG. The coach of Stickville High School promised another exciting season for all the Slug fans. This year, they were going to "really slime them." It was pretty crazy.

The next day I came home from school practicing the school cheers and wearing my new Slugs sweatshirt. It had the team colors: muddy brown and slime green with a silver slime trail running down both sleeves. Dad came out of his study to ask me what all the noise was about.

"The Slugs are famous, Dad! You didn't know that?"

"Famous for what?"

"Famous for losing! Busy told me about a game last year against the East Wallop Hogs—sixty-two to nothing—the Slugs got squished flat!"

"They lost?"

"Sure they lost! They *always* lose! They played nine games last year and lost every single one. They didn't even score a field goal."

"Nine solid games and they didn't score a point? Not even by accident?"

"Nope. That's why they're so famous. The Stickville Slugs haven't won a single game in over forty years!"

Busy and Rocky had told me all about the team during lunch that day.

"The Slugs have lost every single game they've played since 1909. And they don't just lose; they get *smashed*!" Busy said.

"What do you mean?" I asked.

"There was this one game, about fifteen years ago, the Slugs lost by a score of 138 to 3! They only got the three points when the quarterback bounced the ball off someone's helmet and it went through the goalposts."

"That's not really a field goal, is it?"

"Nah," Busy said. "But the referees felt so sorry for the Slugs they gave it to 'em anyway. Then there was this other game where the quarterback came down with the flu so the place kicker had to take over. He didn't know how to throw the ball, so he spent the whole game *kicking* it around the field. The Slugs lost that game 97 to 0."

"That's pretty bad."

"You think that's bad? What about when the Slugs scored three touchdowns for the *opposite team* 'cause they kept running the wrong way," Rocky added.

That's the way it was. Fumbles, broken plays, penalties, bad calls, bad passes—the Slugs always figured out new ways to lose. But that didn't keep the entire town of Boomtown from showing up the night before the big game for a huge rally on the Stickville High School football field. They danced around the bonfire and shot off firecrackers and rockets. They shouted and laughed and told stories about the games they'd seen over the years. Everyone was convinced that *this* was the year the Slugs would finally win a game.

Even Ruth got caught up in Slug fever and went out for the cheerleading squad. She was awfully excited about it when she made the team. She came home after the first week of school wearing her new uniform—a solid brown skirt with green stockings, a silver stripe down the middle of her back, the letter *S* sewn in green felt on the front of her sweater, and bright silver pom-poms.

She brought us into the living room and showed us one of her cheers.

"Give me an *S*!"

"*S*!" we all shouted.

"Give me an *L*!"

"*L*!"

"Give me an *UG*!"

"*UG*!"

"What does it spell?"

"SLUG!"

"What does it spell?"

"SLUG!"

"What does it mean?"

"Slime time! EEEEEUUU! Go Slugs!"

The day before the first game a terrible rainstorm, one of the worst in Boomtown history, blew through town. I'd never seen

rain like that! I had lived my whole life in Southern California, where it rained maybe ten or twenty times a year and even then, not so much. But in Washington, they had more than one hundred words just to describe all the different ways it rained. At the beginning of school I had to learn all of them during a spelling test.

"Hey, Busy," I had said, leaning over to show him my paper, "just look at this list: blowing, blustery, cloudy, damp, dark, drenching, droplets, drizzly, gusty, humid, hurricane, misting, moist, overcast, pattering, pouring, precipitous, raging, rainy, roaring, showery, spattering, spitting, sprinkling, squally, steamy, stormy, tempestuous, tornado, watery, wet, wild, windy. How am I supposed to learn all of these?"

"That isn't even *half* of 'em!" he whispered back. "There's a whole bunch more."

Little did I know that I was going to get to see the rest of the list with my own two eyes. The water came down in buckets. It rained cats and dogs. It rained cows and horses. It was Noah's ark weather. The gutters on the street filled up, and once those were full, the roads turned into streams. Yards turned into ponds. Fields turned into lakes. It was a good thing our house was on high ground. We stood on the porch and watched as Gramma Edna's lawn furniture floated by, followed by Mr. LaPierre's flock of plastic pink flamingos, a watering trough, a picnic table, and a family of plastic lawn gnomes.

"Look!" Sarah said pointing. "Isn't that Mr. Cotton's pickup truck?"

It was. We watched it sail past our front door and disappear down the street.

Mr. Gamelli came around in a rowboat delivering the mail and giving reports as he rowed from door to door. Just as night was falling, I saw a chicken coop sail by with its owner standing on the roof waving to everyone as he went by. But it didn't stop. It rained and rained and rained.

By morning, Boomtown looked like a wet sponge that had sat overnight in a sink full of dirty water. Everyone came out of hiding to start cleaning up the mess, picking up the garbage, rounding up cows and sheep and horses that had gotten loose, propping up fences and signs that had fallen over. Our house wasn't too bad, so we went up and down the street and helped anybody we could. We worked all day up until 3:00 p.m. But at that exact moment everyone dropped their mops and buckets, jumped in their tractors and trucks and horse carts, and headed for Stickville.

Why? Because it was *game time*! Floods, forest fires, earthquakes, it didn't matter. A volcano eruption wouldn't stop Boomtown from watching the Slugs.

"I guess it's time to go, kids," my dad said, heading for the car. "Ruth, get your uniform. Sarah, grab your coat."

So we hopped in the car and joined the caravan. The highway was washed away in several places, but road crews had created some detours. It took awhile, but we made it to the stadium early enough for Ruth to join the cheerleading squad for warm-ups. We sloshed through the gates to the bleachers and got our first look at the football field.

It was a swamp. One of the end zones was completely under water. A flock of ducks swam around in the makeshift pond, and I think I saw a beaver building a dam near the twenty-yard line. The referees were busy dragging branches off to the side. In the middle of the soup were the Stickville Slugs and the Ainogold Giants out on the field and making matters worse. They had already churned the grass into a muddy, mucky, slimy mess.

"Look, Dad," Sarah said, pointing. "The mud is *moving*. There's a *head*! With antennas! Eew, gross!"

I watched a blob of mud as it crawled across the ground. It was filled with hundreds and thousands of slugs. They were in the grass. They were on the benches. They were all over the bleachers. There were slugs everywhere—big ones, small ones, long ones—leaving a spiderweb of silver slime trails wherever they crawled. I figured every last slug in the county must have showed up for the game.

Hmm. They must be Slug fans too!

CHAPTER 10

Touchdown!

A few minutes later I saw Busy and the guys squishing through the front gate.

"Over here!" I waved. "I saved you some seats!"

It was a good thing too. In spite of the nasty conditions, the stands were soon filled with supporters for both teams. The Giants were decked out in bright red and green and gold; it looked like Christmas on the other side of the field. Our side looked like yesterday's lunch. We were dressed in the school colors: muddy brown and slimy green. The school mascot was a teenage kid dressed in a slug costume. He looked like a rotten hotdog with antennas and legs.

The weather matched the scene on the field. The sky was overcast and dark. It was miserable and cold and windy, and the slugs kept crawling over my shoes. The playing field got muddier and sloppier and nastier. But the worse it got, the happier Busy got.

"This is *perfect* Slug-playing weather! We've got a fighting chance—Go Slugs!"

We watched as the referees gathered both teams and their captains in the middle of the field. They flipped a coin and lost it in the mud. After three more tries, it finally came up heads. The Slugs would be first to receive the kickoff.

The advantage hardly seemed to matter. The Giants were exactly that—*giants*. There was one kid who was as big as a refrigerator. He looked like Goliath. Next to him were four more players who were bigger than any of the Slugs. They had arms that looked like truck bumpers. Everyone knew the Giants had better equipment, better players, more practice, smarter coaches, faster runners, better blockers, and fancier plays. The only thing the Slugs had was . . .

well . . . slugs. Lots of them. *Millions* of them. Too bad they couldn't run any faster than the team.

It didn't take long to see how awful it was going to be. The Giants lined up for the kickoff and booted the ball down the field. I watched the ball as it bounced and skidded through the water until it landed in the pond. The Slugs slipped and slid and crawled through the mud until they finally reached it. Four of the players got their legs tangled together and fell in a heap. By the time they finally got their arms and legs sorted out, they couldn't decide who should carry the ball. It didn't really matter. By then the Giants landed on them like a red, gold, and green elephant. The Slugs got squished under the pile.

It went from bad to worse. The Slugs ran three plays and lost fifteen yards. Then the kicker slipped on the mud and kicked the ball into the bleachers. It was worse than I could have imagined, but the guys were going crazy. "This is *fantastic*! This has to be the best they've ever played!" All the other Slug fans were going nuts too.

Then it was the Giants' turn to carry the ball. As they lined up for the first play, a hush fell over the crowd. Then the crowd joined the cheerleaders chanting quietly in the background, "Slugs. Slugs. *Slugs!*"

It was like a slow-motion ballet. The center hiked the ball. The Giants quarterback took the ball in his hands. He stepped back to throw. The slippery mud-covered ball squirted through his fingers and flopped on the ground. A Slug player tripped over his shoes and fell on it. I don't think he even knew what it was.

"Did you see that, Jon? Fumble recovery! The Slugs got the ball! On their own forty-yard line! The first fumble recovery in Slug football history!"

The bleachers rumbled with stomping feet. People waved

their flags so hard that it kicked up a small breeze. Everyone stood up and did the Slug Wave. They squealed, "Eeeeeew! Eeeeeew! It's the Slugs!"

My sister Ruth was right out in front leading the cheers. "It's better to be gross than good! Go Slugs!"

And go they did! As the first half continued, the Slugs managed to fall down at just the right second to trip the Giants. If that didn't happen, the Giants slipped on the mud or dropped the ball or stumbled over each other. Instead of blocking, players were picking slugs off their uniforms. Instead of running, they were squishing. The entire field turned into a grimy, slimy, gooey, sloppy, disgusting mess so that by halftime, neither team had scored a point. And by the final whistle for the last half, the score hadn't changed. The game was tied: 0–0!

The guys and I shouted and screamed and ran around in circles and waved our flags and did the Slug Dance. Slime Dogs (hotdogs dripping in relish) and Slug Slush (shaved ice with lime flavoring) were selling like crazy. Everybody around us was talking and laughing and cheering and slapping each other on the back. As far as the Stickville fans were concerned, the Slugs had already won only because they hadn't *lost*.

But it wasn't over. Both teams stumbled back onto the field. They were so muddy, you almost couldn't tell them apart, except for the size. All around me I could hear the whispers. Was it possible? Could the Slugs actually *win* in sudden-death overtime? Would the Giants lose to the worst football team in the history of high school sports? Maybe. Because no matter how hard they tried, the first overtime ended with the score still tied. Followed by the second. And then the third.

By the time the whistle blew for the fourth overtime, a light rain had begun to fall. Darkness descended over the field, and the lights winked on, glistening off the puddles of water and the backs of the slugs as they crawled through the mud. It was like a dream when the teams took the field for the fourth and final time.

The Giants had the ball on their own twenty-yard line, eighty yards from the end zone and victory. The quarterback took the snap and handed off to his running back. Four more Giants immediately surrounded him and formed a five-man wedge. The wedge was able to keep the running back on his feet as they bullied their way through the mud and the Slug defenders. They covered more than thirty yards before the stunned Slugs managed to drag the five players to the ground.

"Did you see that, Busy? They've come up with a new strategy. If *one* guy can't run down the field, maybe *five* can do it."

We watched as the Giants tried it again. Twenty more yards. Then a third time. Fifteen more. The coach of the Slugs called an emergency time-out, yelling at his players and waving his arms.

"How they gonna stop 'em?" Busy worried. "There's nothing they can do!"

I suddenly popped up from my seat. "No! They can. I got a brilliant idea! Wait here." I pushed between the spectators and made my way down to the sidelines.

"Jonny! Get back here!" Dad tried to grab my sleeve, but I was already gone.

"Don't worry, Dad. I'll be right back."

I squeezed between the quarterback and the coach. Both of them were dripping in mud. The coach had a smear across both cheeks, and he looked exhausted.

"Who are you?" he groaned.

"The name's Captain Marvel, and I've come to rescue you."

"Huh?"

It took a few minutes and he tried to argue, but the more I explained, the more he understood. By the time I was finished, the whole team was laughing. The referee blew his whistle. The squad broke up and headed back onto the field. The coach whacked me on the shoulder, and I ran back up to my seat.

"What was *that* all about?" Rocky asked me.

"You'll see."

On the very next play, the Giants pulled the same trick. They surrounded the ball carrier with a wedge and pushed forward, but as soon as they did, the entire defensive line of the Slugs fell flat on the ground. When the Giants trampled over the top of them, the Slugs reached up and grabbed their legs. The wedge collapsed in a Giant heap with the ball carrier in the middle, like a Slug sandwich drenched in mud sauce. They stopped them once. Twice. Three times.

"You see? I told you!" I announced proudly. "It's the one thing the Slugs are good at—*falling down*."

The Giants were now stranded on the ten-yard line, down to their very last play. But at that distance they couldn't possibly miss the kick. Could they? It still looked like the Slugs were going to lose. They broke from the huddle, lined up for the field goal, and hiked the ball.

"Ten! Fourteen! Six! Hut, hut, *hut!*" The center hiked the football to the holder. When he did, slugs went flying in every direction. The holder threw up his hands to protect himself from the sticky missiles. So instead of catching it, the football squirted past him out onto the open field. Loose ball!

The Slugs scrambled forward, sliding and stumbling and squirming through the muck. This would be their only chance.

Out in front of them was a wide-open field. All they had to do was reach the ball, pick it up, slog their way through the mud, and reach the end zone. Nothing lay between them and victory. Unfortunately, the Giants' place kicker reached the ball first.

He scooped it up, turned around, and looked for anyone who was open. Standing near the goal line, he caught a glimpse of one of his own teammates jumping up and down and waving his arms. *There!* With a mighty heave, he released the ball just as he disappeared under a pile of muddy Slugs.

The football wobbled through the air like a rubber chicken with a broken wing. It had just enough distance to reach the receiver—and it would have, if it weren't for Ruth's pom-pom that came sailing out of the rain-soaked sky like a shimmering cloud.

It all happened in slow motion. The ball flying through the air. The receiver reaching for it. The cheerleading squad throwing pom-poms and falling on the ground in a squirmy pile. Ruth's glittering silver pom-pom fluttering in a perfect arc, down the sideline, just bright enough to distract the Giants player at the fatal moment. He took his eye off the ball. It bounced off his facemask, flipped harmlessly into the air, and plopped right into the hands of one of the Slug defenders who happened to be standing nearby.

The boy looked down and stared at the ball. Where did *this* come from? Busy knew all the players and their statistics, and he said that in this kid's three years on the team, he had played in fourteen games, and in all that time he'd never *touched* the ball. He was a pass defender, but he'd never blocked a pass. He'd never made an interception. He couldn't even catch the ball during practice. Now all of a sudden the entire game was riding on his shoulders, and it looked like he didn't know what to do.

"Run!" Ruth shouted.

The other cheerleaders climbed to their feet and joined in. "Run!"

The guys and I added our voices, "Run!"

The crowd began to yell, "Run!"

The boy's legs finally began to move—fortunately in the right direction.

His name was Waldo Wainwright, number 35, five foot ten, age seventeen, a hundred and sixty pounds, a name and number that would go down in Slug football history. It was the day a Slug slipped and tripped and squirmed ninety-seven yards *untouched* into his own team's end zone. It was the day the Giants lost to the worst high school football team in history. It was the day the wind and the rain and the earth and the slugs joined together and helped lead our team to victory!

I saw it. I was *part* of it! I was there when that big, clumsy teenager tripped and slipped and squished and slid his way down the field and collapsed under the goalpost. I heard the referee blow the final whistle. The game was over. The Slugs had won! *Six to zero!*

The next day there was a parade down Bang Street in Boomtown. Waldo rode in the lead car holding the game ball. Sitting next to him was Ruth on the left and me on the right. Lining the street were thousands of grateful Slug fans. They waved brown and green flags. They ate Slime Dogs and drank Slug Slush. They released a thousand brown balloons into the air. Mayor Akihiro Tanaka made a speech. He proposed making the day an annual holiday in honor of the amazing victory. The celebration ended with a thousand tongues lifting their voices and singing the Stickville High School fight song:

In a state, in a valley, in a town so very small,
Is a place you will find the oddest school of all.
A place where the slimiest of all God's creatures crawl.
The home of the Slugs; we're the Slug capital!
They always leave their mark with a bright and silver trail.
Silently they move, over hump and hill and dale.
Nothing ever stops them; their progress cannot fail.
That's why we love the Slugs! The Slug is what we hail!
GO SLUGS!

After the singing and the cheering and more handshakes than I could count, the crowds began to leave, and we were finally able to make it back home, exhausted and totally happy. The next morning Waldo's picture appeared on the front page of the *Stickville Times*, and right next to it was one of Ruth and me. There was a caption underneath that said, "Three Local Kids Make History." The head-line above that was written in big capital letters: Slugs Slime the Giants.

I don't think I've ever seen my dad with a bigger smile as he sat drinking his coffee and reading the story. Except maybe at the Homecoming Dance a few weeks later, when Ruth was named the Slug Queen. That made him awfully proud too.

CHAPTER 11

Mr. Beedle's Front Porch

The weather continued to change until I was waking up to crisp autumn air, falling leaves, and the sweet smell of our neighbor's burn barrels. Halloween was just around the corner. It meant costumes and candy and running around town with my buddies. Halloween in Boomtown! Exploding scarecrows and pumpkin bombs. I couldn't wait.

As the weather changed, so did the fortunes of the Slugs. They got slaughtered in their next three games by scores of 97–0, 76–0, and, in the rematch against the Giants, 112–0. Not that it mattered. All anybody could talk about was the Slugs' "winning season" and how long the next losing streak would last. Busy said it would last another forty years. Frankie and Tony were predicting ten. I figured it would take another flood and a million slugs for them to win another game—so don't count on it.

Besides football, people were still talking about the day when Whiskers got loose at the church. They wondered if Mrs. Beedle would ever come back. Two of the church elders went out to see her, but she wouldn't answer the door. Dad tried to call her on the telephone over and over again, and he even sent three letters of apology. Mr. Gamelli brought them all back unopened. Dad finally decided there was only one thing left to do. He would go out to the Beedles' farm and knock on the door himself.

"You're going with me," he told Sarah. "And you too, mister."

"Why me?"

"Because you were supposed to watch your sister. And she's going . . . well, you know why she's going. You're both going to apologize. You're going to beg Mrs. Beedle for forgiveness."

Sarah pouted. "She oughta be *thankin'* me. She doesn't need that ol' walker anymore. It's still in a closet at the church."

"That isn't the point and you know it."

"Can we bring some brownies? Maybe that'd help," I suggested.

"That would be very thoughtful."

"And I'll make her a card. I'll draw a picture of Whiskers on it," Sarah said.

"No Whiskers! But the card would be a good idea."

Sarah made a very nice card with a pink ribbon on it, and she promised to be good. We drove to the Beedles' farm, parked the car, pushed open the gate, and walked up to the front door of the farmhouse. As we approached, Sarah pointed and whispered, "I saw Mrs. Beedle in the window! Her wrinkly old face. Right over there."

"Don't point, Sarah," Dad whispered back. The curtains swung shut, and no one opened the door when Dad knocked. He kept at it for a while, calling out Mrs. Beedle's name, but she still wouldn't answer. Dad was about to give up and head back to the car when a man came around the corner from behind the house. He was carrying about a dozen eggs tucked in the loop of his flannel shirt.

"Howdy there! Can I he'p you?"

"Please. Are you Mr. Beedle? I'm Pastor Button—from Boomtown Church."

"Sure thing, Pastor. I know who you are. 'Course, I didn't recognize you at first, not without your three heads and the horns."

"What? Oh, is that what Corine told you? I don't blame her, I guess. She's still pretty upset?"

"No more'n usual." He put out a weathered hand and Dad shook it. He looked like he was about sixty-five or seventy years old, with a friendly smile, black horn-rimmed glasses, a wisp of graying hair, blue overalls, red flannel shirt, and cowboy boots. When he smiled his dentures slid around, but he kept popping them back in place with his tongue. He kept one hand on the eggs and pointed at Sarah with his elbow.

"And this here must be the little miracle worker. Sarah, ain't it? Or should I call you Sorry?"

"That's me! I'm Sorry most of the time," she announced proudly.

"'Course you are." He smiled, shifting his teeth. "I heard all about you."

"You have?"

"Sure 'nough. Healed my old lady, how 'bout that! What else can you do—raise the dead?"

"I don't think so. But I *did* bring some brownies."

"Well, that's very neighborly of you, Miss Sarah. I'm Mr.

Beedle, but you can call me Old Paul. Ever'body does. What else you got there? Is that a card for my missus?"

"Yes, sir! I made it myself."

"It's very pretty," he said, accepting the card. "I'll have to take it in to her, though. Don't think she'll be coming out. That ol' woman is as stubborn as spinach stuck in your dentures. Never been able to get her to do nothin' she don't want to."

"Same as me," Sarah admitted. "I *rarely* do what I'm told."

Mr. Beedle chuckled. "Well, I sure am grateful to you, young lady. Her mood ain't improved any, but she shore is gettin' around a whole lot better. I don't trip over her walker no more. No more silly doctors, neither."

"You sure she won't talk to us?" my dad insisted. "I'd really like to apologize to her. What I mean is that *Sarah* would like to apologize, isn't that right, dear?"

Old Paul nodded his head toward the house. "Tell you what. Why don't we sit for a spell on the porch? When she sees you ain't leaving anytime soon, maybe she'll come out and say somethin'. But I wouldn't bet on it."

He held up the eggs. "I was about to cook breakfast. Why don't you join me?"

That sounded really good, and I was curious about the eggs. They were a strange color, yellowish gray and covered with spots, and the shells looked extra thick, kind of heavy. I'd never seen eggs like these before.

"Are those ostrich eggs or something?"

"These? Nah. These are something a whole lot better. C'mon up here on the porch and I'll show you."

We climbed the steps, pulled our coats a little tighter against the morning chill, and found some chairs. We gathered around the small outdoor stove where we could lean in to warm our hands. Old Paul gingerly placed the eggs in a tray and then poured my dad a cup of coffee out of a dented blue coffeepot. He broke open the brownies and offered one to Sarah, who was more than happy to eat it. Then he carefully picked up one of the eggs and held it out for us to look at.

"Don't touch! You gotta be careful with these babies. Let me show you what I mean."

He walked to the railing and heaved the egg as hard as he could. It crossed the yard and landed near his mailbox. The egg exploded with a nifty blast and sent the box flipping end over end, leaving a small crater next to the pole.

"Wow!" I shouted, hardly believing what I had seen.

"Oh my goodness!" Dad exclaimed.

Mr. Beedle picked up a second one and did it again. This time he was able to knock over the pole.

"I'll have to fix that later." He chuckled, turning to look at our startled faces.

"What was *that*?" I asked in amazement.

"That, my boy, is what ya' call a Hen Grenade."

"A Hen Grenade?"

"Yep! Invented by the world famous fireworks genius Chang hisself. Right there in his own fireworks factory."

"Really? How'd he do it?"

"Nobody knows. It's a carefully guarded fireworks factory secret. I buy mine over at the Red Bird. Keep 'em in my shed. They make delicious omelets, you know—fluffy and extra spicy—but you got to be careful! Crack 'em wrong and you can blow up yer griddle. Done it a few times myself."

We begged Dad to let us throw one, and he finally gave in as long as Old Paul was there to help us. I threw one into a big pile of

Old Paul let me hold one of the hen grenades.

leaves and watched them go flying in every direction. Sarah's didn't go as far, and she blew a hole in the Beedles' sidewalk.

"Don't you worry about that, young lady. I'll plant some flowers in the hole next spring."

"You gotta tell us where these came from," I said, staring at the hole. There were little piles of steaming fluffy white eggs all over the edges.

He asked my dad if he was in any hurry and Dad said no. He wanted to know all about it as much as I did! So we sat down on the porch while Old Paul *very carefully* cracked the eggs and started making omelets. As the eggs sizzled, he told us the story.

"That ol' Chang was always coming up with crazy ideas. One day he started mixing gunpowder with the fertilizer he put in his garden. Not so good at first. He got zucchinis that exploded if you dropped them, pumpkins that carved themselves in the patch, and apples that blew holes in the ground when they fell off the tree. But after a while, he got it figgered out.

"Purty soon he was selling Chang's POPcorn. Every kernel was guaranteed to pop or you got your money back. Then he came up with Chang's Hotcakes; those are pancakes that explode when they get stepped on. It's a great way for getting rid of gophers, and they taste pretty good with maple syrup—the pancakes, I mean, not the gophers.

"But what about the Hen Grenades?" Sarah interrupted.

"Hang on there, missy. I was gettin' to that. Eat your omelet and listen. Is it any good, by the way?"

"It's delicious! Tastes like the Fourth of July."

"Exactly. So here's what happened. Some of the POPcorn got mixed in with the feed he gave to his chickens by accident. One afternoon, one of the chickens tripped in the hen house and BOOM! Nothin' left but scrambled eggs and fried chicken!

"Ol' Chang was simply beside himself with grief. He *loved* that chicken. But it gave him this crazy idea. What if he could turn *regular* chicken eggs into *exploding* chicken eggs? At first, he blew the roof off his shop and knocked over the neighbor's fence. Scared the fur off his dog too. But after some tinkering, Chang got the mixture just right. The eggs ended up looking like this." He held up the last one and showed it to us.

"You see? Yellowy gray with dark speckles and an extra-thick shell. If you handle 'em right, they're more or less safe. But don't drop one!"

For the first time I noticed that each of the eggs had a stamp on it. In black letters: Hen Grenade. And on the flip side: Chang's Famous Fireworks Factory.

Old Paul kept going. "After that, Chang contacted the U.S. Army and did a purty brisk business supplying the military with these little egg bombs. The army used them for years. Very few people know this, but them eggs were an important secret weapon during the First World War. The Allies in France were able to sneak ammunition through enemy lines disguised as breakfast. The Germans never knew what hit 'em."

CHAPTER 12

The Amazing Chang

"Tell us more!" Sarah giggled. Usually she wouldn't sit still for five minutes, but she was sitting quietly on the edge of her chair, munching on another brownie and hanging on Old Paul's every word. I could tell he was enjoying himself too. Probably didn't have too many kids coming out to his farm as an audience—not with grumpy ol' Mrs. Beedle hiding around the corner. So he was more than happy to tell us a few more stories.

"Did ya' know that Boomtown wasn't always called Boomtown? It used to be nothing more than a bunch of tents and shacks thrown together between nowhere and someplace else. It was way back in the days of the railroad, back when all you could find out here were Indians, buffalo, and wild coyotes, and there was only the main railroad line that reached from coast to coast. But with more and more settlers coming out West, they started adding branch lines north and south.

"One day, a Chinese man named Yi Chang showed up. He was a whiz with gunpowder. He'd learned all about it from his father and his grandfather before that and the one before that—I guess it was what you might call a family hobby. All the railroad companies wanted him. He could take the smallest pinch of his homemade gunpowder and blow the spots off a ladybug. That's what they used to say. He was the best in the business."

"What about gold? Didn't they want the gunpowder so they could search for gold?"

Old Paul nodded while he sipped his coffee. "That's what got the transcontinental railroad built in the first place: the California Gold Rush in 1848. A coupla' years later the gold started to run out, but all them prospectors still had gold dust in their eyes. They didn't want to quit looking. So they disappeared into the north, digging for gold up in the hills and mountains all over the place up here."

Old Paul leaned out over the railing on his porch and pointed. "You see up there? Past the river and up over that hill? They call that Rocket Ridge. A feller struck a mighty big vein of gold up there. Word spread purty quick 'til every rock and hill had a mine going—there were so many holes it looked like Swiss cheese! And there was Chang right in the thick of it. He was the main supplier of high-grade black powder for opening mines and blasting tunnels. The Washington gold rush turned Chang into a very popular and wealthy man! Yep, that's for sure."

"Did he dig for gold too?"

"Nah, he was never interested in the stuff. The only thing he cared about was gunpowder. It was 'cause of him this whole town sprang up—shops, grocers, a blacksmith, a school, a church. People came and stayed. Soon there was the prettiest little town you ever saw, nestled on the top of a hill with Chang sitting on top of it, as rich as King Midas hisself. And to celebrate his good fortune, he'd throw a huge party every Fourth of July and invite everyone from miles around. They'd come see his amazing fireworks and rockets and firecrackers. The future was looking bright. Woulda stayed that way if Chang hadn't been so itchy."

"Itchy?" Sarah asked. "He had a rash? I had one of those once. Chicken pox. I was red all over. I couldn't stop scratching. It got so bad—"

I poked her with a finger. "That's not what he meant. Be quiet."

Old Paul chuckled at the interruption. "I meant Chang was always *inventing* things, like the Hen Grenades I told you about. Like this thing over here. C'mon and take a look."

He stood up and took us over to the front door where he showed us his welcome mat. It didn't look so special until I noticed the fuse running underneath the door. "This is watcha' call the Ding-Dong-So-Long. It's an exploding welcome mat—the perfect way to scare off those pesky traveling salesmen."

"Really?"

"Yep. The guy rings the bell. *Ding-dong*. You light the fuse. So long! Works like a charm. Haven't had any of them pests out to my place in years!"

"Wow, Dad. We gotta get ourselves one of these things."

"If you're interested, Preacher, you can pick 'em up from Martin's Mercantile in the main square. Only $4.95 plus tax."

"I'll have to think about it, thanks."

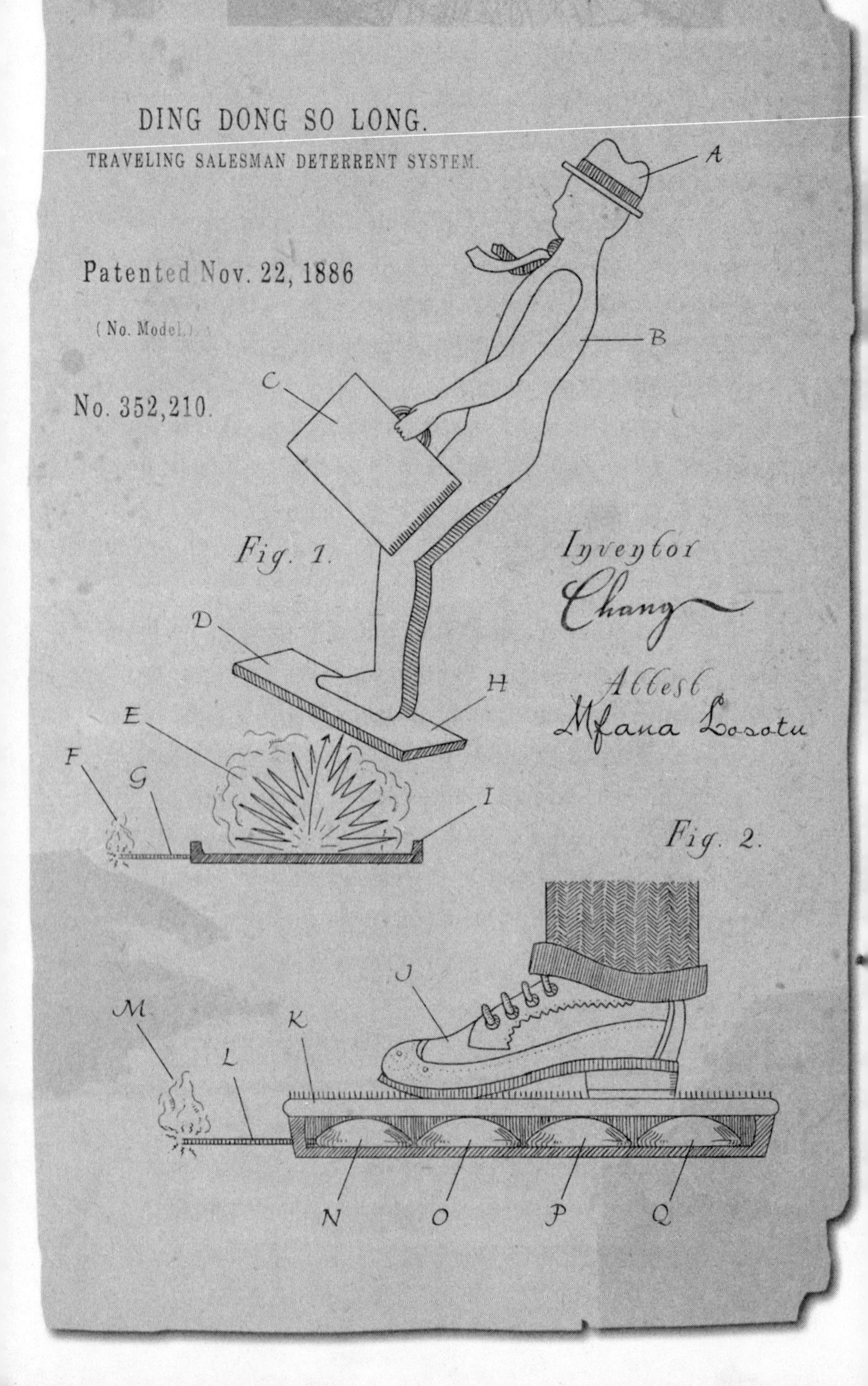
DING DONG SO LONG.
TRAVELING SALESMAN DETERRENT SYSTEM.
Patented Nov. 22, 1886
(No. Model.)
No. 352,210.
A
B
C
Fig. 1.
Inventor
Chang
D
H
Attest
Mfana Losotu
E
F
G
I
Fig. 2.
J
M
K
L
N
O
P
Q

"You think *this* is great, it ain't even the half of it!" Old Paul laughed. "Chang was the one who invented the handy, dandy Drain Gun. No more clogged drains. Put the rubber end against the sink opening and pull the trigger. Pow! I got me one of those too."

"What else? What else?" Sarah demanded, jumping up and down.

"There's the Tree Magician. Drill a few holes, stuff some bomb packets in there, light the fuse, stand back. Guaranteed to relocate the tree or your money back. And Chang's TNT Tea Bags, in convenient two-ounce packets. Instructions say to steep one teabag in a gallon of rubbing alcohol for an hour, then pour and light. Great for starting campfires—or burning down barns—'fraid that's what happened when I used 'em."

My dad wasn't as excited about all of this as Sarah was. "Sounds to me like a lot of the things Chang invented were . . . well, you know . . . *dangerous*. Exploding welcome mats? Blowing up trees? Nitro teabags? What's next? Dynamite to remove warts?"

Old Paul nodded. "Not a bad idea, Preacher! Wish I'da thought of that one! 'Course you're right. Not all of Chang's ideas were good ones. There was that Dandruff Destroyer he came up with—supposed to get rid of dandruff—and it did. Also blew off a person's hair. That was bad.

"And then Chang's BOOMerang. Throw it at crows to scare 'em out of your fields. 'Course the timing mechanism never worked right, and the thing would come circling back around. That was very, very bad.

"And Chang's Bee Blaster. Had a ten-foot pole so you could stick a blast pack into a bee's nest. That one was very, very, *very* bad, take my word for it," he said, rubbing his rear end.

I could tell all this blowing-stuff-up talk was making Dad

nervous. He kept counting the buttons on this coat and glancing at his watch. But I wanted to hear more. I could listen to Old Paul all day long.

"Where'd he get all the gunpowder? He'd have to have a whole mess of it to make all that stuff."

"He cooked it up himself. That was one of the reasons he liked Washington so much. One of the things he needed was sulfur, and with all the volcanoes that used to be around here, it was purty easy to dig up. You know what else he needed?"

"Sure," I answered proudly. "We're learning all about it at school. Charcoal and saltpeter."

My dad sputtered. "You're learning how to make gunpowder in *school*?"

"Why not? What *else* would we learn about in Boomtown?"

"Oh, I don't know. How about different types of birds and all the names of the presidents?"

"Boring. I'd rather learn about gunpowder."

Old Paul continued, "For that you need charcoal, which Chang got from all his neighbors who were more than happy to donate ashes from their stoves and fireplaces. And saltpeter; you need that too. Chang got permission from the miners to gather bat guano from inside the mining caves. Bat doo doo. Really potent stuff!

"With all those ingredients, he started making his own black powder. But the more his inventions caught on, the bigger his business got. In only a few years, his powder factory was the biggest business in town. Everybody wanted it. Chang's Super Duper Bat Doo Doo Black Powder. The railroads, the military, mining companies—they all lined up to get it.

"Our little town just kept getting bigger and bigger until one day, Chang opened up his Famous Fireworks Factory where the best fireworks in the whole world are still getting made. So what do you think of that, you little whippersnappers?"

"I think it's the greatest thing I've ever heard!"

"I think it's fantastic!"

"I think you're all nuts," my dad said.

"Nuts? What do you mean?"

"A whole town, built around *dynamite*? When we moved here I thought it was called Boomtown after one of those places that spring up out of nowhere. You know, a 'boom town'? I didn't think it was *literal*."

"You're right," Old Paul said. "It hasn't *always* been called Boomtown. The original town was founded back in 1878. When the people drew up the town charter and filed papers with the state, they wanted to name it after Chang. They were going to call it Changville or Changtown or Chang City."

"So why didn't they?"

"Chang wouldn't let 'em. He didn't want any credit for himself. He said, 'We built this town together—not just me—*all* of us did it. Call it something else.' So they did. They all took a vote, stuck an *e* on the end of his name, and called it 'Change.' Change, Washington, born on May 18, 1878. They adopted the town motto 'Change Is for the Better' and the chicken as its official mascot in honor of the Hen Grenade that had helped to make the place famous.

"That's why, by the way, you'll find a chicken on the town seal, clutching two sticks of dynamite in its claws. And the statue of Chang in the middle of Town Square. You must have seen it out in front of the courthouse, with two chickens in his lap and one at his feet? It's carved right there on the monument: 'Chang, Founding Father of Change, Washington. September 8, 1830–April 12, 1892.'"

It was a great story. Chang working for the railroad, traveling across the frontier, chasing the prospectors up to Washington, getting rich and famous with all his inventions, and having a town named after him. But I still couldn't figure it out. Old Paul said the town used to be on a hill. But it wasn't on a hill now. The whole town was mostly flat. And it wasn't called Change. It was called Boomtown. *How come*? I wondered.

"Mr. Beedle, can I ask you something?"

My dad stopped me. "We've taken up enough of Mr. Beedle's morning. I'm sure he's got other things to do than tell stories to my kids. Say good-bye and thank him for breakfast. You can ask him more questions later."

We stood up and shook his hand. "But what about *Mrs*. Beedle?" I asked.

Dad shrugged and asked Old Paul, "I was hoping to talk to Corine today. You sure we can't smooth things over before we leave?"

Mr. Beedle squinted and said, "Well, Pastor, I'm sure you know your business better than I do, but some things don't *ever* get fixed. Try as hard as you want, Mrs. Beedle may never come around. She's pretty stubborn."

"I don't believe that. I like to think that you can fix anything if you try hard enough."

Mr. Beedle shook his head. "You think so? I'm not so sure. But I'll tell you what. I haven't been to church in years—but I like you. I'll tell Corine that if she'll go back to church, I'll go with her. That oughta do it. She's been trying to save my sorry soul since before we was hitched. I'll see you this Sunday, Preacher. How's that sound?"

"Okay, sure. I guess so," Dad answered with surprise. "Thank you, Paul. I guess we'll see you tomorrow. I hope so."

Sarah and I waved good-bye from the car window as we drove away, and I started thinking about my dad. He was a lot like Mrs. Beedle. Not sick all the time, not like that, but he could be stubborn. And he was nervous all the time. He always wanted everything to run smoothly. He liked things to be calm and predictable. I remember him telling me once, "If everyone would just follow the rules and behave, then we could live in peace. We'd all be able to get along."

But I wasn't so sure. That sounded too easy. People couldn't always act the way we wanted them to. I sure had trouble doing it. My dad did too. *He* wasn't perfect. What if Old Paul was right? What if some things *couldn't* be fixed? How do you make room for people who don't fit in?

The next day Old Paul was in church and sitting next to him was Mrs. Beedle (without a cane or a walker). Sarah tried to give her a hug, but Mrs. Beedle just frowned and crossed her arms. Everybody was glad to see her and was nice to her and Mr. Beedle. Then after church, we went out to lunch with the Beedles at the Nuthouse Restaurant and had peanut-butter sundaes for dessert. Mrs. Beedle didn't say much during the meal, but she sort of smiled when I told her the story about Dad almost getting smashed by the barber chair, and she gave Sarah the cherry off her sundae, so it looked like she was coming around after all. Then Old Paul led us out into the Town Square to take a closer look at the statue.

There was Chang sitting on a chair and surrounded by chickens. His name was carved on the pedestal just like Mr. Beedle said. The town motto was chipped into the stone right under that: Change Is for the Better.

"What do you think, Dad?"

"What do I think about what?"

"About *change*. Is it better sometimes?"

He looked down at me and seemed to understand what I was talking about.

"Maybe it is, Jon. Maybe it is. I ought to try it—and see what happens."

It felt good to hear him say it—but he probably *wouldn't* have said it if he knew what was about to happen next.

CHAPTER 13

Ghost of Halloween

"Mom!" I yelled.

She popped her head out of the girls' bedroom where she was helping Sarah squeeze into her monkey costume. Sarah didn't fit into it like she did last year; she had grown that much since coming to Boomtown. She was a much bigger monkey than before.

"What is it, Jonny? I've got my hands full in here."

"The fuse on my costume keeps falling over. I can't get it to stay up."

"You'll have to live with it, dear. It's getting too late. Just look outside; it's already dark."

I went back to the bathroom mirror and tried one more time to straighten out the fuse. It kept flopping over sideways like an overcooked spaghetti noodle. I heard the front doorbell ring, followed by the shouting of "Trick or treat!" Too late. I had to get going; the gang would be waiting for me.

Still, I had to admit that the overall effect was satisfying. A big red firecracker smiled back at me out of the mirror. Wait till the guys got a load of this! My face was painted bright red and it matched my firecracker hat perfectly. It went with the firecracker suit that Mom had sewed for me, and I had red pants underneath with black sneakers. And instead of carrying a pillowcase like most kids, my dad had let me take the ash bucket from our fireplace to haul all the candy I was going to get. Mom stopped us at the front door to take our picture before she would let us leave. Then Sarah went off with her little friends, and I went off to join Busy and the other guys. Ruth was too old for trick-or-treating anymore. Instead she had dressed up as a black cat and had already driven over to the Stickville gymnasium with some friends for the Halloween dance. Dad would stay home with Mom and man the doorway.

"Have a blast!" my dad joked as I ran down the sidewalk. "Sarah! Stay with your friends! Don't try and trick anybody! I mean it!"

My first stop was Mitterand's Boarding House where I had arranged to meet the twins, Frankie and Tony. When they saw me coming through the gate, they bundled across the big porch dressed as twin Hen Grenades, shouting as they came.

"KABOOM!" they yelled.

"KERBLOOIE!" I echoed. "Great costumes! Did your mom make them?"

"Yeah. We stuffed 'em with crumpled newspapers to make them rounder. Keeps us warm too."

I had two sweatshirts on underneath my costume, and I was

wearing extra-thick gloves. I was going to need them. I shivered against the chilly October wind that cut along the backside of the buildings that lined the avenue. We walked along Volcano Way to the top of Bang Street to meet up with Rocky, Bobby, and Busy. Damp gray clouds skittered across the full moon, casting eerie shadows into all the corners, turning bushes and trees into crouching wolves and shaded monsters. It was perfect Halloween weather, and we had fun pointing out different costumes as we hurried along.

"Look over there. Frankenstein's monster and the Werewolf!"

"Did you see the two robots? They looked like the Tin Man from *The Wizard of Oz*."

"I think they *were* the Tin Man. I saw Dorothy and a couple of Munchkins going around with them."

"What do you think Busy is going as this year?"

We soon found out. He stood impatiently on the corner, tapping his foot, dressed as a rocket, complete with a pointy hat covered in tin foil and red and yellow flames hanging out of the bottom of his silver tube. The Famous Fireworks logo was painted on the side, and he had a fistful of sparklers to go with his costume. One of them was burning, almost as hot as the look in his eyes. He looked like he might want to explode.

"You guys are late!" he grumbled, gesturing down the street at all the kids running back and forth between the shops. Standing next to him was Rocky, dressed as a matchstick. His red hair was sticking straight up. It was made to look like it was on fire. And next to him stood Bobby, who was made up to look like a smoke bomb, with cotton balls glued all over his black suit. I thought he looked more like a dirty sheep.

"All the good stuff is going to be gone by now! Let's hurry up."

Busy was wrong, though. The shop owners in Boomtown made it an annual tradition to hand out the best candy and goodies every year. This year wasn't any different. At Dr. Goldberg's office, we got licorice ropes long enough to take down a wild mustang. At the Red Bird there were fist-sized jawbreakers. At Top's Soda Shop we each got a huge Hershey bar.

Even at Walt's Barber Shop we got something super. Walt stood out front on the sidewalk, wearing his apron, standing seven feet tall, and looking like a troll. He didn't need a costume. He was scary all by himself. But he was handing out pinwheel lollypops that were as big as tennis rackets. It was going to take a year to eat one of those things!

We made our way back and forth down the street until we reached Town Square. Then we stopped to argue about which direction we would head next. Busy wanted to run over to Mabel's Diner; it was just around the corner behind Martin's Mercantile. She looked like the Wicked Witch of the West every day of the week—she didn't need a costume either. But he heard that she would be giving out cinnamon fire candy—one of Busy's favorites—and he was willing to face her just to get some.

"She'll bite our heads off!" Frankie warned. "I saw her do it once. There was this kid sitting in one of her booths. Said somethin' wrong. She swallowed his head! Snatched it right off his neck. All in one bite."

"She did *not*!" Tony snorted. "She's not all that bad. Just her coffee. My dad says it'll take the paint off a car if you aren't careful."

"I want to head back into the neighborhood anyway," Bobby sniffed. "It's getting cold out here and Mom says she'll have Halloween cocoa for us when we get there."

"What's Halloween cocoa?"

"She puts worms and bugs and snakes in it—and food coloring, so it looks all red and bloody. It stains your teeth so you look like a vampire. It's great!"

We voted to start heading toward Bobby's house, in spite of Busy's complaining. We would have made it too, if we hadn't seen Chang's ghost. We saw him, standing alone in the dark, looking up at his statue in the middle of Town Square. He was dressed all in white and looked exactly the same as the figure in the chair, the same height, the same clothes, the same face. It was spooky how much he looked like Chang. It scared us half to death!

"Look!" Busy cried, pointing at the "ghost." His shout startled the ghost because he hadn't noticed us coming across the square. He gasped in surprise and then spun around and ran away toward Farmer's Park, across the cement and through the wet grass and into the darkness.

"After him!" I yelled, breaking into a sprint. The other guys ran after me—you should have seen it: two Hen Grenades, a rocket, a matchstick, and a dirty sheep chasing a firecracker. Our heavy bags of candy kept banging against our legs.

"It's hard to run in this thing!" Busy panted, stumbling as we crossed over Run for Your Life Road and down Crumble Street.

"Yeah?" complained the twins. "Try running while dressed up as an *egg*! You think that's any easier?"

I held up my hand and skidded to a stop. "*Shhhh!* I think I see him up ahead. Over there in the bushes next to the Nuthouse."

"Yeah, I see him," Busy agreed, huffing and puffing. His hot breath made clouds of steam in the cold air. "Where do you think he's going?"

"He's crossing the street. He's climbing over the fence. That's your dad's farm, isn't it?"

"Yep. He's going out into the field. Let's follow him."

So we did, very slowly and carefully. First we stashed all our candy behind the Nuthouse, and then we headed toward the field. We kept as close to the ground as we could and tried to stay back so he couldn't see us. We went start and stop from one bale of corn stalks to another that were standing bundled in the fields like dried out scarecrows in the darkness. All the while the lurking figure remained out in front, turning past Mr. Gunderson's barn, past the windmill, and heading toward the black powder factory in the distance. We could see the dark stain of smoke spreading lazily across the sky as it crept out of the twin cones, casting a fingery shadow over the moon.

"Where's he going?" Bobby hissed nervously, pulling on my sleeve.

"I think he's headed out to the fireworks factory."

Busy whispered, "He must be going there to haunt it!"

"Huh?"

"It's Chang's ghost. He's going back to his factory. That's what ghosts do."

"There's no such thing as ghosts," I insisted.

"You don't think so? Well, *I* do. Where did we see him first?"

"Out in front of Chang's statue."

"And what was he wearing?"

"A white robe."

"And who did he look like?"

"Chang—sort of."

"He looked *exactly* like Chang." All the guys nodded in agreement.

"And where is he going now?"

"To Chang's factory."

"Exactly! I rest my case. He's a ghost."

I looked at my friend and frowned. Busy's eyes were shining with excitement in the moonlight, but his costume was a mess. He had left his pointy hat back by the Nuthouse. Rocky's hair was sticking out more than ever. The twins weren't round anymore. They had left a trail of crumpled newspaper all the way back to Town Square, same as the little cotton droppings that had fallen off of Bobby's costume. All of us wanted to keep going, but I could tell they were scared of the ghost.

"I think all of you are crazy. I'm telling you, there's no such thing."

"What difference does it make? He's getting away! We got to catch him!"

We raced over the field, jumped the fence, and ran across Dynamite Drive. We saw the white outline of our quarry float around the corner of the main fireworks factory and out of sight. We ran past Popgun Pond and across the little bridge with our feet pounding and our hearts thumping. Gasping for breath, we came up into the shadow of the huge brick building. We poked our heads around the edge and looked around. He was gone.

"How'd he do that? Look. There's no place to hide. It's all wide open back here."

We walked out into the large parking area and tried to find him. The moon shone down from overhead like a giant spotlight. Nothing. He had disappeared.

"You see!" Busy claimed with satisfaction. "I told you so! He vanished into thin air. He's a ghost. He *has* to be."

I just stood there scratching my head and peering into the darkness. Maybe Busy was right. Maybe he *was* a ghost. It sure was spooky, that's all I've got to say!

CHAPTER 14

Stake Out

The next morning was Tuesday, and we had to go to school. I was tired all day, after being up so late and chasing phantoms through cornfields and eating too much candy. But as soon as the school bell rang I shot out the door with Busy, and we ran all the way to Tebs's Salvage Yard. The twins and Rocky and Bobby caught up with us at the entrance to our secret hideout.

In the alley just behind St. Bernard's Lutheran Church there was a loose board that let you in through the fence. You couldn't see it hidden behind the blackberry bushes that bordered the edge of the driveway, and it was too prickly for most people to crawl in. But if you did, you could push aside the board, and it would let you into Mr. Tebido's salvage yard. Everyone called him Tebs for short.

Busy had found it one day while he was playing Hide and Seek. After that he and the guys worked on making a tunnel through the old car parts and piles of tires and stacks of wood until they reached the middle. There was an old rusty potbelly stove buried under the pile, so they kept moving the stuff around to create a kind of a room. They put up some canvas and tarps for a roof. They laid out cinderblock and some boards for benches. Once you got the stove going it was pretty cozy in there. That's where we met to discuss our next step.

"We got to say the secret oath first," Busy insisted.

"Can't we skip it this time? We got a lot to talk about."

"No. We *got* to say the oath. That's the rule."

"Oh, all right."

We stood with our backs to each other like a circle of wagons guarding a camp. Then we hopped up and down on one foot as we turned like a wheel until at the end we were all facing each other. We pointed our fingers like a gun, finished the oath, and then punched each other in the shoulders. I never liked that last part.

"Scoot, boot, hide the loot,

North, South, East and West,

Tell the secret and we'll have to shoot,

Swear it now on pain of death. OUCH!"

It wasn't a very good rhyme and Busy always punched me too hard, but he was the one who came up with the oath so you had to do it or else you couldn't be in the gang. I rubbed my shoulder and found a seat near the warm stove.

"So what are we going to do? Who was he, do you think?"

Busy answered, "You already know what I think."

"Let's not start *that* again. He was a real person and you know it. We found his footprints in the dirt. Ghosts don't leave footprints."

"They do if they're trying to trick you. Ghosts are like that."

Rocky interrupted the argument. "I think he's the one who's been taking all the stuff from around town. My dad says stuff's gone missing from out in back of the Mercantile."

"And our lawn mower was stolen right after we moved in."

"We can't find our bicycles," the twins both said.

"And Dad says somebody took all the wood for the new fence he was going to build," Busy admitted.

"So he's probably the one taking stuff—he must be stashing it out somewhere near the factory."

"But why?"

"That's what we're going to find out," I said. "We're super heroes, remember? And super heroes catch bad guys."

"Let's not be super heroes this time," Frankie said. "Let's be FBI men, out to track down John Dillinger."

"Yeah," Tony added. "We can all wear hats and pretend to carry Tommy guns."

"And we can take down clues in a notebook. I got a magnifying glass. That'll help."

"And I got a pair of fake handcuffs. We'll need those once we catch the notorious outlaw."

"Sounds great!" we all agreed. "So here's the plan."

We spent another couple of hours laying out the details and then spent the next few days getting ready. That Friday night I climbed down the walnut tree as quiet as a mouse and snuck across the back lawn and over the fence. I had on a felt hat pulled down over my eyes to make me look mysterious, and I was wearing my dad's overcoat and my rubber boots. I also carried a wooden pistol that I carved out of a hickory branch. You can't be too careful when hunting criminals!

I found the other guys right where we planned, hiding in Busy's barn. All of them were dressed like FBI agents. Busy had a sheriff's star cut out of an old tin plate. It was pinned to the shoulder of his coat. The twins were both wearing their cowboy holsters with their cap pistols. Bobby and Rocky had painted red scars on their necks.

"Makes us look tough," Rocky said, "so the bad guy won't mess with us when we catch him."

We snuck out of the barn and headed over to where we had last seen the "ghost." Frankie and Tony hid in the shadows by the corner. Busy and I took our spots at the opposite end. Bobby and Rocky went across the parking lot and hid in the bushes. It was pitch black that night—no moon at all—so it was going to be hard to see. But we had carefully practiced our hooting. If any of us saw or heard anything, we would make a hooting sound, like a night owl, and the rest of us would come running.

Now all we had to do was wait. It was awfully cold sitting there hunched in the dark. It had rained earlier that day and looked like it was going to rain again. The ground was all wet, with puddles glinting dully on the asphalt and fog rolling in off the river. It was eerie, like a scene out of Sherlock Holmes. We were like detectives searching the streets of London, trying to catch a world-renowned jewel thief while all of Scotland Yard had failed. It was only a matter of time before he struck again and stole the crown jewels!

"What do you think, my good Watson?" Busy whispered in his fake English accent.

"I'm not sure, Holmes. We should have seen something by now."

That's when we heard hooting coming from the bushes on the far side. The branches began to rustle, and out from between them came our mysterious man, dressed this time in a thick flannel shirt and pants, with boots on his feet and one of those miner's caps on his head. He quickly covered the beam with a gloved hand and turned it off, glancing left and right to see if anyone was watching. Then he stepped out onto the cement, crossed the open deck, and slipped across the road.

As soon as he was gone, we all hooted at the same time and ran out into the middle for a powwow.

"Did you see that? What are we going to do?"

"He's gone for now. Let's go into the bushes where he came out and see what we can find."

We ran to the spot, and Busy flicked on a flashlight. We found a trail through a thicket of bushes. We followed the line of fresh footprints that were filled with muddy water.

"There!" he hissed when his light fell against the wall of a brick building. It was low, only one story high, with a metal roof, rotting and rusted, and trees growing up through the holes. The walls were covered in a blanket of ivy and moss, and most of the windows were missing their glass. We stumbled along the edge of the wall until we came to a heavy wooden door with wheels at the top. On the ground were fresh tire tracks that led through the bushes. Branches had been dragged into place to hide the exit, but it was obvious. This is where our "ghost" must have been coming in and out.

It took four of us to slide the heavy door to one side. We expected the door to stick or at least squeak from all the rust on the wheels, but it glided silently along its tracks as though it had been freshly greased. As soon as it was open, the flashlight reflected off the bumper and license plate of a pickup truck that was sitting waiting for its driver. We looked inside and found the keys in the ignition. The bed of the truck was filled to the top edge with dirt.

"This is Fred Cotton's truck!" Frankie exclaimed. "I'm sure of it—he's given me rides in it lots of times."

"I thought it got lost in the rain storm."

"That's what the newspaper said—but here it is!"

We walked around behind the truck and were met with an even bigger surprise. Lying open on the cement floor were two large doors with hinges on them. Coming up out of the hole was a conveyor belt of some kind, leading up out of the darkness and into the back of the truck. Next to that was a ladder leading down into the pit, with an old kerosene lamp sitting on the edge.

"What do we do next?" Tony whispered nervously.

"What else? We climb down," Busy answered.

"We do? Not me. *You* go first."

"Huh? Somebody's got to stay up here on lookout. I'm not going."

"How about Captain Marvel, then? This whole thing was his idea in the first place."

"Me? Why me?"

We stood there arguing for a few minutes, none of us brave enough to climb down a ladder into a pitch black hole that was being dug by a dangerous outlaw who had already stolen a truck and a whole bunch of other stuff. Who knows what he was doing down there? We probably would still be standing there fighting about it if he hadn't come right up behind us and scared our pants off.

"Ahhhh!" I screamed.

"Oh nooooo!" the twins shouted.

"Don't kill us!" Rocky cried.

What a bunch of fraidy-cat FBI men we turned out to be!

Fortunately for us, Busy kept his head and pulled out his cap pistol and tried to sound brave. "Don't move, mister. You're under arrest! Go ahead, Bobby. Put the cuffs on him."

"*You* do it!" Bobby shouted, throwing them at his feet. They fell into the hole and disappeared. Bobby backed away with his hands sticking up in the air.

"Don't be afraid," the man whispered. "I'm not going to hurt anybody."

"Afraid?" Busy sounded offended. "We ain't afraid. You oughta be afraid of *us*, 'cause as soon as we get out of here we're gonna tell the cops what you been doing!"

The man's headlamp was on, and the bright light was making it hard to see. I was getting a little bit braver myself and said, "Take off your helmet so we can see your face."

He reached up, took off the helmet, and shone the beam onto the ground. In a few seconds our eyes began to adjust, and I could get a better look at him. It was definitely the same man—the one we'd seen on Halloween standing in front of Chang's statue. He looked more like Chang than ever! The same exact face as on the Famous Fireworks logo—it was almost like looking at a photograph.

"Who *are* you?" I asked, swallowing hard and checking to see the exit. We could probably all make it if we bolted at the same time. I started counting to ten and got ready to yell.

"I'm . . ." He paused, blinking his eyes and glancing back and forth at each of us. "I'm nobody important," he finally answered. "I'm just looking for something."

"Looking for something? For what?"

He passed a tired hand over his forehead. For the first time I noticed how thin he was under his thick shirt and pants. He was covered in dirt and mud from head to toe and was not really much taller than I was, with dirt under his fingernails and smudges on his face. His skin was smooth—he didn't look that old, maybe thirty or forty—and his black hair was pulled behind his head into a tight ponytail that ran down the middle of his back. He didn't look dangerous at all. He just looked sad. And very, very tired.

"Something that was lost a long time ago. Something that belongs to me."

"What is it?" Busy repeated.

"I can't tell you. It's a secret."

"Well, at least tell us your name."

The man looked like he was about to tell us but then changed his mind. "I guess that's a secret too."

Busy took charge. "Come on over here, guys." We walked over into the corner and put our heads down in a circle.

"I don't know about any of you, but he looks like he could use our help. Did you see him? He looks half starved. I'll bet he hasn't had anything good to eat in months."

"So what do you want to do?"

"I think we should help him. Help him find whatever it is he's looking for. It must be pretty important—or he wouldn't be killing himself to find it."

"But what about all the stuff he's stolen? He must be hiding it down there in the hole."

Busy shrugged. "So we found it already. It isn't missing anymore. It's still right here in Boomtown. He's just *borrowing* the stuff, if you see what I mean. And if we help him, then it'll be like Boomtown is helping him. That's what my dad would say."

"Do you think we should ask your dad about it?"

"No! We don't tell anybody anything! We'll help this guy find what he lost and then we'll see. Who knows? We could end up as heroes! That's what we've always wanted, right? Here's our big chance!"

So we took a vote and decided right then and there to help him, but I still wasn't so sure. Was this a good idea? You'll have to keep reading to find out.

CHAPTER 15

Wrong Turn

From that night on our little group took turns in shifts helping our nameless ghost dig his hole. My mom and dad started to notice. Morning after morning they found muddy footprints on the back porch, and my clothes were always filthy dirty.

"What is it that you boys are doing out there?" my mom asked.

"What?"

"Look at you! You're tired all the time. Your clothes are a shambles. There's always dirt in your hair and mud in your ears. And your arms. Just look at your muscles. You must have gained ten pounds—and you eat like a horse."

"It must be a growth spurt, sweetheart," my dad suggested. "He's what? Eleven years old—almost twelve now? It happens at about this age."

"But look at him! *Nobody* can eat that much." I guess she had noticed all the missing food from our pantry. I was getting worried.

My dad measured me with his stare and scratched his head. "He does seem taller, maybe half an inch. It could be the water here in Boomtown. And all that fresh air. He never comes inside anymore. What do you say, Jon?"

I smiled sheepishly and tried to hide my guilty feelings. "That must be it. I drink a lot of water. And I breathe all the time. And the guys and me, we're always doing something. Climbing and running and stuff. Boomtown is like Popeye and spinach—chock full of vitamins! I'm sure that must be it."

They let me go, but I still caught Mom looking at me sideways whenever she had to wash another load of my muddy laundry or sew up the holes in my pants. I tried to be more careful after that. I didn't want to raise any more questions than I could answer.

They were right, of course. With all the digging and hauling we were doing, I could feel the muscles in my arms and legs getting stronger. Busy and the other farm kids had worked hard since they were little. All this lifting and digging was new for me, but after the first six weeks I could keep up with any of them.

Not that all we did was dig. There were mostly whole sections of tunnels that didn't need any digging at all. The digging was just in those places that had caved in. All we had to do was clear out the dirt and rocks and shore up the ceiling. I asked Busy about this one night while we were helping our silent leader fit new beams for the ceiling.

"So where'd all these tunnels come from in the first place?" I asked, wiping my forehead and leaning on a shovel. Our "ghost" didn't say anything—just like always—but I could tell that he was as interested in Busy's answer as much as I was.

"These? They've always been here. Well, not always. But since back before Boomtown was called Boomtown."

"Oh yeah, I remember Old Paul telling us about that, about all those folks digging for gold. But he never said why they changed the town's name."

Busy grabbed the water jug, took a drink, and then sat down on a big rock to tell me the story.

"This whole town used to be on top of a hill. It was filled with holes all over the place—from all the prospectors. It looked like a swarm of woodpeckers had attacked it. I've seen the old pictures."

"So where'd it go? The hill, I mean. This town seems awfully flat to me."

"Way back then, Chang needed a place to store all of his gunpowder and fireworks and dynamite. He couldn't leave it lying around in his *kitchen*, you know! One spark and he could blow the whole town to smithereens. So he started putting it underneath the ground in all these old mining shafts. It was a pretty good idea too. Plenty of room and as dry as a cigar box."

"That *was* a good idea."

"That's what he thought at the time—and then the chicken got loose."

"The chicken?"

"Yeah, one of his Hen Grenade chickens. Got loose down here in the tunnels and Chang went chasing after it. He caught up with it, but by the time he did, it had already laid an egg. Guess it was one of those extra-powerful ones, 'cause when it went off so did all the dynamite and the fireworks and everything else. It went up like a Roman candle—KER*woosh!* That must have been something to see! Anyway, it blew the whole town inside out. When the dust cleared, there was no more hill—just a flat spot where the town used to be. And worst of all, Chang was gone too."

"So that's why they changed the name!"

"Yep. After Chang was gone and the town along with it, they had to rebuild most of the buildings. So much had changed, they decided to change the town name from Change to Boomtown. Made sense. They still had the fireworks factory and the black powder plant—and we still liked blowing stuff up. It's a perfect name, that's for sure."

Late one Friday night while the "Other Chang" (that's what we'd started calling him, since he wouldn't tell us his real name) was out dumping dirt, we found this spot where the tunnel was all boarded up and covered in a layer of dust and cobwebs.

"Hey! What's this?" Frankie asked excitedly.

"I don't know. It's not on the map." Tony held up his kerosene lamp so he could study the paper closer.

It wasn't much of a map, just an old scrap of paper with some lines and some *X*s on it that the Other Chang had given to us. It showed the river and next to that the fireworks factory. That was the starting place. Then a few crooked lines and a mark written in Chinese that was supposed to show the secret entrance to whatever it was we were looking for. We'd been up and down the tunnels looking for the entrance, but hadn't had any luck, not so far anyway. But now there was this boarded-up detour. Maybe we had found it!

"Are there any marks on the wood? Anything that looks like this thing on the paper?" I wondered.

We put our lamps in a circle and inspected the wood for any

telltale clues, but we didn't find anything that looked like Chinese lettering.

"So what do we do?" Rocky asked Busy. "You're our fearless leader. Do we wait for the Other Chang to come back or what?"

"Nope. Let's surprise him. If this is what he's been looking for, he'll be super happy if we open it up. Let's get to work."

So for the next twenty minutes we tore down the wood. It was pretty easy since it was rotten from termites over the years. A lot of it just broke off in our hands. We had it open in no time flat. Then we all stood there, staring down the long dark tunnel, disappointed and sweaty because we didn't find a golden statue with huge red rubies for eyes. That was what Busy kept saying we were looking for. He saw it in a book once.

"Where is it? Shoot! I thought this was gonna be it!"

"Maybe it's down there," Rocky said, pointing at the tunnel.

Busy held up his lamp and took a few steps into the opening. "Guess there's only one way to find out. You comin' or what?"

At first it twisted and turned like some of the other tunnels we'd seen. Then it straightened out and went on for what seemed like miles. There were a few spots where it widened out. There were some side tunnels, but those didn't go anywhere. We went down them, but they always came back to the main path. We kept plodding along until we reached a spot where water dripped from the rock ceiling over our heads and the floor sloped downward and ran away into the dark.

"Do we keep going?" Tony shivered, his question echoing along the wet passageway.

"Why not? We've come this far. It has to go somewhere. Maybe to the treasure chamber—or to a secret laboratory—or to where the Minotaurs are hiding."

This is the tunnel under the river we found. – *Jonny*

"You've seen too many movies." I sniffed, wiping my runny nose on a sleeve. It was cold and wet down there. "But you're right. We should keep going. This is the longest tunnel we've ever found."

Rocky was in charge of marking our trail with paper plates. He put another one on the ground and made it stay with a rock. It had been his idea—and a pretty smart one at that—to mark our path with plates that had a crayon arrow drawn on them so we could find our way back. As soon as he was finished, we kept on walking, clinking and clunking down the trench carrying our shovels and picks and lamps.

The trail went down and then back up again. As it did, the dripping stopped, and it started to get a little warmer. I was glad for that. There were a few more turns, and finally we came to a cave where we plopped down on some rocks and broke out some crackers and cheese and took a drink from our canteens. We were all starting to get tired, and I realized that we had completely lost track of time. I looked down at my watch. It was morning already. I couldn't believe it! We had been out all night! Mom and Dad were going to be pretty angry when they found out. But it was too late to turn back now. Might as well keep going and take my punishment when I got home.

Overhead we could hear the squeaking of bats. We could see the glitter of their eyes as they hung upside down from their perches, watching us suspiciously.

"Hey!" Bobby shouted. "Look at these!"

He was pointing at the rock wall, and we scrambled over to see. All up and down one side of the cave were paintings, bright red and yellow and orange, pictures of horses and buffalo and Indians chasing them with their bows and arrows. One picture showed a circle of Indian braves dancing around a fire with the moon overhead. Then there was a row of symbols—none of us knew what those meant—and finally a painting of a man doing a handstand on the back of a galloping horse, and another one doing a back flip while shooting arrows at a target.

"That's weird," I said.

"No it isn't!" Busy exclaimed. The instant he said it a beam of morning sunlight hit the wall and lit up the cave. "Don't you know where we are? I should have guessed it already." He checked his compass and then made his way toward the light. "Look! The cave opens up right over here. I'm such a dope."

"What are you talking about?"

"The long tunnel, the dripping water. It went down and then up. We crossed under the river! Don't you see it? We're all the way on the other side! And now it's morning—and I can smell a campfire. Come on!"

We followed Busy around the corner and out into the open field, shielding our eyes because it was so bright after being in the dark for so long. It had snowed in the middle of the night, so the morning light was even brighter bouncing off the fresh snow. I looked around and couldn't believe what I was seeing! It was like walking into the middle of a cowboy movie, except there wasn't any popcorn or cowboys.

"How'd we ever end up here?"

"Who cares? Let's go!"

CHAPTER 16

Flaming Dive of Death

"*Flaming Arrow!* Over here!"

Busy raced across the snow, almost tripping over his shovel as he ran. In the distance I could see a circle of tents arranged around a central cooking area where about forty men, women, and children were busy roasting breakfast over the fire. They all looked up when they heard Busy shouting. One of them stepped forward and waved. It was a boy about our age, wearing buckskin pants and a fur-lined coat. He had long, jet-black hair and a pair of eagle feathers hanging down over his left ear. He came quickly over the snow to join us as we approached.

"Busy! Where did you come from?"

"The cave over there, just behind the trees."

"That's the one that goes under the river? You came all that way?"

"Yep! We found the entrance at the other end all boarded up. It goes all the way back into Boomtown. We'll have to show it to you."

The boy put out his hand and offered it to me. "My name is Flaming Arrow. What's yours?"

"I'm Jonny. This is Frankie and Tony; they're twins. That's Rocky and Bobby. And I guess you already know Busy."

"Sure, we're old pals, me and Busy. Known each other since we were just kids, isn't that right, Running Nose?" He laughed.

I gave Busy a strange look. "Running Nose?"

"That's what he calls me. He thinks it's pretty funny, don't you, dummy?"

"It *is* funny. And it fits you. Do you need a hanky?"

Busy's nose *was* running. We were all freezing after being under the river and now shivering in the snow. My teeth were chattering, and I was starving.

"Come on over to the fire and warm up. We were about to have breakfast. You can join us."

As we walked toward the fire, I asked, "So, is Flaming Arrow your real name?"

"Nah, it's just my circus name. Everyone gets one when they join the act. We think they are fun, so we just go by them most of the time."

Flaming Arrow introduced us to his parents and then sat us down beside a very old Indian. His grandfather, he said, Chief Knife Thrower. He looked really, really old. His face was all wrinkly, and he had dark, intelligent eyes. He wore a brightly decorated blanket around his shoulders and this really neat beaded breastplate on his chest. He had a feathered arrow in his right hand; we were told it was the symbol of his office. He didn't say anything while he sat silently by the fire, and I tried not to stare.

While we waited to eat, the thing that really caught my eye was the huge tent in the distance. It had three sections with a bunch of smaller tents surrounding it. There were horses tethered out front, and I saw men and women going in and out. There was a man who was leading a grizzly bear on a rope. I saw another man juggling tomahawks that were on fire. The women were dressed in fancy costumes covered with feathers and bells so that they jingled when they walked.

"What's all that?" I whispered to Busy, tilting my head in the direction of the big tent, as he accepted a plate of cooked deer meat with roasted corn on the side and some blackberries to go with it. It was served on a plank of bark, and they gave each of us water to drink in tin cups. I wolfed down my food and enjoyed the flavor of the strange meat as Busy explained.

"These are the Hopontop Indians," he said between bites. "Hopontop isn't their real tribal name; it's their circus name. My friend here, Flaming Arrow, he's part of the circus. He does trick shooting. You ought to see it. He can put a burning arrow through the middle of an apple when you throw it up in the air. Maybe he'll show you."

"I'd be glad to—after we finish eating," Flaming Arrow said proudly. "That's nothing. You ought to see me shoot an arrow into a Hen Grenade! KaBOOM! That's how I got my name. All of us chose names based on the tricks we can do. My father over there—he's called Back Flip on Buffalo. And my mom, her name is Wolf Tamer. We're all in the circus."

"*What* circus?"

"The Hopontop Traveling Circus. It's *famous*! Haven't you ever heard of it?"

"Nope. I'm new to Boomtown."

"We go all over the place in the summer. Not now, of course. We stay home and practice during the winter. In fact," he said, jumping up and getting all excited, "this morning we're trying out a new act. Want to see it? Maybe they'll even let you help! Stay here and I'll ask."

Flaming Arrow ran over to where his father was standing, and while they were talking, I asked Busy what was going on.

"The Hopontops got started way back before the pioneer days, way back when the only things you could find out here were Indians and trees. Actually, they weren't originally called the Hopontops. They started out as part of the Chinook tribe.

"Sometimes fights would break out between the tribes. They

would fight over the best places to fish or the best hunting grounds. Some Indians who didn't want any part of the fighting would get caught in the middle. So in order to keep things calmed down, they started putting on a show. They were real good at trick riding and acrobatics and target shooting using bows and arrows and stuff like that. So anytime there was a full moon, they'd gather all the local tribes together and entertain them with their tricks."

"No foolin'?"

"No foolin'. They got so popular that tribes would come in from all over the place to see them, and sometimes they'd travel around with the show. After a while, prospectors and trappers and settlers started moving in. They started putting on the show for them too. Along the way they changed their name to the Hopontops, and called their show the Hopontop Traveling Circus. They've been doing it ever since. They've been all the way to Washington, D.C., to perform for the president! They're famous, just like Flaming Arrow says."

Just then Flaming Arrow came running back over with a big smile on his face. "Follow me! My father says you can hold some of the ropes. This is going to be great!"

We stood up and headed on over to the tent where we saw a team of ten horses hitched up to a big metal tub on a cart with eight wheels. The tub was filled with water all the way to the top.

"What's that for?" I wondered.

"You'll see."

Flaming Arrow led us through the flap of the tent and inside. My eyes popped open wide when I saw. The tent had to been more than a hundred feet tall, with three sections supported by massive poles. Each pole was carved with Indian pictures, and up above were ropes and rigging and nets for the high-wire acts and small platforms at the tops of each pole. The canvas walls were painted with elaborate scenes. Flaming Arrow said they were of Hopontops performing some of their more famous acts. There was a painting of Dark Cloud the Magician wrapped in a cloud of smoke and another one showing an Indian diving into a burning pit of flames.

"What's that?" I asked, pointing at the picture of the fire.

"*That* is what we're practicing in here. It's called the Flaming Dive of Death. And you get to pull on some of the ropes. Follow me!"

We headed across the ring to where a series of ropes were hanging. Flaming Arrow put us in teams, two each on a rope. He called it a *longe*—it sounded like "lawn" with a "g" sound at the end—he said it was a French word that meant "guide rope." While we waited I kept looking around. Wooden bleachers, ten rows high, surrounded the edges of the tent. At both ends and toward the middle there were flaps so that circus acts could go in and out. The dirt floor and the three rings were covered in fresh sawdust. The sharp pine smell was making my nose itch.

"What are we supposed to do?"

"You see the boys on the other side? Just do the opposite of what they do. When they pull—you wait. When they stop—you pull. It's that easy. I'll let you know when."

Just then, the tent flap flew open and horses came galloping in carrying whooping riders on their backs. They were dressed in full Indian costumes, with eagle headdresses and fringed buckskin pants, beaded moccasins and leather necklaces, with bells on their feet and wristbands—it sounded like thunder and rain. Next came the eight horses pulling the metal tub—three feet deep and eight feet across. The horses strained against the heavy load as they pulled it to the center ring.

HOPONTOP
TRAVELING
CIRCUS

SINCE 1892

STARRING THE
FLAMING
DIVE OF
DEATH!

NATIVE
DANCERS

TRICK RIDING

ROPE TRICKS

MYSTICAL
MAGIC

WORLD RENOWNED SHARP SHOOTING!

The riders jumped off their horses and did somersaults in the air. Then they ran over to grab a large rope that hung down in the middle. It went straight up and passed through a series of pulleys that were connected to all the other ropes that we were holding.

"Here he comes!" Flaming Arrow announced.

We heard the sound of pounding drums followed by a man who came galloping full speed into the tent standing on the back of a black mustang. He had feathers along his arms and down his back. He had on an eagle headdress with a curved wooden beak and glass eyes. He thundered into the ring, leapt from his horse, snatched the rope in midair, and hooked it to his belt. He soared up and out in a high arching circle, arms spread and feathers flapping.

"Pull!"

We each took turns yanking on the ropes. The more we pulled, the higher and faster the Indian flew. The circle got wider every time he came around. He looked just like a huge eagle circling in the sky.

Then an Indian with a bow shot a burning arrow across the tent and into the pool. It hit right in the middle, and the water burst into flames. The flying man swung directly over the pool, released the rope, and stretched his arms out in a swan dive. He did one, two, three, four somersaults in the air, and disappeared headfirst into the tub in an explosion of smoke, water, and flames. The splash was so big that it put out the fire, and for a few seconds, all we could see was a cloud of steam rising up from the dark pool.

He was gone!

"Where'd he go? Flaming Arrow? How'd he do that?"

Before he could answer, the same mustang from before came galloping back into the tent. On his back was the same Indian, completely dry, wearing the same costume. Not even one of his feathers was wet or on fire.

"C'mon! How'd he do that?"

Flaming Arrow just crossed his arms and gave us a smug grin. He wasn't going to tell.

"It's a Hopontop Traveling Circus secret. If you ever want to see it again, you'll have to buy a ticket just like everybody else."

And I did. That next summer our whole family went out to see the very first performance of the year, held special just for the people of Boomtown. I sat in the front row with Busy on my right and Rocky on my left, just so I could watch it all over again. We never could figure out how he did it.

How about you?

CHAPTER 17

You Better Watch Out!

School was out for Christmas vacation. Mom was over at the church helping the ladies finish up their plans for the big Christmas service that was to take place in a couple of days. Ruth was out in the front yard helping Sarah build a snowman. I was eating toast with Dad at the breakfast table while he read the morning newspaper and worried about one of the big headlines: RASH OF BOOMTOWN ROBBERIES CONTINUE.

"You see this, Jonny? Take a look at the list of things that have been stolen."

He pointed to the list that included some of the following:

Lazy Gunderson's fence, Tom O'Grady's thresher blades, eight trees from the north end of André Soisson's property, two bicycles from in front of Martin's Mercantile, forty-two railroad ties from the train yard, three hundred feet of track, Farmer Higgins's posthole digger, six hundred feet of Christmas lights (off the trees in front of the courthouse), not to mention miscellaneous pickaxes, shovels, pry bars—and our lawn-mower.

"That's not all. My winter coat has gone missing," Dad complained. "You know the one, with all the buttons down the front? I had to go out and buy a new one. What's going on around here?"

Dad looked at me suspiciously, like he'd been doing ever since that night the guys and I didn't come home. Mom and Dad had called the other parents and were pretty upset to find out that all of us had run off without permission. We had cooked up an excuse and said we were working on our tree fort and fell asleep, but they didn't seem convinced. I felt like a dirty rat, lying to my parents like that. But I would feel even worse if I ratted on the Other Chang. So I changed the subject.

"Is it stealing if all the stuff isn't really gone?"

"What do you mean?"

"I mean if, let's say, whoever is taking this stuff is only *borrowing* it. Let's say they give it all back once they're done using it."

"How is that any different? It still doesn't belong to them."

"Yeah, I know. But what if it's for a good reason? Like if a family was starving or something like that?"

"You mean if they needed food just to survive? That might be okay, but they should still ask. There're a lot of good people who would be glad to help. Nobody should *have* to steal. But I suppose it happens for that reason sometimes. Why are you asking?" He studied me curiously.

"Umm . . ."

Thank goodness the doorbell rang before I had to make something up!

I ran to the front door and opened it to find two men standing on the porch. One was dressed all in black and the other was dressed all in gray, and they looked about as opposite from each another as wet is from dry.

The first man was as wide as he was tall, round and red like a ripe tomato. He took off his hat and tipped it, showing a circle of white hair like a crown on his head. He looked a lot like Santa Claus, with his red nose and thin wire frame glasses. All he needed was a sack of toys.

The man standing next to him was so tall I had to bend my neck to see his face. He was as skinny as a string. He had a thin face, gray eyes, black hair, and long bony fingers and arms. He was as white as a snowman. He opened his mouth to say hello to my dad, who had joined me at the door, but the other guy jumped in and started talking a blue streak. I don't think he stopped to take a breath for five minutes.

"Hello, hello, we meet at last! The name's Peter Platz, pastor of St. Bernard's, and this is Reverend Timothy Tinker, from First Presbyterian, and so sorry, we should have come over the instant your family arrived, but we've been so busy with our own church things, and after all, with a new minister at Boomtown Church, you never know, always pays to wait, some of them don't survive the first month so it's nothing personal, you understand, but Timothy here has buried so many of your pastors over the years, it's almost a full-time job; isn't that right, Tim?"

He giggled and elbowed the other minister good-naturedly. The thin man just pulled his overcoat tighter and didn't crack a smile.

"Would you gentlemen like to come in?" Dad asked. "It must be pretty cold out there."

Pastor Peter Platz and Reverend Timothy Tinker.

Pastor Platz rolled through the doorway followed by his tight-lipped partner, both stomping their feet and rubbing their hands trying to get some feeling back into them. "We should have driven instead of walking, that's for certain," he barreled on while they followed Dad into the living room and sat down. "Hope you didn't mind my comment, there, Pastor

Button, about the curse and all. I'm sure you'll be fine. You've survived the first few challenges, right? You seem quite healthy, and I'm sure you've been forewarned. My advice is to keep your eyes open and your head down, and I'm sure you'll be just fine."

"Thanks," my dad muttered. "I think."

"So, enough of that, down to business. The reason we're here. Got to get you up to speed on the Living Nativity and all. Got to do your part. Everyone's counting on you."

"Pardon me?"

"The Living Nativity! Two days from now! On Christmas Eve! The Hen Grenade and Hotcake breakfast in the morning out at St. Bernard's, then the whole town marching down Boom Boulevard at night. There'll be the Christmas Chickens hanging from every pole, the lights twinkling in the windows, Mary and Joseph on their donkey, and the three wise men on their camels. We circle around and form up in Farmer's Park. And then after the living nativity and the reading of the Christmas story, we head on over to Boomtown School for the fireworks. It's an annual tradition! Santa Shooters! Rocket Reindeer! Exploding Elves! Those are always my favorite."

My dad's eyes just kept getting bigger and bigger. "What are you talking about?"

"Oh my goodness, I am so sorry. This is entirely my fault," Pastor Platz said, wringing his hands. "I really should have called you sooner. There's an advertisement in the paper—you didn't see it? I'm sorry. All my fault."

My dad got up and went back into the kitchen and started flipping through the newspaper. He found the ad at the bottom of page 4. This is what it looked like:

24th Annual

Living Nativity

hosted by

Pastor Peter Platz
ST. BERNARD'S LUTHERAN CHURCH

Reverend Timothy Tinker
FIRST PRESBYTERIAN CHURCH

Pastor ____________
BOOMTOWN CHURCH
(if he is still alive)

December 24 ~ Christmas Eve

Procession begins at the Town Hall at 7 pm
and ends at the Boomtown School playfield at 8 pm
with the annual "Lighting of the Santas"

Bring your lamps and candles!

HEAVY WINTER SNOWS PREDICTED

He walked back into the living room carrying the paper. "I notice that my name isn't mentioned in the ad. Is there a reason for that?"

"Well, we use the same ad every year, and we got in the habit of just leaving a space for the pastor at Boomtown Church. We had to keep changing it all the time."

Dad frowned. "Fantastic. And I also see that the ad talks about the 'Lighting of the Santas.' What's that all about?"

"The best part! The highlight! The crescendo! People wait all year for the big moment. You'll see! It's spectacular! Marvelous! Explosive! Jim Dougherty's boy, Rocky, took the big prize last time. One hundred and seventy-five feet, who'd have believed it? My money's on him, same as last year. Or maybe Guenther's boy—he came in a close second. Too top heavy, I think."

"*What* was too heavy?"

"Santa Shooters! We're talking fireworks, son. *Fireworks!*"

"Fireworks on Christmas?"

"Of course, of course! Got to have fireworks. That's how this town got its name. Every holiday: Christmas, New Year's, Groundhog Day, St. Patrick's, Easter, May Day, Mother's Day, obviously the Fourth of July, and . . . well, you get the idea. The bigger, the better."

My dad turned and looked at me with a scowl. "Did you know anything about this?"

"The Living Nativity? No. But the Santa Shooters? Sure. I wanted mine to be a surprise. Hold on. Let me go and get it."

I ran up to my room and carefully carried my creation down the stairs. I was very proud of it—a paper maché Santa Claus with his arms stretched over his head like Superman. I had painted it bright red, with black boots, and I had glued on paper strips for a beard and made a pointy hat. He had on a pair of airmen's goggles over his eyes and a yellow comet painted on his hat and the words *You Better Watch Out* painted on his chest.

Pastor Platz was very impressed. "Why look at that! One of the finest Santa Shooters I think I've ever seen."

I showed Dad how it worked. "His hat comes off like this so you can pack rocket propellant down this tube inside the body. The fuse comes out here at the bottom. When the fuel finally reaches his head--BOOM! It blows off in a big ol' ball of fire. Our blast is going to have red and green trailers with gold sparklers in it. Isn't it super?"

My dad looked shocked. I think he was having trouble breathing. "When did you make this?"

"At school."

"You built this in *school*?!"

"Yeah, me and my buddies, in science class."

"But this is dangerous."

"No, it isn't. Our teacher taught us all about it. The ingredients are stable. You have to put a match to it to make it explode—and there aren't any matches allowed in class. We learned all about chemistry and physics and math and all kinds of other great stuff. It isn't boring like most schools. We learn by doing all sorts of really neat things—and we have a lot of fun doing it. I *love* school!"

I could tell Dad was confused. He wasn't happy about the rocket, but he'd never seen me excited about school either. I was having so much fun in math and science classes that I thought I might grow up to be a rocket scientist or maybe an inventor, and I told him so. Still, he was worried.

"This is *nothing*. Most of my friends learned how to do this kind of stuff in kindergarten. This is *Boomtown*, Dad. This is what people *do* here."

After the two pastors left, Dad talked to Mom,

and she calmed him down. He seemed to be feeling better, and on Christmas Eve, he was right out front leading the parade with the other pastors. We marched down Boom Boulevard, and we sang carols and sipped hot cider and followed Mary and Joseph and the wise men and the shepherds and the sheep down to Farmer's Park. Bringing up the rear was a whole army of kids dressed like angels, with Sarah singing at the top of her lungs and carrying a sparkler on top of a long pole to represent the Christmas Star.

"Sarah? As an *angel*?" my dad whispered to Mom as he watched her sing. "That's quite a stretch, don't you think?"

"Don't be an old poop, Mr. Button," Mom replied. "Just look at her! She's having the time of her life!"

We all did. After the living nativity and the reading of the Christmas story, we went out to Boomtown School just like Pastor Platz promised. First came the Exploding Elves, with long fuses sticking up out of their pointy hats. *Boom!* Off with their heads! Then eight tiny Reindeer Rockets with Rudolph pulling the sleigh. *Woosh!* Then came the climax of the evening: all the science classes lighting up their Santa Shooters. My class got to go second.

Busy, Frankie, and I were on the same team. Busy and Frankie lined up our rocket, and they let me light the fuse; then we ran for cover. It was amazing! It shot up into the air—fifty, one hundred, one hundred fifty, two hundred feet—right into the record books! That's what they kept shouting. But then, without any warning, our wonderful Santa rocket got caught in a cross breeze and made a perfect one-hundred-eighty-degree U-turn. It came right back to earth, straight down to the same exact spot where my dad was watching. It blew up in a gorgeous shower of green and gold sparks—and had just enough power to pick Dad up off his feet and blast him over the fence.

It was about twenty minutes before Dad woke up. Mom was checking his forehead. Dr. Goldberg was checking his pulse. I was accepting congratulations from my team members—along with their condolences. Reverend Tinker was working on Dad's funeral arrangements. He seemed pretty relieved when Dad's eyes opened up and the doctor said he was going to be okay.

His quick recovery brought happy cheers from the worried crowd. A lot of them were our church members. I think they were happy because they wouldn't have to start searching for a new pastor. Dad was happy just to be alive. Everyone else was glad because we could finish shooting off the rest of the fireworks.

Mom helped Dad over to the car, where they could sit and

watch the rest of the launches from a safe distance. I felt a little guilty that my Santa had almost blown up my dad, so I sat with them too. We could see Ruth with her high school friends leading Christmas carols for the children. Sarah was in the front row with a bent halo, dressed as an angel and trying her best to act like one. We watched as the last of the Santas shot into the sky looking for good little boys and girls. And it was nice for me to stand next to my mom and dad who were holding hands and enjoying the show.

"Merry Christmas, Mr. Button," Mom said, giving him a kiss on the cheek.

"And a Merry Christmas to you, Mrs. Button," he answered, kissing her back.

Then she gave him a little push and laughed. "I guess I better wish you a Happy New Year too. You know, just in case you don't live long enough to see it."

"Oh! *Very* funny!" Dad groaned, handing her the car keys and limping around to the left side. "And since you think you're so funny . . . you can drive us home."

CHAPTER 18

The Boomtown Museum

Dad tried to make the best of it, but after being chased by a rocket, almost smashed by a flying barber chair, and almost blown up by an exploding Santa Claus, he was more nervous than a balloon at a porcupine's birthday party. One night my mom dropped a dinner plate, and Dad almost jumped out of his socks. He stayed in his study for the rest of the evening and wouldn't come out until it was bedtime.

Dr. Goldberg stopped by the next day and prescribed two days of rest followed by a family outing—something that didn't involve any fireworks. "Have you been out to the museum yet? That's always a lot of fun. It's at the far end of town on Losotu Lane. Can't miss it. Huge Victorian mansion. Glass conservatory. No explosions."

Following doctor's orders, Dad hid under the covers for two

days, and then early Saturday morning, we bundled into the car and drove through the deepening snow out to the Boomtown Museum.

The first things we saw when we drove through the wrought-iron gate were the house itself, three stories tall, wrapped with porches all around, and the glass-enclosed conservatory with all its thousand windows glittering in the winter sunlight.

"What are all *those* things?" Sarah gasped.

On the roof were wires and antennas and gizmos and gadgets with little windmills and wheels spinning in the icy breeze. Steam drifted out of large and small chimneystacks that poked through the shingles creating a mist that hung over the mansion like a steamy hat. Every now and then a whistle would blow, releasing a blast of steam into the air. As we walked up the sidewalk, we could hear all kinds of strange noises coming from inside, like the house itself was breathing. And when we rang the doorbell (it sounded like a foghorn) the door hissed open all by itself!

Just inside waiting for us was a beautiful woman, dressed in what we learned later was the traditional costume of her tribe: a purple turban, a yellowish red shawl, a bright red skirt, a beaded necklace, copper arm bands, and woven grass anklets. She didn't have on any shoes. She bowed deeply as we entered and introduced herself as Samora Losotu, the granddaughter of Dr. Losotu.

"You're so pretty!" Sarah said.

"Thank you. So are you," she said graciously.

"I'm Sarah—people call me Sorry, but don't worry. I promised Dad I would behave myself. That's him over there. I'm nine. This is my mom and Ruth and my dopey brother, Jonny. He's older, but I'm smarter."

"Really? Then you should be able to read what it says under

this painting. Can you read it for us?" She was pointing to a large painting showing a young black man wearing glasses.

"Doctor Mffunny Lootootoo," Sarah tried to read the strange spelling. "That isn't right, is it?"

Samora smiled and showed her teeth. "No, but you're close. You pronounce the *M* and the *F* separately like this: Mmm-Fah-Nah. And the last name like this: Low-Sew-Too. All together, you've got the name: Doctor Mfana Losotu, famous inventor and explorer."

"He was an inventor? We should have guessed that from this crazy house."

"He was a *lot* of things: an archeologist, a paleontologist, an astronomer, a chemist, an engineer, a biologist, a writer, a musician, a teacher—but mostly an inventor. He built this house and all the things in it. Do you want a tour?"

"Yes!" Sarah spurted. "We want to see everything!"

Samora took her hand and led her down the hallway, and we all followed. "So let's start in the kitchen, shall we? It's just down this corridor."

"The kitchen?" I complained. "That sounds boring."

"You think so?" she answered mysteriously. "We'll just have to see."

She led us through two shiny metal doors with porthole windows and into the brightly lit kitchen. She was right. It wasn't like anything I'd ever seen before. There was a conveyer belt wrapped around three of the sides, with stainless steel garage doors in the walls and pipes and tubes hanging down and strange machines with wheels and metal grabber hands and gears and belts. In the middle was an island covered in more machines, not like coffee pots and toasters, but huge metals monsters with movable tracks and swinging arms and flashing lights.

"Anybody want some cocoa?" Samora asked.

"I do!" Sarah answered. We all did.

"Then go ahead and push the COCOA button. Five times—one for each of you. And push the one for WHIPPED CREAM if you want any."

Just to the left of the swinging doors was a console with activator buttons. The top row said: LIGHTS, HEAT, WASH, DRY, VACUUM, DISPOSE, LIFT. The second row said: TOAST, EGGS, BACON, SAUSAGE, JUICE, COFFEE, and COCOA. The third row said: SOUP, SANDWICH, SALAD, CASSEROLE, FRUIT,

LEMONADE, and TEA. Seven buttons in a row. Ten rows. Seventy buttons all together.

Sarah got to push the COCOA button, and I got to push the one that said WHIPPED CREAM. In a couple of seconds, the conveyor belt started moving and one of the garage doors slid open. Five cups on saucers were pushed onto the conveyor belt and started moving down the row. Like a line of little cars, they each parked under one of the hanging pipes. Steaming hot cocoa was shot into the cups. They stopped again to get a squirt of whipped cream. Then they continued around the room and came to a halt right in front of where we were standing.

I stood there with my mouth open while everyone else sipped cocoa. They all said it was delicious and hot and chocolaty. But all I wanted to know was how it worked.

"My grandfather came to Boomtown back in 1882, back before it was even called Boomtown," Samora explained. "Our ancestors originally came from South Africa, but they were among the few from that part of Africa who were taken as slaves and brought to this country illegally. Mfana's parents were slaves in Georgia. That's where he was born, but when he was fourteen years old, he was able to escape through the Underground Railroad—Harriet Tubman herself helped him do it!"

Sarah wiped chocolate off her lip. "We read about her in school."

Samora nodded. "She helped a lot of people to escape, including my grandfather. He was smuggled up North to Delaware where a man named Thomas Garret took him in. He was the one who taught my grandfather to read. After he learned how to read, there wasn't anything he couldn't learn. It turned out that Mfana was a natural-born genius."

J.
HOPONTOP HIGHWAY
K.
L.
I.
H.
M.
RIVER
A.
B.
C.
D.
E.
F.
G.

OKANOGAN
BOOMTOWN MUSEUM
N.
B
LOS
ECHANG
Legend
A. Museum
B. Conservatory
C. Nursery
D. Bowling Green
E. Fountain
F. Lily Pond
G. Geothermal Plant
H. Water Pumping Station
I. Telescope Hill
J. Hoponover Bridge
K. Pear Grove
L. Apple Grove
M. Cherry Grove
N. Water Tower

"So why'd he come here?" I wondered.

"A lot of the inventions Mfana dreamed about building needed steam—*lots* of steam. He wanted to find a place where he could dig down deep enough to reach the earth's heat—maybe a place that used to have a lot of volcanoes. That way the heat would be close up to the surface. So he searched and searched until he found this place. It was perfect. It had a river right next to where he wanted to build. It had natural hot mud springs, like the ones at Yellowstone Park. The people who lived here were happy to let him do it. And then there was Chang, of course. That made it all possible."

"Chang?" I asked.

"Certainly. Both of them were inventors, and so when they met, they became best friends. Chang had all this money, and Mfana had all these ideas. They teamed up and worked on a lot of them together. I'll be showing you some of those on the tour."

"So you're saying this whole house is driven by steam?"

"Yes. Let me show you."

We put the cups on the conveyor belt, and she pushed the WASH button. The cups were carried away through a hole in the wall. We could hear the whooshing sounds of water and steam washing up the dishes.

"You see? Way down deep under our feet, down in the lowest basement of the house, there's a huge steam farm with pipes and tanks and pumps and turbines. That's where the house gets its power. In addition to that, out by the river, Mfana built the Boomtown Geothermal Plant, basically a larger version of the geothermal generator that runs the house. The turbines produce enough electricity to power the entire town—with some to spare. You probably noticed that you don't receive an electric bill at your house?"

My dad nodded. "I wondered about that. The steam plant runs the whole town?"

"Every last bit of it. It was my grandfather's gift to the people who loved him. When he died, he bequeathed the power plant to Boomtown in his will, along with this house and everything in it. He was a very generous man—and he loved Boomtown very much."

We followed Samora out of the kitchen and around the corner until we were standing in front of two black cage doors. She pushed a button on the wall, and the doors slid open with a hiss. Lights flickered on inside, and we could see that it was an elevator, with red velvet cushions for sitting on and glass windows on every side.

"Instead of *talking* about what my grandfather did, I'd rather *show* you. We'll be able to see everything from in here."

"We will?" my dad said doubtfully, stepping inside and taking a seat. "What do you mean, 'see everything'? And what are these for?"

We crowded into our spots and wrapped the belts around our waists. "They're safety belts, Dad."

"Safety belts?" he muttered, starting to count his buttons. "In an elevator? Why would you need safety belts in a . . ."

He never got a chance to finish because all of a sudden Samora shouted, "Hang on!" and she threw the switch. The elevator shuddered, and then it lurched, and then it hummed and hissed, and then five, four, three, two, one—it blasted off like a rocket.

"*Whaaaaaaah!*"

The elevator shot up and up, and I thought we'd be smashed into the ceiling except all of a sudden the roof popped open and the elevator kept going, up and up, ten stories into the sky, until it

stopped with a jerk almost as fast it had started. The safety belts knocked the wind out of us when we slammed to a halt. I was laughing my head off; Sarah was giggling; Mom and Ruth thought it was fantastic. Dad looked like he was going to throw up.

Samora took off her safety belt and tried to look apologetic. "I'm sorry; I probably should have warned you. But it's more fun to be surprised, don't you think?"

"Yes! Yes! Yes!" we all shouted. "Do it again!"

"No!" my dad groaned, turning green. "I want to go DOWN! Right now. Except . . . wait! Can we do it *slowly*?"

"No problem," Samora answered, pulling the lever back, causing the elevator to descend with a hiss. It turned slowly as it dropped, like a merry-go-round. It was great! We could see everything from up there. The steam plant, the glass roof of the conservatory curving away, the reflecting pond and the fountains, the apple fields and Rocket Ridge in the distance, the Boomtown School, the Hopontop village, the smokestacks at the fireworks factory, and even our house and my walnut tree.

"The elevator is on a telescoping pole so we don't go flying off into outer space," she explained. "My grandfather built it for my sister and me. We used to ride on it every single day. I still don't get tired of it. Are you sure you don't want to do it a second time?"

Dad held on to the railing and moaned. "Just get me to a bathroom. No hurry. Soon as we can, thank you."

We rode the elevator down until we were back inside, and the roof closed behind us. With a hiss the elevator slid to a stop, and the doors opened. Dad stumbled into the hallway, and Samora showed him to the closest bathroom. While we waited, she told us about the bedrooms all along both sides.

"Every room has one of these control panels," she said, showing us a silver box on the wall by the door. "Push these buttons and the bedroom will clean itself."

"Really? Can we do it?"

I pushed the button that said VACUUM, and we watched as a vacuum cleaner popped out of the wall and began to whisk around in circles. The bed and the nightstand and a small couch rose up off the floor on silver pistons so that the vacuum could get underneath. In about a minute, it finished its job and raced back into its little garage.

"That's amazing!" my mom gasped. She liked the idea of a house that cleaned itself, especially with Sarah around. Dad looked impressed too. He'd come out of the bathroom, and the color was coming back into his face.

"You can change the sheets, wash the windows, and do the dusting with these other buttons," Samora remarked proudly.

Dad asked, "Does the bathroom clean itself too?"

"It does. It has a control panel next to the door. Do you want to see?"

She crossed the hall, lifted the small door, and pushed the red button. "The door seals shut so none of the steam escapes. The system will clean the toilet, the sink, the shower, the floors, and the walls. It even has a lemony scent to make everything smell nice when it's finished."

The sounds of shooting steam could be heard coming from behind the door—and then we heard another sound—a thumping noise.

"Is it supposed to do that?" my mom asked.

"Sarah!" Ruth shouted. "Where's Sarah?"

"Oh no! She must be in the bathroom! Turn it off!"

Samora looked sad. "I wish I could, but there isn't an Off switch. You aren't supposed to go *inside* the bathroom when it's being cleaned. Oh my. I hope she'll be all right."

My dad was pounding on the door. "Sarah! Sarah? Can you hear me?"

A few more seconds passed, and then we heard the sound of blowing air—and laughing. When the door popped open, a burst of steam came pouring out. We couldn't see anything at first, and then the mist cleared and there was Sarah, perfectly dry, hair straight, with a huge grin on her face, and looking cleaner than I've ever seen her in my entire life.

"That was fun!" She laughed. "What else can this crazy house do?"

All my dad could do was stare.

CHAPTER 19

Dinosaurs!

"Really. I'll be fine. I'm just going to go sit in the car. You go ahead."

Mom was trying to talk Dad into staying, but he had seen enough. "Doctor Goldberg said I needed *rest*. No more excitement, that's what he told me. I've had plenty enough for one day. Enough to last me a lifetime! Don't worry. I'll turn on the radio. I'll practice my sermon for tomorrow. I'll take a nap. Go have fun. Take your time."

Even though Dad's eyes were blurry, he could see we were having a great time at the museum. He didn't want to spoil it for us. He was worried about Sarah, of course, about what she might do next. But Samora patted him on the hand and told him about another one of Dr. Losotu's inventions. "It's called a Naughty Nanny. It has a belt with a big magnet on it. You can put it around your kid's waist and stick her to the refrigerator until she promises to behave. I could let you borrow it."

"Sounds perfect," my dad agreed, looking sideways at me. "Can I have two of them? One for each?"

Dad walked out to the car while Samora took us back toward the center of the house. We stopped in front of a large pair of glass doors. The words *Great Room* were etched in tiny scrollwork in the glass. This was surrounded by drawings of prehistoric animals and birds, fossils, hieroglyphs, gears, motors, and flying machines.

"Through these doors are some of Doctor Losotu's greatest discoveries and magnificent inventions, not to mention his collection of historical documents, books, city records and archives, photographs, paintings, and drawings. And a big surprise—just for the kids."

"What is it?" Sarah whispered.

"It's a *surprise*," was all Samora would say. "Let's go in."

She pushed open the doors, and we walked into a room that was as big as a school gymnasium. It had a crystal chandelier hanging over the center, about the size of a small car, three stories up and glittering like the stars. The walls were covered in red velvet wallpaper, but there weren't any windows. Nothing but a big, empty space.

"That's it?" I said, looking disappointed. "Where are all the inventions? Where are the dinosaurs? Is *this* the surprise? An empty room?"

Instead of answering, she led us across the polished wooden floor to the center of the room where there was a small table, the only other thing we could see. On top of the table was a silver box, and on top of the box were five buttons. SHUTDOWN. DINOSAURS. INVENTIONS. BOOKS. The fifth one was blank.

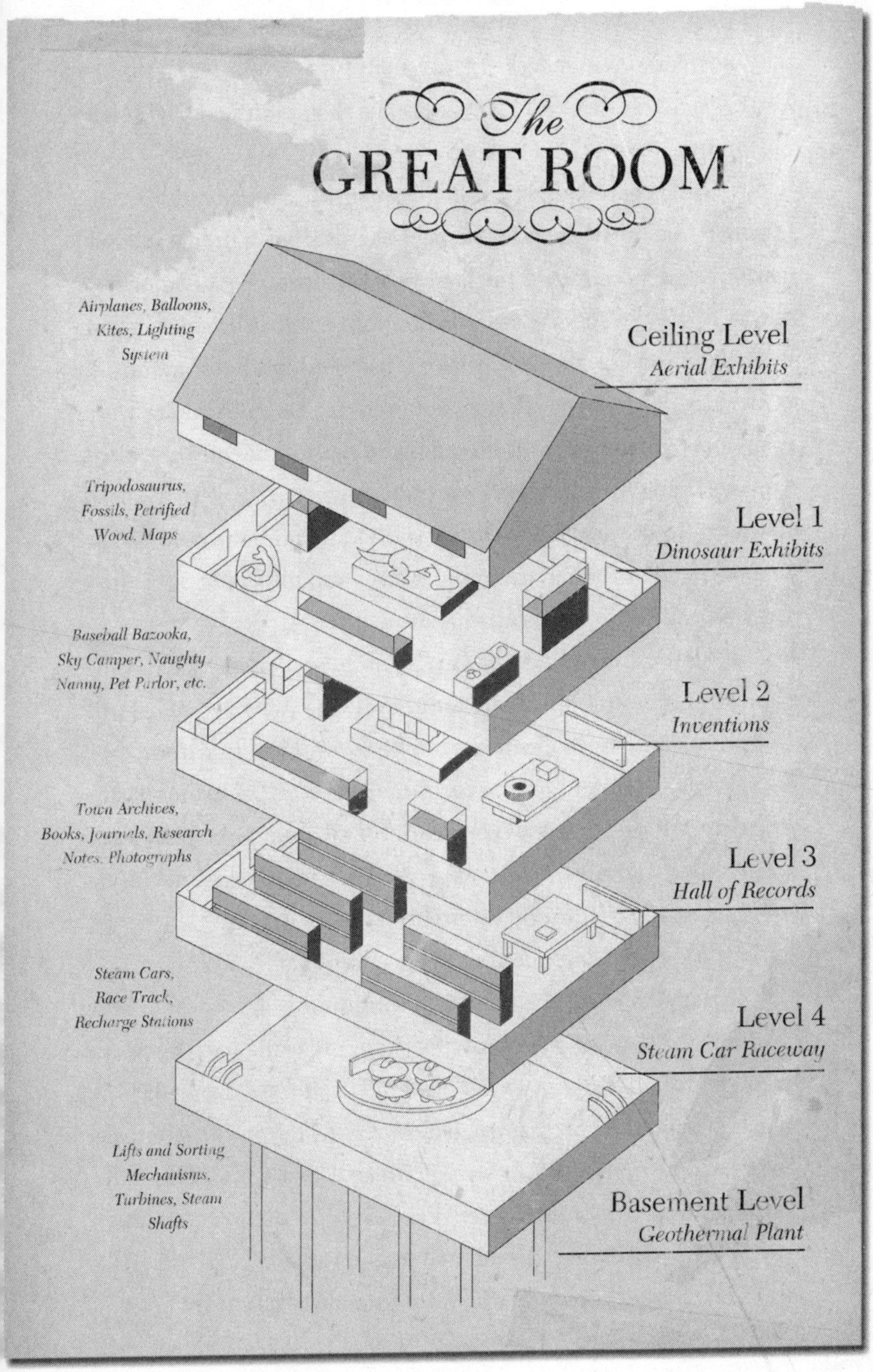

The GREAT ROOM

Ceiling Level
Aerial Exhibits

Airplanes, Balloons, Kites, Lighting System

Level 1
Dinosaur Exhibits

Tripodosaurus, Fossils, Petrified Wood, Maps

Level 2
Inventions

Baseball Bazooka, Sky Camper, Naughty Nanny, Pet Parlor, etc.

Level 3
Hall of Records

Town Archives, Books, Journals, Research Notes, Photographs

Level 4
Steam Car Raceway

Steam Cars, Race Track, Recharge Stations

Basement Level
Geothermal Plant

Lifts and Sorting Mechanisms, Turbines, Steam Shafts

"Push one. Whichever one you want."

I reached for INVENTIONS, but Sarah got to the DINOSAUR button first.

Nothing happened at first, but then we heard a hiss and a grinding noise and the floor started to tremble. Overhead, the chandelier started to sway, and the crystals made a little tinkling noise as they vibrated. All of a sudden the wooden floor erupted. Doors popped open like a jack-in-the-box. Display cases and exhibits grew up out of the floor like weeds. Panels slid open in the walls. There were maps and photographs and drawings and charts. The ceiling opened up, and flying dinosaur skeletons and other fossils were lowered down on ropes and cables. On my right was a miniature landscape map with rivers and mountains and lakes and little red flags showing where different dinosaurs had been discovered.

While we caught our breath, Samora explained, "The dinosaur exhibit is stored in Basement Level One. When you push the button, steam power pushes everything up here into the Great Room. Push another button and everything goes back into storage and gets replaced by the next exhibit. It's all done with pistons and wheels and movable tracks—that way all four of the different exhibits can fit in this one room. Pretty neat, isn't it?"

"It's the greatest thing I've ever seen! What's *that*?"

I was pointing at the huge dinosaur on my left. It was at least ten feet high and about twenty feet long. It had a long neck and tail, a fat round body, and a flat head full of short teeth. And it only had two legs at the back and a useless dangly leg on the front. The brass plaque on the railing said "TRIPODOSAURUS." The translation underneath said, "Three-Legged Dinosaur."

"A *Tripodosaurus*?" I said. "There's no such thing."

"Of course there is. It's standing right there in front of us."

"That's not what I meant. I mean there's no such thing as a three-legged dinosaur."

"This is the only one ever found. Chang discovered it accidentally during one of his mining digs. He showed it to Mfana, who finished digging it up and brought it here. He found lots of dinosaur bones over the years—it was one of his favorite hobbies. But this is the only dinosaur anyone has ever found that had three legs."

"But how did it walk?"

"My grandfather believed it used its head as a fourth leg. You see how flat the head is on top? The Tripodosaurus would bend its long neck down and shuffle forward using its head."

"That doesn't really make any sense."

"Well, maybe not, but it probably couldn't move very fast so it wouldn't be able to run away from other predators. That's probably why there's only one of them."

I looked at the weird bones and the painting of the dinosaur next to the plaque. "Maybe the doctor made a mistake. Maybe he just couldn't find the fourth leg when he dug up the skeleton."

"Don't be silly." Samora laughed. "Who ever heard of a *four-legged* Tripodosaurus?"

Sarah thought it was very funny. I still thought it was dumb.

Ruth had wandered across the room and had stopped to stare at an umbrella hanging from the ceiling. At least, it *looked* like an umbrella, with all of the cloth removed. Hanging underneath the skeleton was a small picture of what the artist thought it would have looked like with all its skin. The wings looked like dragon wings. And when they were stretched out, the creature looked like a kite made out of greenish-gray leather.

In Latin it was called a "*MURIS FUGAPENNAMID*." In English it was called a "Batkite."

Sarah said, "It looks just like a kite—without the string."

"That's right," Samora agreed. "With the wings folded in, the batkite looks just like a closed umbrella, with its small body wrapped inside like a tent."

"I wonder if cavemen used it like that? Wouldn't that be funny? Cavemen running around using batkites for umbrellas?"

"Who knows? Maybe they did."

"How did it fly?"

"My grandfather wrote a scientific paper all about it. He thinks that the batkite would sit around waiting for a strong wind. Then it would open its wings, and the wind would snatch it up into the air like a kite. It would dart back and forth and catch flying insects for food. When the wind stopped blowing, it would land on the ground or in a tree."

"That's so weird."

We continued to wander around the room, looking at all the strange dinosaurs and ancient pottery and other things that Dr. Losotu had found until we came to a large brown and grainy photograph hanging on the wall. It showed him standing next to Chang with a big grin on his face. Behind them was the excavation where the Tripodosaurus was being dug up. The picture showed a date: June 12, 1890.

I kept staring at the picture, because every time I looked at Chang it was like looking at our mysterious stranger. The same face, the same eyes, the same build—it *couldn't* be a coincidence.

"Did Chang have any children? Was he ever married?"

"No. People always called him the Gentleman Bachelor. He never had a wife and children."

"Are you sure?"

Mom looked at me funny. It must have been the way I asked

the question; she always seemed to know when I was hiding something.

"Why are you asking? Did somebody tell you he had children?"

"I, uh, umm . . ."

Just then my friends came bursting into the room, slamming through the double doors and running between the displays.

"Jon!" Rocky said, bouncing to a stop with Bobby and Busy next to him. "We've been looking all over for you!"

"Where're Frankie and Tony?"

"It's their turn today . . . they're out helping . . ." Rocky stopped himself just in time. He slapped his hand over his mouth when he saw Mom and Samora standing there. Busy poked him in the ribs with an elbow.

"They're helping at the boarding house . . . um . . . shoveling snow off the sidewalk. That's why they couldn't be here," Busy explained, glaring at Rocky.

"So what are *you* doing here?"

"We heard you were at the museum. We wanted to come. Have you seen the inventions yet?"

"We've seen a lot of stuff, but we haven't seen the ones in this room yet. We were about to."

"So what are you waiting for?" Busy asked. He moved over to the control panel. "Push the button!"

We all gathered around the silver box and made sure that everyone was in the clear. Then I pushed the button, and we watched the dinosaurs disappear back into their caves. *Whir. Clank. Buzz. Hiss.* Then a whole amusement park of strange machines started coming up out of the floor and dropping out of the ceiling. I almost couldn't believe my eyes! I'd never seen anything like it!

CHAPTER 20

Baseball Bazookas
(and Other Crazy Gadgets)

The first thing I noticed was the airplane hanging from the ceiling. I mean, it sorta *looked* like a plane, though it was more like a bathtub with wings on it.

Samora must have read my mind because she said, "It *is* a bathtub." She chuckled. "It's the wooden one from an old bathhouse we used to have here on the property. My grandfather added the wood and canvas wings. He put a seat inside the bathtub and then added the gears and pedals from a bicycle and put tires on the side so it would roll for takeoff."

"Why did he build that?"

"Mfana started trying to build an airplane as soon as he heard about the Wright Brothers. You know about them, don't you? They accomplished the first manned flight at Kitty Hawk back in 1903. I'm afraid Mfana wasn't quite as successful as they were."

Sarah asked, "You mean he couldn't get it to fly?"

"Oh, it flew all right. It was *landing* that was the problem. You see the puffy wings on the sides—with the empty balloons hanging down? That was Mfana's big idea. He thought if the wings were filled with helium it would make the whole airplane lighter than air. Unfortunately, he was right."

"What happened?"

"The airplane went *up*, but it wouldn't come *down*! Not for a whole week! He nearly starved to death before enough helium finally leaked out. He landed about three hundred miles south-east from here—in Horseshoe Bend, Idaho. He's considered a bit of a folk hero down there. But he stopped trying to fly after that because my grandmother was so upset about the ordeal."

Samora led us across the floor over to a flat platform covered in what looked like a deflated hot air balloon or maybe a parachute. She bent over and flipped a switch. We could hear the sound of air being pumped, and we watched as the balloon began to inflate. As it filled up, it took on a square shape, like a huge slice of bread, about ten feet square and two feet thick. It quickly rose into the air with ropes hanging down underneath.

"Mfana's trip to Idaho gave him plenty of time to think. Without food or water or a bed to sleep on, he thought about how nice it would to float up in the sky—*if* there was a way to bring some supplies and *if* there was some way to come down when you wanted to. That's how he dreamed up the Sky Camper. Jonny, why don't you take the first turn? Go ahead. Climb aboard."

I scrambled over the edge of the platform and through the door of the camper. The flat balloon floated up to the ceiling and took me with it. Underneath was an expandable room that unfolded as it rose up. It had small, net-covered windows and a helium-filled floor. A tether hung down through a hole in the floor and was anchored firmly to the platform. I waved from the window at my mom, who was looking very worried.

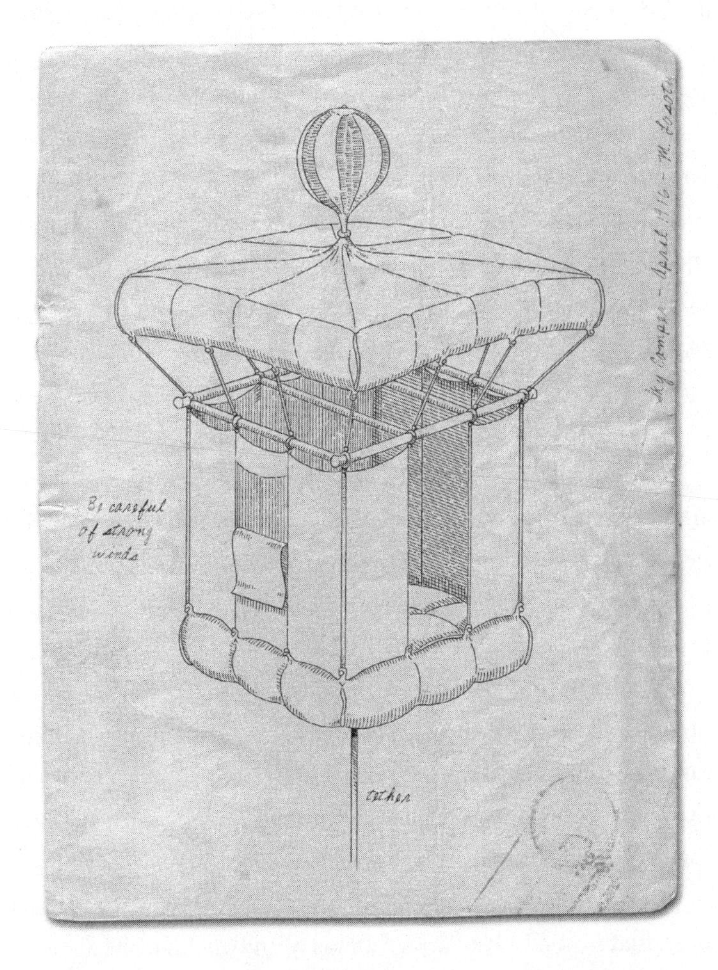

Samora touched her arm and explained, "It's safe, as long as you keep the front door zipped shut. The Sky Camper is perfect for one average-sized person. Inside are enough supplies for an overnight stay. The balloon and helium tanks are portable, so you can travel out to a campsite, fill the balloon, climb aboard, and enjoy an evening up in the clouds."

I was already testing the anchor rope. By pulling on it I was able to make the camper go back toward the ground. There was a place to tie it off so you could go in and out. That would be handy if you needed to . . . you know . . . in the middle of the night. I came down and let Sarah have a turn. She let go of the rope and popped back up to the ceiling. "Whoo-hooo!"

"You see how the windows zip down so you can look out. And the balloon acts just like a roof to keep you dry in case it rains. It even comes with a battery-powered lantern so you can read at night."

"Mom!" Sarah yelled hanging out the front door. "We have to get one of these!"

"I don't think your dad would like it very much," Mom answered Sarah and then turned back to Samora. "What would it be like if it started getting windy?"

Samora rubbed her hands together. "That's when it *really* gets exciting!"

While she was busy putting the Sky Camper back to bed, we ran around the room looking at all the other amazing things. I didn't know what to ask about first. I stopped in front of a glass case with three objects inside. We huddled around and stared while Busy told us all about them. He had been to the museum lots of times.

"That first one there—the one that looks like a giant lunch box—that's called a Pet Parlor." It was round on top with latches on the side. It had a round opening at one end and a fan on top. "You put your dog or cat inside. The head fits through that hole. You plug in a hose and pump in hot, soapy steam. It's like the self-cleaning bathroom. The air fan turns on, and your dog comes out clean and dry as a whistle."

Sarah frowned. "I don't think Effeneff wouldn't like that very much."

"Does it come in a sister-size?" I asked.

Both Sarah and Ruth punched my arm.

I rubbed my shoulder and pointed at the second thing. "I can guess what *those* are—they look like rocket shoes."

That's what they were. They each had four wheels and an adjustable frame so they could fit different people's feet. Lying next to them was a picture showing a man with a tank strapped to his back and tubes running from the tank to each of the shoes. In his fist was a starter cord. I could see how it worked. Pull the cord and blast off!

"Now *that* looks like fun!"

Samora had joined us by then. "It would have been fun if it had worked. Unfortunately, the person wearing the shoes would usually flip upside down. The shoes would go flying off in every direction. One pair flew across the river and kicked such a big hole in a boat that it sank! Another pair zoomed down the road and smashed a berry field into berry juice! A third pair blasted into the Town Hall, chased the mayor up the stairs, and kicked him over his desk!"

The Rocket Shoes may have been one of Mfana's failures, but they still looked like a lot of fun. I wondered if Samora would let me borrow them.

We moved on to the next invention. "Now this one was definitely not a failure," Samora said as she took a little key and unlocked the cabinet. She picked up a long, metal tube that had a silver tank at one end and a trigger in the middle, just like one of those guns that the army uses. From a storage closet underneath, she pulled out a canvas bag and handed it to Busy.

"Let's put everything away so we can have some room."

We moved back into the center, and she pushed the SHUTDOWN button. We watched while all the exhibits disappeared into the floor. In a minute, it was an empty room again. Busy was already busy handing out the mitts, and Rocky ran around laying out the bases.

"This," she announced, "is called the Baseball Bazooka! You load the baseballs in here. The tank at the end is filled with compressed gas. Turn this knob, and you can change the pitch into a curve ball or a fastball or a sinker. Then all you have to do is point the bazooka, pull the trigger, and *BANG!* You're the greatest pitcher who ever lived! Want to try it?"

She handed me the Baseball Bazooka, and I ran over in the pitcher's spot. Rocky grabbed a bat and got ready to hit. Bobby was the catcher. Mom and Ruth and everyone else manned the field. I turned the knob and picked Fast Ball. I lined up the sites and fired. *WHUMP!* It jerked in my hands, and the ball whizzed over home plate and smacked into Bobby's glove.

"Steeeerike One!" Samora shouted.

I tried a few more pitches, and Rocky struck out one, two, three. Then it was his turn to pitch and my turn to bat. I swung through the first two shots and then caught one on the sweet spot of the bat. *SMACK!* It flew across the room and bounced off the back wall.

"HOME RUN!"

I ran around the bases to the cheering of the crowd, blowing kisses to all my fans and taking a bow at home plate.

"You got lucky," Rocky complained. "I'll get you next time."

We played Baseball Bazooka for a while until my mom glanced at her watch. "We've really got to be going," she said. "Your father is all alone out in the car, and it's past lunchtime."

"But we haven't pushed the last button yet!" Sarah cried. "Samora said there was a surprise. Just for us kids!"

Our tour guide smiled. "I did say that. I have been saving the best for last."

"Please, Mom, *pleeeeeese!*" we all begged. Even Ruth wanted to stay.

"Okay," she surrendered. "But after this, we go."

We quickly gathered up the baseball equipment and stood still, waiting for Samora to push the button. Busy and the other guys knew what to expect—but we didn't. What could be better than a Sky Camper or a Baseball Bazooka? It didn't take long to find out.

Side compartments in the four walls popped open. Inside were large canvas bags that began to inflate. In seconds, a soft, cushioned wall of air surrounded the edges of the whole room. A short wall, also filled with air, rose up from the floor to form a center ring with an opening at each end. Then up out of the floor popped these four little cars. They looked like marshmallows on wheels. They were all puffy and squishy, with padded seats and fenders. Finally, in one corner of the room, a narrow driveway with padded guardrails on each side slid into place.

"Welcome to the Boomtown Racetrack!" announced Samora with a wave of her hand. "Who's first? Jonny? Sarah? Ruth? How about you, Mrs. Button? Come on over and pick out your car."

"Really? A *racetrack*? And we get to use it?" I asked.

"Sure," Samora answered. "Climb in!"

STEAM POWERED RACE CAR.

AUTO-RECHARGE SYSTEM.

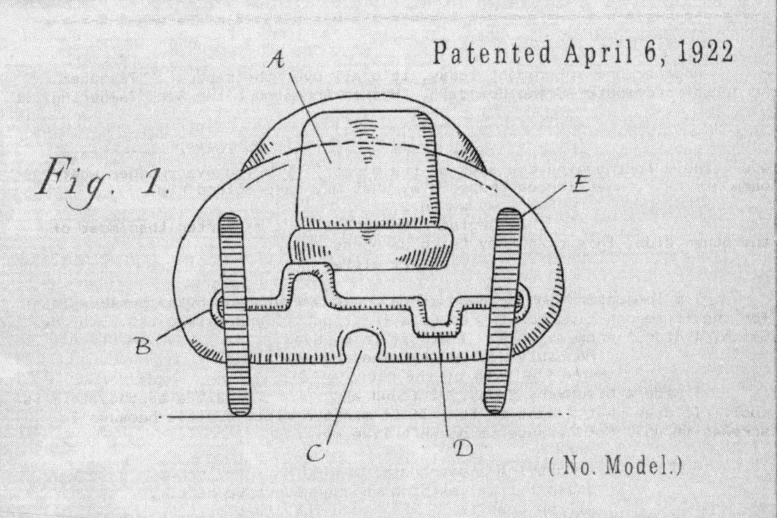

Inventor
Mfana Losotu

No. 408,112

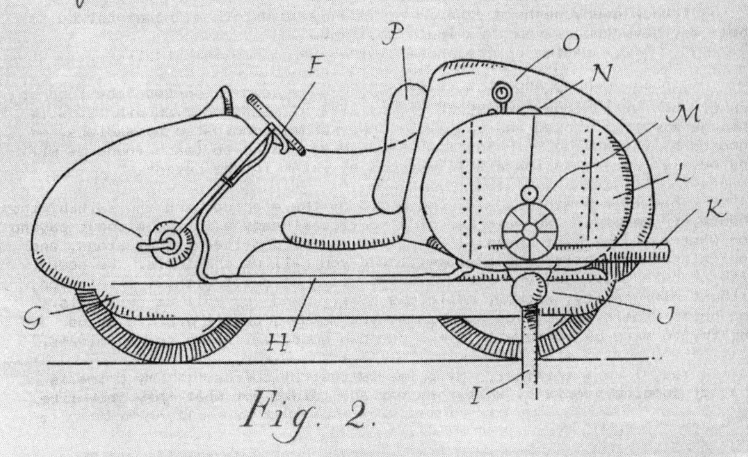

We ran across the floor and jumped into our cars. Each one had its own number and a padded steering wheel. There was an accelerator and brakes and sitting on the seat was a soft helmet. We put on our helmets and safety belts and waited impatiently for Samora to tell us what to do.

"These cars are driven by steam power," she explained. "Each has a tank with pressurized steam. Squeeze the handle on the steering wheel to make the car go forward. The harder you squeeze, the faster you go. Release the handle and use the brake to stop. You can only drive in one direction, beginning at the starting line. You have to go ten laps to win, but the cars will only go about seven laps on one tank of steam. That's what the station in the corner is for."

Samora pointed and said, "When you feel your car beginning to slow down, you can pull into the station to refuel. The station will automatically capture your car and bring you to a stop. A steam hose is guided through a slot underneath each car, and a fresh load of steam will be injected into your tank. It's up to you to decide when to recharge your car—in the fifth, sixth, or even seventh lap.

"But don't wait too long! Only one car can refuel at a time, and you might run out of steam short of the station. If that happens, you have to move the car using the bicycle pedals down there on the front axle. You don't want to have to do that!"

My mind was racing. "Do you have to wait for a full charge—or can you take off out of the station before it's full?"

"Good question. You can take off anytime you want. Just squeeze the handle. Winning a race depends on making good guesses and perfect timing. It's not about how fast you go, but how *smart* you go."

We pushed the cars over to the starting line. Rocky was

holding the green flag. He raised it and shouted, "On your mark, get set . . . *GO!*"

I took the early lead, but Ruth was a close second. We circled the track, once, twice, three times. Ruth and I were neck and neck, and Mom was in third place. Sarah was way behind, but she pulled over after only five laps to recharge her car. Ruth pulled over after six. I waited too long because my car ran out of steam at the beginning of the seventh lap. I had to pedal my car into the station. By then, Sarah was way out in front with her fresh tank. Busy was there to wave the checkered flag. Sarah was the winner!

"I won! I won! I won!" she yelled, jumping up and down.

We pushed the cars into the station and recharged all the tanks. This time it was me and the other three guys. I learned my lesson from the first race; I pulled over early and got a full tank of steam and crossed the finish line before anyone else. Winner! Ruth took the third race. Busy wo n the fourth. By then it was almost 2:00 p.m., and we hadn't had lunch. We were starving.

We watched as Samora put the room back together, and then all left the museum together. We thanked her for the tour and waved good-bye to her as we walked to the car. I promised the guys I would catch up with them after dinner. We woke Dad from his nap, and we couldn't stop talking about all the amazing things we had seen. We couldn't imagine ever again having so much fun.

Of course, we hadn't been to the Spring Fever Festival yet. Now THAT was a blast and a half!

CHAPTER 21

CHANG'S FAMOUS FIREWORKS

Spring Fever Festival

Winters in Boomtown can be pretty brutal—for *grown-ups*, that is. The town is just east of the Cascade mountain range and only eighty miles from the border of Canada. Early snow can start falling in October, and ice can be on the ground until as late as April. The poor grown-ups get trapped inside for maybe five months, and by the end of winter they start climbing the walls from cabin craziness. But not kids like me. We *never* run out of fun stuff to do in the snow. Especially when we've got someone as smart as the Other Chang helping us. One day during the holiday break from school I met the guys out at Slippery Slope and showed them what the Other Chang had built.

"Hey, Jon, watcha got there?"

"It's a rope. Got it from the Reynoldses' farm."

"It's really long. What's it for?"

"Let's go up to the top, and I'll show you."

Busy and Rocky and the twins followed me as we hiked up Slippery Slope. This was a long hill on Lazy Gunderson's farm—you know, Busy's dad. By the second or third day of January, after two weeks of sledding during the winter school break, the hill-side was already a solid sheet of ice, one foot thick and slick as glass. It glittered like a jewel in the cold winter sunlight. The ice slide was on the shadow side of the hill and shaded by pine trees. Depending on the weather, Busy said sometimes it could last all the way into May.

Most kids in Boomtown made their own sleds out of whatever they could lay their hands on. One favorite was to build some run-ners and a deck out of scrap wood—mount an old chair on top and away you went! Another popular trick was to take a pair of your father's overalls, soak them in water, and hang them on the clothesline overnight. By morning, you'd have a rock-hard sled with shoulder straps for handles. Take it out to Slippery Slope, and you could go as fast as a horse buggy on a windy day.

Those rigs were fun, but nothing like what our gang had built that year. It was an ice schooner! Busy named it the Flying Icicle. We took grain sacks and filled them with snow and left them outside until they froze like giant bricks of ice. We tied them underneath two thick sheets of plywood and put ropes on top to hang on to. It was big enough to fit four guys at a go. It was a scream to ride on—but it weighed a ton! It took almost eight kids to drag it back to the top of the hill.

"What's this contraption for?" Rocky asked when he saw what we had rigged up. It was an old garden digging machine that was upside down and strapped to a tree. The tiller blades were taken off and a wheel hub was in its place. There was a smaller rubber tire bolted to the tree. With Bobby and Frankie helping, I was able to loop the rope around the wheel.

"It's a ski lift, like they got at ski resorts," I answered. "You know, one of them rope pullers that can pull you up a hill?"

"That's really swell. You build it? Where'd it come from?"

I glanced around to make sure there wasn't anybody close enough to hear me. "I got it from *him*. He helped me move it here and set it up. It was *his* idea."

"Wow," Rocky whispered. "So where did *he* get it?"

"Don't know. Probably the same place he got all the other stuff. I didn't ask and he didn't say."

"He's pretty smart, isn't he? Inventing all kinds of things—like the conveyer belt down in the tunnel."

"And did you notice how he got hooked up to the electricity from the factory? I don't know how he did that either."

"Or his underground camping room. Have you seen it? It's all warm and cozy. I wish *I* could live there."

We tried out the ski lift machine, and it worked perfectly. All the other kids started using it too, and we became local heroes. That whole winter there was a line of kids on sleds and skis and frozen overalls zipping up the side of the hill. A lot of times our parents would show up. There was often a large bonfire blazing near the bottom of the ice ramp. Moms and dads would bring out boxes of sticky buns for the kids, and folks would pass around coffee and steaming hot cocoa with marshmallows and watch us play. Blue sky, green trees dripping in snow, a brisk snappy wind. It was great.

On the other side of town was Fred Cotton's place. We went out there one morning for the Snow Wars. Like most things in

Boomtown, sooner or later explosives were involved. And like so many other things, Sarah was right in the middle of it acting as the general.

"We'll build our fortress right here," she ordered as her small troop snapped to attention. "There's lots of snow, and it's on a little hill. That'll be good."

"We'll dig the trenches," her lieutenant replied.

"And we'll make a wall, General Sir Ma'am." Another soldier saluted.

"Excellent plan. And after that, we'll build our army. Let's get to work!"

That's how it was done. One team built walls and battlements and snow trenches at one end of the field. Behind that they lined up their army of snowmen—two feet tall, thirty snow soldiers in all. At the opposite end of the field was the other team making ice balls. They were about eight inches around, and inside of each one was a Hen Grenade. Fred Cotton was always around to make sure we were safe.

Some other adults got in on the fun too. Fred Cotton was the one who had stretched some old bicycle tires between two big trees. The tires had a leather pouch set in the middle. Ice grenades were loaded into the catapult and flung across the field to try and blow up the snowman army and its fort. That's what my team was doing that morning.

"Ready! Aim! Fire!"

It was pretty neat to watch our frozen egg missiles fly across the field and devastate Sarah's snow fortress. *Kaboom!* Stick arms and snow heads and carrot noses flew in every direction. If you wiped out the army in ten shots or less, your team was the winner. That was the whole point of the game—blowing stuff up. That's what Boomtown was all about.

Which was also the entire point of the Snow Castle the kids got to build every year. Captain Trudeau, a retired captain from the navy, hosted the castle on his property. He was in charge of overseeing safety. We spent two months building the castle and its surrounding walls and moat. It took thousands of ice blocks, which were made from snow packed into wooden frames and left overnight to freeze. The bricks of ice were stacked and bonded together with wet snow to create walls, doorways, bridges, towers, stairways, and battlements.

Our castle that year was a beauty! Towers on each corner with two extra-tall ones in the middle, an arched doorway, an icy ramp over the moat, and bright red flags blowing in the breeze. When it was hit by cold beams of sunlight, it glittered like a million diamonds. I couldn't wait to see it get blown to smithereens.

That was always the official beginning of the Spring Fever Festival—the day that all the frozen-weather, cabin-crazy grown-ups looked forward to. They would stand at their windows and check the thermostat, waiting for the temperature to climb above thirty-two degrees. It was the first day the ice on Lake Caona cracked—the day the creeks and streams began to run again, the day the steady *drip, drip* of melting icicles was heard all over town. That's the day the Snow Castle would go up in flames and the festival would begin.

It was a Saturday morning when everyone in town gathered in the field to watch the mayor of Boomtown push down the plunger and set off the dynamite and fireworks embedded in the ice. What an explosion! The ground shook, and the sun got covered up by all the flying snow. Glittering fragments of ice rose into the air colored by sparkling rocket bursts and shooting flares and cannon blasts as it all went up at once. The crowd cheered and cheered, but not as loud as the kids who had built the castle. I stood there with Busy and watched the explosion with great pride.

"Pretty neat," I said.

My best friend slapped me on the shoulder and grinned. "And this is only the beginning! There's a whole *week* of stuff like this! Let the games begin!"

CHAPTER 22

The Great Grand Slushathon

During Spring Fever Week, the gazebo in Farmer's Park features performances from local choirs and musical groups like the Boomtown Bombers—that's Sheriff Ernie's jazz band. They're really good. Booths are set up all over the place where you can buy roasted chestnuts, hot cider, homemade cookies and pies, hot dogs on a stick, and sparklers and firecrackers. Folks gather in knots to catch up on news. The kids have snowball fights in the streets. Everyone is in a good mood.

The Slush Olympics are held on the first Sunday afternoon. There's a whole list of events where you can win white, blue, and silver medals (silver being the best). The hardest event is probably the Slush Swim. The outdoor public pool in Chang Park is filled to the brim with slush, and competitors have to swim laps in the freezing slushy water. The swimmer who lasts the longest is the winner. It was our neighbor, Mr. LaPierre, who won that year. He looked like a blue popsicle when he was finished. I think he must be nuts.

Another big event is the Slush Pull. Busy invited me to join him and his dad for that one. It was simple, really. Build any kind of sled you want, strap it to a horse, and off you go! You can use anything you can find—something as simple as a sheet of plywood with rope handles—as long as you build it yourself.

For instance, there was this one team that took the hood off a car and welded runners and wheels underneath. Mr. Gunderson used his aluminum fishing boat. We pounded out the bottom until it was as flat as a pancake, and then we polished it with wax, and Busy painted stripes on the side. We'd tested it a few times by tying it to Mr. Gunderson's fastest horse, and we flew along like a feather in a hurricane.

We lined up at the starting gate for the race. *Bang!* Sheriff Ernie shot his pistol straight in the air and we were off. Starting from Farmer's Park, we had to loop around the statue of Chang in Town Square and then head west on Boom Boulevard. Zoom past the hardware store—zip past the Nuthouse—turn right on Blasting Cap—right on Dynamite Drive—zing past the factory and keep on going!

"*Whoooohooooo!*" we screamed, slush splashing in our faces and wind whipping in our frozen ears. Mr. Gunderson cracked the whip and pulled on the reins to make the turns. We almost tipped over coming around the sharp loop at the black powder factory, but Busy and I leaned to the right and got us back on the ice.

"They can't catch us now!" Busy's dad shouted. "It's straight on to the finish line!"

We finished the race with a quick dash along the river and

ended at Chang Park. People lined both sides of the street cheering on their favorite team. They shot off firecrackers and Roman candles when we reached the finish line, and all the rest of the week I got to parade around with a silver medal hanging around my neck. But that still wasn't the best part.

There were inner tube races over at Slippery Slope. There was the Slush Eating Contest, where people tried to eat as many bowls of lime-flavored slush as they could without getting up from the table to use the outhouse. Then there was the Slush Bucket Relay, where teams of four people scooped up buckets of slush and took turns running back and forth from the starting line until one team was the first to fill up the bed of a pickup truck. Then there was the Slushbarrow Race where two people fill a wheelbarrow with slush; then the musher pushes it and a slusher rides on top, as they dash through a slushy obstacle course. There was also Slush Hockey where teams of six players with straw brooms try to score goals by swatting a block of ice past the goalie.

By Saturday of Spring Fever Week everything was starting to wind down, but there was one big event left to go: the Great Grand Slushathon. Racers had to complete a three-mile racecourse riding on bicycles. Each bike had a studded tire on the back for traction and a short ski on the front for sliding. It was a father-and-son race. My dad wasn't too happy when he found out about it. I probably should have warned him before I pushed our bikes over to where he was standing.

"What's this thing for?" he asked.

"It's your Slushcycle. And your helmet. For the race."

"*What* race?"

"The Great Grand Slushathon. This is our number . . . 13. Not very lucky. Too bad."

"I'm not riding in the race!"

"But you *have* to! All the pastors are doing it, Dad. The Reverend Tinker. Even Pastor Platz. The mayor's gonna race. So's Burton Ernie."

"Maybe *they* are, but *I'm* not. I'm a pastor, not an athlete. I'll sit this one out. Besides . . . it looks dangerous."

"It's not *that* bad. Well, maybe a little bit. That's what makes it fun."

"No thanks. I have already had too many close calls. I am not going to go asking for trouble."

I was going to give up, but Pastor Platz was standing nearby and overheard what we were saying. He patted me on the shoulder and pulled my dad over to the side.

"Listen, Arthur, don't be nervous. I do this every year—I never finish, but I always start. My people expect it—so do yours. Right now they've got a pool going. You're not doing too badly. If you survive, they expect you to come in third or fourth place."

"If I *survive*? I can't ride one of those contraptions. I *won't*."

"Then you'll be the first pastor from Boomtown Church who hasn't ridden in the race for the past twenty-two years. At every festival, the pastors ride in the race and their whole congregations cheer them on."

"But why? What's the point?"

"You know how it is—people think their pastors are somehow different, like we're better than they are, more perfect. The mayor and a lot of the other community leaders were having the same problem. So we came up with this race just for us—the mayor and the sheriff and the pastors and their boys. It makes people feel like they can trust us because we're just like them—because we go out and make fools of ourselves and laugh about it. Do you see what I mean?"

My dad couldn't argue with that. He was always worried about what people were thinking. People expected pastors and their families to be perfect, but we were far from that. We tried to be good, but it was hard. Dad didn't want people to think we were any smarter or better than anybody else. So if this crazy race had a way of changing the way people thought about us, wasn't that worth it?

"Dad, I really think we should do it."

He looked at me, and his shoulders slumped in resignation. "So do I." He sighed heavily. "Give me the number."

We spent the next few minutes trying out the Slushcycle. I had the hang of it in no time, but Dad was having a lot of trouble. As soon as he started to pedal, the front ski skidded to the right. The back tire spun on the ice. He got his pant leg caught in the chain. His foot slipped off the pedal, and he banged his shin. Oh boy. This wasn't going to be pretty.

The warning gun sounded, and somehow Dad managed to slip

and slide and slosh through the slush with his "bicycle death machine" (that's what he kept calling it) over to the starting line with the other racers. Burton Ernie was there with his older son, Vernon, who was home from college for a visit. Busy was there with his dad. Frankie, Tony, Bobby, and a bunch of the other boys I knew from school and their dads were all lined up and ready and raring to go.

Then there was *my* dad, soaked up to his waist, a rip in his pants, and shivering from the cold. I was having trouble hearing the announcer over his chattering teeth. Captain Trudeau waved his arms and signaled the excited crowd for silence.

He shouted through a megaphone, "Attention, racers! The three-mile course is marked by red flags along the route. Any deviation from the course will result in automatic disqualification. Observers must refrain from assisting or hindering the racers in any way. Riders may dismount and push their bicycles whenever necessary. The first complete team to cross the finish line here in Town Square is the winner. Any questions?"

My dad's shaking hand slipped into the air.

"Yes? Pastor Button? You have a question?"

"Has anyone ever *died* doing this?"

The Captain laughed and so did everyone else. "Not yet, Arthur! Don't worry. We'll keep an eye on you. A *thousand* eyes. Just stick to the course."

Then the Captain raised the green flag. "On your mark . . . get set . . . MUSH!"

In a spray of ice-cold water, the racers took off to the cheers of the crowd—everybody except Dad. I was out in front with Busy; the twins were on our left; behind that came the main pack, but I had to stop when I heard Mom calling my name from the sidelines.

"Jon! *Jon!* Look behind you."

Pastor Platz and his son skidded past me, followed by Reverend Tinker who looked like a toothpick on wheels. Burton Ernie was long gone and so was everyone else. Dad was still frozen at the starting line.

He was wrestling with the handlebars. The back tire was spinning in the ice; the harder he pedaled, the faster it spun. Sarah came bursting out of the crowd and gave him a push. As he came down the street, I could see that he was starting to figure it out, even though he was still kinda wobbly. But by the time he reached me, he was feeling more confident, and he passed me with a grim look of determination on his face and a crooked smile.

"Watcha waitin' for, slowpoke? We've got some catching up to do!"

"Good job, dear!" Mom called. "See you at the finish line!"

After that, we were doing pretty good. We passed Pastor Platz on the side of the road with his face as purple as a summer grape. Next we passed Reverend Tinker who had crashed into a snowman on the side of the road; his son, who was almost as tall as his dad, was trying to get the two of them untangled. Next came the mayor; the ski on the front of his bike had fallen off. His team was out of the race. Then we passed my math teacher and the school principal and even the fire chief. All along the way our church members were there to wave us on, cheering my dad's name. "Button! Button! Can't catch the Button!"

"Hey, we're doing pretty good, aren't we?"

Dad was breathing heavily, but he coughed out an answer, "Yeah. I think I'll survive. Did you see all our people? I even saw Mrs. Beedle!"

I think that's when Dad understood how important the race really was. Not to win—there was no way we'd ever catch Sheriff

Ernie. We were too far behind. But to *try*. People wanted something to cheer for. They wanted to cheer for *him*—and he needed it too. It was a chance for him to act like a kid again.

"C'mon, Jon!" he said, leaning over his handlebars and pumping his legs. "Let's catch up to Lazy! I think I see him taking a nap on the side of the road!"

We whizzed past Lazy and Busy who were taking a breather at one of the comfort stations. These were spaced apart about every half mile where riders could stop, change wet socks for dry ones, get a hot or cold drink, dry off with a towel, and then keep on going. By the halfway mark riders were strung out all over the course. According to one of the station attendants, we were only in tenth place!

"Did you hear that, son? Only nine other teams in front us. Maybe we can catch up to a few more." He pulled on his other sock and tied his boot. He looked exhausted but determined.

"But we've still got to get through the toughest part. TNT Trail. You up for it?"

I was talking about the highest and muddiest part of the course, the trail out behind Lazy Gunderson's property. By the time we reached it, the other nine teams had churned it into a sloppy, lumpy, bumpy mess. There were tire and ski marks from where they had passed, and it was tough trying to avoid the holes and puddles and tree roots—not to mention the low-hanging branches and the piles of snow that kept falling on our heads as it melted from the trees. The sun had come out by then, and we were actually getting hot from working so hard. But we kept on going, even though we were covered in slushy muck. Dad looked like a mud snowman! He was having so much fun that he couldn't stop laughing.

Until I suddenly heard him yelping, "Look out!"

He was sliding around a corner and had to turn his handlebars almost sideways to avoid hitting the man who had come out of nowhere and was standing right in the middle of the trail. He had stumbled out from between the trees and didn't see us coming.

"Ahhh!" my dad screamed, crashing through the bushes and disappearing over the edge. I skidded to a stop and looked to see where he'd gone. Oh no. We were right at the top of the slide! There was our ski lift. There were some of our sleds parked on the side. And there was Dad, heading over the brink and down the solid ice surface of Slippery Slope, picking up speed as he went.

"What are *you* doing up here?" I gasped, shocked to see the Other Chang standing there, in broad daylight.

He shrugged and gave me a sheepish look. "I wanted to see the race."

"Well, you've got to go and hide. And I got to go and catch up to my dad!"

I threw my Slushcycle in the bushes and grabbed one of the sleds—but it was way too late. By then Dad was going like lightning, faster and faster, the front ski slithering back and forth as he shot down the hill, ice powder flinging up from the back tire, arms flailing, scarf flapping in the wind. He looked like one of our Hen Grenade ice balls flying through the air—with a big explosion at the end.

"Dad!" I wailed. "Fall down or something!"

I'm not sure that would have helped, but it seemed like the thing to say. He was going so fast by the time he reached the bottom that even some piles of dirt at the bottom of the slope didn't stop him. I guess the Other Chang had dumped them there during the night—they weren't there before. Instead of breaking his slide, they were more like a ramp. He flew past the bottom of the hill and up and over the piles. It was just like a ski jump. He was launched thirty feet into the air—head first toward heaven and glory—although he probably wasn't seeing it that way. His eyes were closed, and he was shouting something. I could only guess what it was.

"How did he die?" visitors would ask when they saw my dad's picture on the wall with all the others.

"Oh, him? He died at the bottom of Slippery Slope with a Slushcycle ski buried in his forehead."

"You don't say?"

"Yep! Too bad. Nice man. Tough way to go."

But then, miracles of miracles! Instead of crashing to the ground, my dad sailed high enough to land in the branches of a nearby tree, covered in nice soft snow. They caught him just like a mother would catch her baby, two arms spread wide. Then he bounced a couple of times and slid down until he went *plop* in the snow. The Slushcycle kept on going, though, and wrapped itself like a wet pretzel around the trunk of the tree. *Crunch!* That shook all the snow loose, and it buried my dad up to his neck.

By the time I dug him out of the snow bank, the race was long over, and it took almost another half hour to walk back to the finish line. People had sent out search parties, and they were very happy to find us alive. Dad got wrapped in blankets, and they set him down by a huge fire to get warmed up. Dr. Goldberg checked him over while I stood by waiting. Of course, Dad didn't look very happy.

It had gotten really late, so Mom went to get the car. Everyone else had drifted off home. Finally, it was just Dad and me. He looked me hard in the eye and frowned. "That man—on the trail. The one who nearly got me killed. He was wearing my coat. And my *hat*. Do you have any idea why?"

"Because he was *cold*?" I suggested.

Not exactly the answer Dad was looking for.

CHAPTER 23

Burton Ernie Investigates

The whole town was buzzing after the discovery of the "mysterious mounds" at the foot of Slippery Slope. Folks went out to marvel at the Slushcycle wrapped around the tree and talk about how Pastor Button had almost died for what—the *fourth* time now? Amazing. The guys and I listened while the adults stood around swapping their best theories about what the dirt piles could mean.

"It's Space Gophers, that's what I'm telling you," Mr. Gamelli insisted.

"Space Gophers?" Lazy snorted.

"You know, huge alien gophers from outer space. They came down in their gopher space ship, and they're diggin' around for who knows what."

"You're nuts! I say it's a government conspiracy."

"What, like spies? Secret agents?"

"Why not? Maybe they're digging a hidden base underground so they can conduct secret government experiments."

The mailman laughed. "*Now* who's talkin' crazy? Did you dream that up while sleepin' on your tractor?"

Of course there were no secret agents or Space Gophers. But no matter how hard anyone looked, they couldn't find any signs of digging, other than the mysterious mounds that appeared all over town. After the snow finished melting, there were piles of dirt dotting the landscape from one end of Boomtown to the other. And then there were all those burglaries. It was driving Sheriff Ernie bonkers.

He knocked on our door early one morning because he wanted to talk it over with my dad. They had become close friends. Burton Ernie sang in our church choir and played the saxophone. Mom and Dad had been invited to their house for dinner several times.

They played cards together on Tuesday nights. I'd heard them talking in the kitchen and knew that Dad was trying to encourage the sheriff even though his attempts to solve the crime spree in Boomtown had failed miserably.

I really don't think Sheriff Ernie was trying very hard to solve the case. It seemed to me he was enjoying all the trouble and gossip. Up until then, all I'd seen him do was drink bad coffee at Mabel's Diner and take naps in his police cruiser. There was hardly any crime in Boomtown. The occasional mailbox, among other things, was blown up by teenagers. That would have been a problem anywhere else but, quite frankly, it was encouraged here. Sometimes Sheriff Ernie had to give out a speeding ticket and warn a few jaywalkers. Of course, there were the random fires caused by stray fireworks. Other than that, Boomtown was as quiet as a church—not *our* church, of course—but as far as crime was concerned, things were pretty uneventful.

But that particular morning, I could tell that he was nervous as he stood on our doorstep and asked to come inside. He twirled his police cap in his left hand while he scratched his forehead with the other. He greeted Mom and accepted a cup of coffee while he sat at our breakfast table and waved good-bye to Sarah and Ruth as they went off to school. My dad told me to sit. The sheriff wanted to ask me a few questions.

"Don't be afraid, Jonny," he said with a friendly smile. "I've been around to talk to all the other boys and their parents. I'm gonna ask you the same things I asked them."

I wasn't too nervous. Everybody liked Burton Ernie, even though he wasn't a *real* policeman. I'd heard he hadn't gone to policeman's school or anything like that, but twenty years earlier, after the Bank of Boomtown got robbed, the mayor decided we needed a sheriff. He asked forty-seven other people until he got to Mr. Ernie. He said yes. Before that, he had worked at the fireworks factory. Ever since, he'd been the sheriff.

"I don't know anything," I said. "About the robberies, I mean."

"Your dad thinks he saw one of the men who might be involved up on Slippery Slope, just before his slushcycle accident. He says the man he saw was wearing his hat and coat."

I swallowed hard. "Did you see his face, Dad?"

"No, I didn't. I was too busy sliding down a hill to what could have been my untimely death, if you'll remember."

Inside I heaved a sigh of relief. "Oh. That's too bad." I paused, trying to think of a way to steer the questions away from me. "Have you found any other clues about the dirt?"

Sheriff Ernie shrugged. "I went up on top of the hill. No footprints—I mean, too *many* footprints. It's a real mess up there. I've been around to all the places to see the dirt piles. There must be about a hundred of them, but the same problem. Too much mud and rain and slush and whatever. Can't follow the tracks. But speaking of mud, that's the other thing. Each one of your friend's parents—Busy, Frankie and Tony, Bobby, Rocky—they all say the same thing. Your dad too. He says you've been coming home for months covered in dirt. Tracking mud into the house. Pants torn up. Tired all the time. What about that?"

The guys and I had planned for this. We had been out to Left Foot Island a bunch of times to leave some evidence. We figured we'd use the same story as when we'd been out all night.

"We've been working on a new fort—out on the island. We started it all the way back in October. You oughta see it! We're trying to get it finished before school lets out." I held my breath and waited.

Sheriff Ernie twisted his lip and studied my eyes. "That's what all your friends said. I went out to the island. It's a pretty good fort, you're right about that." He sipped his coffee and glanced sideways at my dad. "Nothing else you want to tell me?"

"Nope."

Burton Ernie stood up and pushed his chair away from the table with a scrape. "So, Arthur? Are you coming with me like we discussed?"

"I am. Just let me get my *new* hat and coat." He stood up and kissed Mom on the cheek. "You too, Jon. Get your things. You're coming with us."

"I am? But what about school?"

"It'll hold for today. We're going to sniff around with Burton here. We thought maybe you'd have a few ideas to share as we go along."

I gulped down my milk and tried to hide my excitement—and

my fear. I suspected that Dad was suspecting *me*. If we got close to where the Other Chang was hiding, or if we found something related to the robberies or some other clue, Dad would see it in my face. Like a game of Hide and Seek. If we got "warm" or "warmer," I would give the secret away. I was going to have to be very, very careful.

We walked out the front door and down the sidewalk to the steady drizzle of springtime rain and climbed into the sheriff's police cruiser. It was great—the other guys were going to flip when I told them about it. The white and black car had BOOMTOWN SHERIFF painted on the door with a star in the middle. The seats were gray leather, and there was a cage between the front and back. It had a searchlight and a siren and a red light on the roof. Sheriff Ernie let me play with all three of them. I gave the siren a good, loud squeal as we drove down the street and headed out toward the fireworks factory.

"So where are we going?" Dad asked.

"I was at the library talking to Helga Knutsen. Have you met her?"

"Sure have. Nice woman."

"Anyway, I went to see her because she knows everybody in town. Everyone has a library card. People are in there three or four times a month. She hears all the local gossip. Same as Mabel out at the diner. If they don't know something, nobody knows it."

"So what did she tell you?"

"She wondered if I'd been out to see Denk."

"Denk? What's a Denk?"

"Volodenka Sviatoslavova," Sheriff Ernie stumbled over the name. "Nobody can ever pronounce it—especially me—so we just call him Denk. He lives down by the river—just him and his kids. He doesn't come into town much. But he goes all over the place, hunting and fishing, at night, early morning, that sort of thing. Helga wondered if he might have seen something."

Dad nodded. "Worth a try." He turned to ask me. "What do *you* think, Jon? Think maybe Denk has seen something? Maybe people sneaking around at night? People doing things they aren't supposed to be doing?"

"I don't know. Maybe."

I stared out the window as we drove along, my hot breath steaming up the glass as we went. I drew a frowny face with my finger. It stared back at me with guilty eyes.

Let's hope that Denk can't see or hear so good, I thought as I put my nose close to my frowny friend, *or I'm going to be in big trouble!*

CHAPTER 24

The Mysterious Letter

So what can you tell me about this Denk person?" my dad asked as we turned off Dynamite Drive and bounced down a muddy side road filled with rocks and dirty puddles.

"It's a sad story, actually," Burton Ernie answered, trying to keep his cruiser from crashing into the nearby trees. "Denk had lived with his wife and seven children down by the river west of town for as long as anyone could remember, same as his father and his grandfather before that. But about two years ago his wife died of pneumonia. He's been on his own ever since."

"He's been raising seven children all by himself?"

"He's got the help of the older kids. He's managed, same as always."

We pulled up in front of a ramshackle cabin. It kind of looked like the fort we were building—a bunch of junk nailed together and tucked under a tin roof and patched with tarp and sheets of bark. A pencil-thin trickle of smoke rose from a river-rock chimney. There was a flicker of light showing through one of the window openings that were covered in thin, plastic sheeting.

Two of the kids were out in the front yard tending a sow with her piglets. A third girl was feeding the chickens. A huge man I assumed was Denk was to the far right of the house splitting wood. An older boy gathered up the pieces after they went flying under the powerful swings of his giant father. He stopped and shouldered the ax and watched us as we climbed out of the cruiser and walked over to where he stood waiting.

"Morning, Denk. Wasn't sure if you'd be home. Thought you might be out hunting."

Denk was almost taller than all of us put together. Two icy blue eyes stared suspiciously out of the nest of his long hair and scraggly beard. A puff of steam curled up from his beard in the cool, morning air. He was wearing a patchy cloak made out of different kinds of animal skins, and a wide leather belt around his waist held a huge bone-handled hunting knife in its sheath. He had on deerskin pants and heavy boots and a thick, cotton shirt. He looked just like a Viking. He even had the axe.

He answered in a thick Slavic accent, "Got me a moose two days ago. That'll do us for now." He gestured with his thumb toward the animal hanging dead on a hook from a tree. It was as big as a truck. The horns looked like the two hands of a giant.

"That's a big one," Sheriff Ernie said. "No doubt about it."

Denk gave us an icy stare, and it made me shiver.

"So, Denk," Sheriff Ernie asked nervously, "the reason we came out . . . maybe you've heard about the robberies we've been having around town? And the mysterious mounds? Thought maybe you'd seen or heard something while you were out hunting or fishing."

"Nope."

"No unexplained noises? No strangers sneaking around?"

"Besides you, no."

"Find anything unusual? Tracks? Tunnels? Anything like that?"

He stood silently for a minute, like a giant Viking tree that had no place to go. He scratched his beard and then nodded toward the shack with his head. "Found me a piece of paper. Want to see it?"

We stomped through the mud and followed Denk into the house. A single kerosene lamp lit the dark room. In the dim light, I could see three more girls sitting on benches and gathered around a thick, hand-carved table. One was reading, the oldest was sewing a loose hem on a dress, and the youngest was perched in a high chair and playing with a rag doll. They stared at us silently as we stood dripping in front of the fireplace. Something was cooking in the big black pot over the coals. It didn't smell very good.

Denk reached up and grabbed the paper that was propped behind a framed picture of a blonde woman. She was pretty and had braids and looked a lot like the older girl. It must have been his wife. Sheriff Ernie took the paper, and we carried it over to the lamp. It was all crumpled with age and folded across the middle, on some kind of very thin parchment. It crinkled as the sheriff studied what looked like a letter. Even though the paper was yellow and faded with age, I could still see the Chinese characters written carefully in black ink and a red stamp at the bottom.

Denk grunted. "Can't read it. Don't care. You can have it."

"Where did you find it?" Sheriff Ernie asked.

"Down by the river, back of the fireworks factory. It was stuck on a branch. 'Bout a week ago."

Dad peered over Sheriff Ernie's shoulder and tried to make out the words.

"We'll have to get it translated. It's all written in Chinese."

The sheriff shook his head. "Nope. I can do it—I'm a little rusty, though."

"You can read Chinese?" my dad asked surprised.

"I used to work at the factory, remember? I picked up quite a bit from my buddies down there. Like right here, the first line, it says 'follow directions' and 'map.'"

"What map?" I gasped but then tried to cover it up with a cough.

由我給了，你應該沒有的
指揮引起在找出快取方面
的困難，迄今仍然是秘
密。向沒人提及這，雖然
應該你從來做出旅程，你
可能相信我的在變化中的
朋友。我只能希望這件禮
物將補償我的忽略，雖然
沒什麼東西以他的父親的
損失可以償還一個兒子。
我祈求這封信找到朝往你
的手的路徑，懷著最好的
願望，愛和榮譽，你的父親

"I don't know. I just started reading. But next it says 'find hidden' or—I'm not sure about this word—I think it means 'secret.'"

My dad was getting excited. "It sounds like instructions on how to find something that's been hidden. You follow a secret map to find it? Maybe something that's buried. That would explain a lot."

Sheriff Ernie continued translating. "I think you're right, Arthur. Look here. This next bunch of words. First a warning: 'Tell no one.' Then 'journey,' 'friends,' 'trust,' 'town.'"

"What's it all mean?"

"I think it's saying that whoever is making the journey isn't supposed to tell anyone—except maybe for the friends who live in the town. I suppose the letter means Boomtown."

"Well, if it is talking about the people of Boomtown, it's true. The people I've met certainly can be trusted. We've seen that, haven't we, Jon?" Dad smiled and put his hand on my shoulder. "But who's the letter for? Who's making the journey? What's hidden? What are they looking for?" I was wondering all the same questions.

"The letter doesn't say—but look at what it DOES say." The sheriff pointed at the words. "'Gift.' 'Return.' 'Father.' 'Son.' 'Sorrow.' 'Love.' 'Honor.'" Then it says 'father' a second time and then this!"

"What?"

Sheriff Ernie has his finger on the red box at the bottom of the letter. It was a carved stamp with intricate markings placed in the lower right corner.

"That's a signature. It's called a 'chop.' I'd know that mark anywhere. That's Chang. That's Chang's signature!"

"*Our* Chang?" my dad exclaimed.

"The one and only! Do you know what this means?"

Of course we didn't. Both of us just stood looking at Sheriff Ernie like he had four heads.

"It means," he announced proudly, "that our Gentleman Bachelor, our dear old Chang, may have been a *father* after all! This letter came from Chang. Maybe he was writing to his son, and he was inviting him to come to Boomtown to search for something hidden. He was supposed to keep the journey a secret, but when he got here, he was supposed to ask for help from the town."

Chang's *son*! Of course! That's why the Other Chang looked so much like the statue and the photos—it was his *father*.

"But that's impossible," my dad objected. "You said Chang lived alone his entire life. He didn't have a wife. He didn't have any children. He died almost sixty years ago. That would make his son more than eighty years old! How could he be here in Boomtown? Digging holes? Sneaking around stealing lawnmowers and Christmas lights? He'd have to be in pretty good shape for that . . . or . . ."

My dad stopped abruptly and turned to look at me. ". . . or he'd have to have an awful lot of help, isn't that right, Jon?"

I almost tripped over my feet as I backed away. "Hey, don't look at me! I haven't seen any eighty-year-old robbers lurking around town."

All of a sudden, Sheriff Ernie glanced at his watch and shouted, "But I have! I can't believe I forgot! Look at the time! I'm going to be late!"

Dad and I ran after him as he dashed out the door carrying the letter flapping in his hand.

"Late? Late for what?"

"For the bank robbery! It's Tuesday! It's almost 11:00! We got to skedaddle!"

CHAPTER 25

CHANG'S FAMOUS FIREWORKS

Another Near Miss

Burton Ernie was already in the car with the engine running and the front window rolled down. "C'mon, boys, hurry up!"

I ran around to the passenger side, but Dad hung back to talk to Denk, who stood towering in the road with two of his children at his side. They looked so forlorn and damp and poor standing there. I guess that's why Dad had to say something.

"Denk, we weren't really introduced. My name is Arthur Button. I'm the new pastor out at Boomtown Church." He put out his hand, and Denk stared at it like it was a rotten fish.

"I . . . um . . . I was just thinking. With your situation and all . . . the kids . . . you've got your hands full. We've got some great programs at the church. We could help with some food—maybe with the children. The men could fix your roof. Maybe I could come back tomorrow and we could talk about it?"

Denk looked like he was going to grab Dad's head off his shoulders and hang it next to the moose. He sure could have done it if he wanted to. Instead, with a loud grunt he spun on his heel and stomped back into the cabin with his children in tow. The door slammed with a *bang* and he was gone.

"Ah, nerts, Arthur! Now why'd you go and do that for?"

"What?" my dad complained, climbing into the car. I slipped in beside him, and the sheriff pressed down on the accelerator angrily. We bounced back down the muddy road and out onto the street with the siren blaring.

"You *insulted* him! After he helped us and all! That was really too much."

My dad still didn't get it. "What did I do? I just offered to help. You saw how they were living. It's only the Christian thing to do."

"You think so? You think you know how Denk lives? You could tell that just by *looking* at him?"

"Well, no . . . I mean . . . I just thought . . ."

Burton Ernie turned left on Blasting Cap and raced down the street. "You didn't think, that's the problem! That man was almost ripped in half when his wife died. I never saw a man cry so much. But after a while, he pulled it all together. He had to. He had seven kids to take care of—he's done it ever since. Did you know that his girl is the number one student in her class at Stickville? His boy makes practically all As. He hunts and he fishes and he feeds them. They work together as a family—they ain't rich, but they ain't poor neither."

"I was just trying to help," my dad murmured.

"Sometimes the best way to help is to mind your own business.

Right now, the best thing to do is jump out of the car. We're here!"

Burton Ernie came screeching up in front of the Bank of Boomtown, slammed on the brakes, leaped out of the car, and ran up onto the curb. There was already a small crowd gathered, but with the arrival of the sheriff, more people came running. They burst out of the stores and shouted to their friends across the way, and by the time Dad and I got onto the sidewalk, there must have been a hundred people waiting outside, looking toward the bank.

"What's going on, Burt?" Dad asked.

"I told you!" he shouted. "The bank is being robbed."

"But how do you know?"

"Because it's *Tuesday*! The bank is *always* robbed on Tuesday."

Before he could say anything else, the front doors of the bank burst open and out stomped the bank robber. He had a bag of money in his left hand and a gun in his right. He looked like he could be about eighty, and he was wearing a jean jacket, a red flannel shirt, gloves, and a black stocking hat and glasses. He wasn't the least bit surprised to see the police car or Burton Ernie with his gun drawn or the crowd of people who'd been waiting for him to come out. Instead, the old man threw the bag on the ground, pointed at his watch, and started yelling at Sheriff Ernie in a disgusted voice.

"You're late! It's *two minutes* after eleven. I had to stand in the lobby of the bank and *wait* for you!"

"Hey, I'm sorry, Frank," Sheriff Ernie apologized. "We got tied up down at Denk's place."

"You know this was my first robbery since the doctor removed my cast. I was all excited, and then I had to stand here like a dope waiting for you to show up!"

"Really, I'm so sorry."

"Well, don't let it happen again." He stood there with his

hands on his hips and tapped his foot impatiently. "So? I'm *waiting*. You gonna arrest me or ain'tcha?"

"Oh! Right! Almost forgot. I got the handcuffs right here."

Burton Ernie put his gun back in his holster and walked over to the bank robber.

"Burton! What are you doing? Aren't you going to take his gun?" Dad shouted, pointing at the black revolver still in the robber's hand.

"Oh yeah—'suppose I should." He reached out to take the revolver and then stopped. "Hey, Frank, that's not your usual gun, is it? The other one's smaller, if I remember right."

"I got my favorite down at Guenther's Gun Corral. Gettin' the sights realigned and the pistol grip recovered. This is my backup piece. Nothin' to worry about, though. It ain't loaded or nothin', same as always."

Just to prove it, he twirled the gun and pulled the trigger. He sure looked surprised when the gun went off—*Bang!* All the people standing around screamed. The sheriff dropped the handcuffs. I almost fainted. But poor old Dad—he felt the bullet go whizzing past his ear. I think it must have missed him by only a few inches.

Dad jumped backward and tripped over his feet. He bounced off the fender of the cruiser. He slipped down onto the cement with his eyes as big as two donuts. Just over his shoulder, the bullet had made a perfectly round hole through the *o* in the No Parking sign. Neat shot!

"Frank!" Burton Ernie hollered. "I thought you said it wasn't loaded!"

"It wasn't!" the robber cried, looking at the smoking gun. "At least, I *thought* it wasn't loaded. Musta' missed one."

He shrugged his shoulders, handed the gun to Sheriff Ernie, put his arms out, and let the sheriff cuff his hands. "Sorry 'bout that, Preacher. Nothin' personal."

Dad was flat on his backside, clutching his chest and counting his buttons. "One, two, three, four . . . that's the FIFTH time I've almost been killed! I'm running out of buttons!"

Sheriff Ernie opened the car door and pushed Frank into the backseat. Then he came over and checked to see if Dad was okay.

"I think your guardian angel has been workin' overtime."

Dad bellowed, "My guardian angel is going to quit his job and go on vacation! Before I got to Boomtown I never even had a paper cut! Whoever thought that being a preacher could be this dangerous?"

We helped him to his feet and tried to brush off some of the mud. "Wow, Dad! Look at the parking sign. That coulda been you."

People had come running at the sound of the gunshot. There had to be more than two hundred folks by then. Everybody was talking at once and swapping their version of the story. Dad was getting more and more upset. I guess he had a good reason.

"Can you *please* explain what is going on?"

"Sure 'nough, Arthur," Burton Ernie answered. "You see that feller in my backseat? That's the notorious Frank Cavenaugh! You ever hear of him—Frankie the Banker? Made a name for himself about twenty years ago."

"Sure, I remember hearing about that. He robbed about thirty banks before they caught him, isn't that right?"

"That's him! He's the same one who came to Boomtown and robbed our bank—he's the biggest reason I got made sheriff! Anyway, he was doing a job down south of here and got himself arrested. He was convicted, served fifteen years in the state penitentiary, then got released four years ago with time off for good behavior. He's been living here ever since."

NAME FRANKIE "THE BANKER" CAVANAUGH (ADDRESS)

INTERMEDIATE
REC ALGOA,WA.
1536

DATE OF ARREST
CHARGE Bank Robbery
DISPOSITION OF CASE
RESIDENCE
PLACE OF BIRTH Mo.
NATIONALITY Amer.
CRIMINAL SPECIALTY
AGE 38 BUILD Slender
HEIGHT 5-5 COMP. [illegible] HAIR [illegible]
WEIGHT 109 EYES Sp Blue
SCARS AND MARKS [illegible]

CRIMINAL HISTORY

NAME	NUMBER	CITY OR INSTITUTION	DATE	CHARGE	DISPOSITION OR SENTENCE

RECEIVED 11-3-33 FROM Spokane COUNTY TO SERVE 20 YRS.

FROM 10-28-33 FOR THE CRIME OF Bank Robbery

Record By....V. T. Adamson, Superintendent,
Bureau of Identification,
State Penitentiary.

"But why here?"

"Frank came back after he got out of prison and told me that while he'd been staking out the bank in Boomtown, he decided he really liked the place. Nice people. Fireworks. His kind of town. So after the fifteen years, he wanted to come back here. The folks were glad to have him. He's what you call a local celebrity, the only man to ever commit a major crime in Boomtown. They let him ride in the Fourth of July parade. And he teaches classes at the library on firearms safety."

"Firearms safety? You're pulling my leg, right?"

"No sir, I'm not. He's usually a lot more careful."

"And now he robs the bank on Tuesday? *Every* Tuesday?"

"That's right—a little deal me and him worked out. It's about the only thing he really knows how to do—rob banks. And without him, I don't get to arrest anybody. It keeps both of us sharp. Good practice. And besides, it gives our town a little more character. The neighbors pay him a small salary for the show. Keeps a roof over his head. Keeps him out of jail—except for today, of course. Guess you didn't know about it 'cause last fall he broke his leg something awful, and it's been in a cast for months. He just got the cast off, and Doctor Goldberg gave him the okay to start up robbing again."

"You know what I think? I think all you people are loony."

Sheriff Ernie just shrugged his shoulders and took Frank to jail. He got released the next day and promised to be more careful in the future. From then on Sheriff Ernie tried extra hard to make it to the bank on time. The No Parking sign was removed and installed in the lobby of the library. When visitors saw it, someone was sure to tell the story about Arthur Button, the man who *almost* got shot by Frankie the Banker.

After that Dad stayed inside the house for almost a month, except on Sundays. He kept the door locked and his head down. He even gave up shaving. He told me that he was afraid of a horrible shaving accident. He stopped asking me any questions about the dirt or the mysterious man or the robberies, which meant that my buddies and I had a lot more freedom to move around.

But was that the end of it? Not by a long shot.

The Fourth of July

The first chance I got, I confronted the Other Chang about the letter. I figured he must have lost it during one of his trips out into the open. The guys gathered around while I questioned him, anxiously waiting to find out the truth. This time he couldn't deny it, but he kept his face turned away in the dim candlelight of his cavern hideaway and answered in a halting voice. I think he was afraid.

"It's true," he admitted. "My name is Xian Chang. You can call me Xian."

"Huh?"

"SHE ON," he pronounced it slowly. It sounded like Shawn. Or even my name, Jon, except the *J* sounded like a "she." We all practiced saying it: *She-on*. Xian.

"What the letter hinted at is true, although Chang was *not* my father. He was my great-grandfather, born in China more than one hundred and twenty years ago."

"But how? Everybody says that Chang was a bachelor. He didn't have any kids."

"Chang didn't *know* he had a child," Xian explained. "My great-grandmother, Wen, was pregnant when Chang escaped from China. He was only seventeen years old—he didn't know that his wife was going to have a baby. Otherwise, I don't think he ever would have gone."

"But why did run away in the first place?"

Xian's dark eyes glittered in the flickering candlelight. "It was a terrible time in our country, during the rule of an evil emperor named Daoguang. He persecuted men such as Chang's father who was a professor of history and a fine gentleman. He was against violence and refused to fight in the emperor's many battles.

"Daoguang's cruelty bred rebellion like mushrooms after the rain. He was always at war fighting neighboring lands, but especially our own people. One day he sent troops to our home village to force the young men living there to join his army. Chang's father confronted them at the gateway to the village and refused to let them enter. He was arrested, but it gave Chang enough time to escape."

We were absolutely fascinated by Xian's story. Even though it was cold and damp in the underground hideout, we could have sat listening to him for hours. Busy asked the next question.

"Why didn't he take Wen with him?"

"There wasn't enough time. He told her that he would find a safe place for them to live. As soon as he did, he would send for her. But a year passed and then another and yet another. Word never came. His son was born, my grandfather, Hui. Years went by and after a while, my family assumed he must be dead. We believed that until the letters came."

"Right!" I exclaimed "The letter! The page that Denk found. There's more to it, isn't there? More pages? *And the map*? Where did that come from?"

Xian's face looked sad. "It is a very long story, and I have digging that must be done. There is a new place—I think it is the tunnel I have been looking for."

"Please tell us," I pressed him. "What are you looking for? The letter said it was a secret—that you weren't supposed to tell anyone—*except* the people of Boomtown. That's us! *We're* the people of Boomtown. You're *supposed* to tell us."

But he wouldn't say anything more, no matter how many times we asked him. Instead, he worked even harder trying to dig through a new caved-in area he'd found. He worked so hard over the next few months that he started to lose weight and was showing signs of a fever. He would cough a lot and wipe his sweating forehead with a rag. He almost never talked when we came to help, except to beg us to keep his secret. He was *sure* he was getting close. But I think he was starting to lose hope.

Months went by as spring turned to early summer and school ended for that year. Not only were we busy helping Xian in the tunnel, the guys and I had also been super busy working on our float for the Fourth of July parade. It was a fire-breathing dragon on wheels, complete with wings and a mouth that opened and flames and smoke that shot out of the mouth. It was Busy's idea to rig up a microphone and speakers. We took turns pedaling the cart, flapping the wings, swooshing the tail, blasting the smoke, and shouting into the microphone with snarls and growls. We were very proud of the results.

The Fourth of July parade was, of course, the biggest bash of the year for Boomtown. People would travel from miles around to watch it, some from as far away as Seattle and even Spokane. They came not only to see the floats and hear the bands, but also to see the most spectacular fireworks show in Washington. Chang's Famous Fireworks Factory hummed twenty-four hours a day in order to get all the fireworks made on time—nine *tons* of rockets, shells, firecrackers, Roman candles, cherry bombs, gerbs, and girandoles for the big fireworks show they hosted every year in Chang Park. The launching platform was built on the shores of Left Foot Island, and a brass band would play music during the blast off. Meanwhile, red, white, and blue bunting waved in the breeze along every street in town. Everyone was dressed in patriotic costumes. There were booths and displays and noisy activity wherever you went. Everybody was excited.

It was always a busy time of the year for Boomtown. The month of May was for planting the fall crops. June was set aside for bringing in the winter wheat harvest and cherry picking. But none of that kept anyone from dropping their rakes and shovels to have a little fun. They made plenty of time to build fancy floats, sew costumes, iron uniforms, practice band music, build grandstands and booths, bake cakes and pies, and make caramel apples and cotton candy for selling. The Hopontop Circus was in town for that week and so was the Bonitelli Brothers' Traveling Carnival. That meant rides and rodeos to go along with all the blasts and booms. I was in hog heaven. I never had so much fun in all my life.

The big day finally arrived. Helga the librarian was in charge of getting everyone lined up for the parade. She ran up and down the line, handling any last minute emergencies, checking on the musicians, straightening ribbons and bows, and telling everyone to smile, smile, *smile!*

BOOMTOWN

52ND ANNUAL

FOURTH OF JULY PARADE

FIREWORKS

IN CHANG PARK AT SUNSET

COME and JOIN THE FUN

BANG STREET & BOOM BOULEVARD
STARTING AT NOON SHARP

Mayor Tanaka and his wife, Kyoko, rode in the lead car waving to the crowd. It was followed by a float that looked like a battleship on fire. The float had a cannon on it that the mayor's son kept blasting off. It was so loud it rattled the windows. I didn't mention it before, but our mayor was a famous war hero. He saved five men trapped inside a burning ship by blasting a hole in the deck with a bag of gunpowder. The people in Boomtown loved that sort of thing, so when he came back wounded from the war, they made him mayor.

The mayor's float was followed by the Stickville Slugs marching band, dressed in their slime green and brown uniforms and playing the school fight song. Right after that came the Slug Queen Float with my sister, the Slug Queen, and her giggling gaggle of Slug Princesses. She sat proudly waving from her Slug Throne in the middle of Slug Grotto. Perched on the front was King Waldo holding the muddy game ball from the historic win over the Giants. Marching alongside was the entire muddy football team clomping along in their muddy cleats.

Next came the Root Beer Float. It was sponsored by St. Bernard's Lutheran Church and had all the members from the church serving ice cream and root beer to the crowd as fast as they could scoop.

Then the Back Float, built by Carlson's Chiropractic.

The Goat Float, built by Fannie's Fleece and Feathers.

The Coat Float, built by Kellogg's Clothiers.

And the Note Float, built by the Boomtown Music Store.

Finally, it was our turn. We rolled down the street, snarling and blasting, surrounded on every side by all the kids from the fifth and sixth grades at Boomtown School. The boys were dressed as knights. They had cardboard shields covered in tin foil in one hand and wooden swords and lances in the other. The girls were dressed as young princesses, and they kept squealing and running away from the dragon while the knights tried to cut off its head with their swords. It was a big hit with the crowd. I could hear them cheering from inside the dragon. It was awfully hot in there, but it was worth it!

The parade rolled noisily on, winding its way up Bang Street, back around along Volcano Way, until it turned at Farmer's Park and ended in Town Square. That's where the finale would be—the detonation of the Founder's Float—an annual tradition that signaled the official ending for the parade. I'll tell you about that in a minute—it was the blast that changed everything. But not yet.

Next in the parade came the Hopontop Traveling Circus with their trick riders and jugglers and dancers. Sheriff Burton Ernie in his cruiser, blaring his siren. He was followed by the proud faces of the war veterans dressed in their uniforms and medals and led by the color guard and the Marine Corps band. Then the clown cars driven by the Bonitelli Brothers' clowns. Then the banging, clanging, clonking, bonking BangOnBuckets Band led by Gus Odegaard—that was Bobby's dad—owner of Gus's Gas-N-Go. Anybody could play, as long as they brought a frying pan or a bucket and something to hit it with.

That was followed by the Boomtown Museum float, with Samora and her sister riding in a pair of inflated Sky Campers being pulled along by a steam-belching machine on huge metal wheels. The two ladies were throwing cinnamon-flavored candy to the kids in the crowd. These looked like small sticks of dynamite with black licorice "fuses" coming out of the top and tasted like fire in your mouth. And then the Hog Callers Club calling "SoooWHEE! SoooWHEE!" And the Miner's Float. And Chang's Fireworks Float. And the Farmer's Float.

The parade rolled on and on . . . inching closer and closer to the fiery flaming finale when our perfectly imperfect plan blew up in our flabbergasted faces. The explosion was unlike anything Boomtown had ever seen.

We never saw it coming—unfortunately neither did my dad.

CHAPTER 27

A "Hole" New Problem

The day before the parade, there was a knock on our front door. It was Pastor Platz and Reverend Tinker again, this time with some news about the Fourth of July.

"Oh, didn't anyone tell you, Arthur? The three of us, we're the Masters of Ceremony."

"Since when?"

"Since *always*! It's a Boomtown tradition, dating all the way back to your fifteenth predecessor—his name was Daniel Weaver or something like that. The ministers of Boomtown take the stage and announce all the floats and bands as they march through Town Square. We're the ones who signal the ignition of the Founder's Float. It's a very important responsibility—and a great honor."

Dad backed away and started to count the buttons on his shirt.

"One, two, three, four, five! I've been nearly killed five times already at one of your Boomtown events. I don't want any part of this one!"

"Oh, don't be ridiculous, Arthur. What could possibly happen in the middle of Town Square? You'll be surrounded by thousands of people! You'll be safe up on the stage. Timothy and I will be standing right next to you. What could be safer than having two ministers at your side?"

Dad argued for a while, but finally gave in. Ruth borrowed a Slug football helmet and gave it to him. He could wear it during the parade. Besides that, both pastors made sure the stage was extra sturdy, and they added an extra-thick railing around all the sides. The stage was built right in front of Chang's statue in the center of Town Square. Every precaution was taken to keep Dad from getting hurt, but that didn't make him feel any less nervous. The whole idea of being surrounded by rockets and sparklers and firecrackers and exploding parade floats made him shake in his shoes.

"It's okay, Dad. Mom will be there watching. And Sarah will be right next to her."

"Yeah, Dad! Don't worry. I'll watch out for bank robbers and flying barber chairs. No problem."

"Very funny," my dad grumbled. "But *you're* not the one who's in danger. *I* am."

Still, the next day he was on the stage with the other two pastors, wearing his football helmet and announcing the floats as they came rolling down the street. I peeked through the crack between the body and the wing and saw him cringe when our fire-breathing dragon got close. But I could tell he was impressed, even if he was scared. We pedaled our contraption out to the field at the Boomtown School and then ran all the way back to Town Square.

We didn't want to miss seeing the Founder's Float being blown up. That was supposed to be pretty great.

We weren't disappointed. The display was built on the back of a flatbed pickup truck. Lazy Gunderson got to build it that year, and he also got to drive the truck. Captain Trudeau was in charge of the explosives. Some of the ladies from our church helped with the models.

The Founders Float was a reenactment of the day when Change, Washington, blew itself inside out. There was a plaster of paris mountain painted brown and green with little plastic trees and rocks and sand glued on top of it. The old town—before it was destroyed—was built in little miniature reproductions of the shops and buildings and farmhouses. There were little plastic miners in front of mineshafts, pushing wheelbarrows or carrying pickaxes and digging holes looking for gold. On the side of the mountain was a sign that said Founder's Day Float and on the other side another one that said Boomtown 1894–1950. There were American flags flapping from the roof of the truck, and Lazy was waving to everyone as he parked about ten yards in front of Dad's stage.

By then, Busy and me and Rocky and the twins were all standing and waiting for the big moment. I was close enough to hear Dad, even over all the shouting and clapping.

"Does he have to park that close to us? Look how many people are standing around it," he pointed out.

"Not to worry," Pastor Platz assured him, patting him on the shoulder. "Burton will take care of it. Besides, that's not the real problem, anyway."

"It's not?"

"No. It's the *Captain*. He's the one who rigged up the explosives. He always tends to overdo it on the dynamite. Keep your eyes peeled—and your head down."

Burton Ernie was in the square waving everyone to get out of the way. "Back up! Back up!" he shouted. "At least fifty feet! Back behind that rope over there."

While Sheriff Ernie handled the crowd, I tried to look around and make sure that Dad was out of danger. After all, it *had* been five times already. I didn't want him to get hurt. That's when I noticed the crack.

"Hey, Busy. What's that? I don't think that was there before."

"What?"

"The crack. Right there in the street. You see? It starts from underneath the Founder's Float, and it kind of wanders over to here—and then look—it goes underneath the stage and up to the statue of Chang."

He followed me around as we traced the crack. It started out in the street, but it reached all the way to the edge of the curb and followed the edge all the way around to the back. It kept going after that—and it was getting bigger!

"Oh no!" I shouted. "*Dad!* Dad! You've got to get off the stage!"

I ran around to the front waving my arms and yelling his name. Pastor Platz heard me and saw what I was pointing at. Reverend Tinker did too. They headed for the steps and tried to get Dad to listen, but he was confused by the shouting of the crowd. He saw my frantic arms waving, the sudden departure of his pastor pals, and people scattering. But before he could get his legs moving there came the sound of the Founder's Float exploding. The miniature city lifted off the ground and shot straight up into the sky in a blaze of fire and cloud of smoke.

KABOOM!

I ducked as a piece of the miniature Boomtown Museum went flying over my head. The other small buildings disappeared in a whoosh of fire. In less than a few seconds, we were being showered by a white cloud of plaster as it rained down on our heads. There had to be more than two thousand people in the square that day, all of them clapping and stomping their feet. The earth shook from their stomping, but even without them, the Captain had made sure the ground would quake with all his extra explosives. The back end of the truck had been smashed into the street—and that's all it took. The crack opened up wide and shot straight to where my dad was standing on the stage. He never knew what hit him.

I had to run away like everyone else as they felt the road begin to shift. Pastor Platz passed me on the right, rolling along like a bowling ball down a steep hill. Busy and Rocky ran screaming, along with a thousand other people, as the street trembled, then cracked, then opened up wide like the mouth of a whale. My poor dad was trapped in the middle like Jonah, and was swallowed up whole—the stage, the microphones, the speakers—nothing was going to stop it.

Behind him was the statue of Chang. It had to weigh more than ten tons—all the cement and the bronze chickens and Chang on his chair. It tipped forward and down. I watched my dad disappear in a cloud of dirt and flying asphalt. The last thing I saw was the look in his eye. *Good-bye, son. It was nice knowing you.*

It took almost five minutes for the dust to clear. By then the volunteer fire department had arrived. They weren't far away; they had been part of the parade. Doc Goldberg was standing by, waiting for them to scramble down into the hole to pull Dad out of there. He stood clutching his black bag anxiously—he didn't look very confident. Mom was there too, and Ruth with her Slug tiara and slime green dress—both of them crying. Even Sarah was worried; she ran around and tried to get the firemen to hurry up.

"Get down there!" she ordered. "Get down there and help my dad! Or I'll go get him myself, you slow pokes!"

They dropped down a ladder and threw in some ropes and got ready to scramble down into the hole. But before they could, a loud gasp rippled through the crowd. By then the dust had settled enough, and the sun had managed to break through the gray gloom. It shone down on a scene that no one would ever forget. I can still remember it like it was yesterday.

There at the bottom of the hole was the statue. Sitting in Chang's lap was my father, bruised, battered, covered from head to toe in cement dust—almost as gray as the statue he was laying on. He was just beginning to open his eyes—and what did he see standing next to him? The living, breathing mirror image of the man portrayed on the statue.

Xian had come running down the tunnel when he heard the explosion and felt the ground shaking and caving in. He told me later that when he saw my dad was in trouble, he forgot all about hiding. All he could think about was saving my father. I sure appreciated him for trying to do that.

Xian looked up from the hole and squinted into the bright sunshine. He saw the hundreds of people looking down at him. His gaze circled the faces until he saw me. He shrugged and gave me a weak wave. Everybody standing around—my mom and Sheriff Ernie included—gaped at me with their jaws hanging open. And then my dad's mouth dropped open; I guess he just figured out what was happening. He was staring at me too.

Now I had a whole new problem. I still didn't have any idea how bad it was going to get before it got better. But I was about to find out.

EXTRA! STICKVILLE  T

JULY 9, 1950

With Eyes Wide Open and Pens at the Reac

PARADE GOES BUST IN BOOMTOWN

4TH OF JULY CAVE-IN REMAINS A MYSTERY

BOOMTOWN — The citizens of Boomtown remain stunned over the unexplained cave-in that followed the climax of the town's annual 4th of July parade. The crowd, estimated in the thousands, stood by for the explosion of the Founder's Day Float which apparently opened a crack in the street surrounding Town Square. The statue of Chang, founding father of Boomtown, plunged downward into a hidden, underground chamber. Pulled along with it was the most recent minister of the Boomtown Church, the Reverend Arthur Button, who has already survived five other spectacular accidents over the past ten months, includi...

Town Square remains cordoned while a full investigation continues. Sheriff Burton Ernie is in charge and has since dispatched volunteers to trace the tunnel back to its origin. So far, nearly all of the stolen items (recently reported missing by this newspaper) have been recovered.

This is what is known for certain. The entire scheme was carried out by a single man working alone. Digging during the day and dumping dirt under the cover of night, he single-handedly dug a tunnel from Chang's Famous Fireworks Factory, approximately two-miles due east to the underground chamber.

As to the identity of the "Mysterious Mole" as he has come to be known, reports allege that his name is Xian, the great-grandson of Chang, although his true iden-

MAN TWO GET

GO
surprisi
John Fis
with two
announc
undergo
reverse
doctor
George
agreed to
controvers
When finis
will have
back leg.

When a
motivation,
he was tired
around in
natural resul
having two l
travel const
direction.
can't wait
things norm
ing back a

"People
walking for
he said.
trying to wa
mailbox and
to go around
tire block jus
there."

Mrs. Fi
was very
the future ho
regains the
straight line
was quoted a
now on, whe
the store, h
and down
ket with a

CHAPTER 28

Trial of the Century

Boomtown was buzzing with the news like a beehive on a hot summer day. All anyone could talk about was the trial. It was scheduled to start on July 25, exactly three weeks after the cave-in. And, of course, *everyone* wanted to be on the jury. Mayor Tanaka's office was swamped with phone calls morning, noon, and night, and there was a line of people snaking out his door and down the hall and into the street. Normally you couldn't pay people to be on a jury. But this was Boomtown's trial of the century. This was *history*.

Since the town didn't have its own prosecutor or defense attorney, it had to borrow both of them from Stickville. Likewise, the circuit judge, Maria Rodriguez, would have to sit in for the trial; she was given a temporary office down the hall from Mayor Tanaka. She couldn't get a moment's peace either.

The first problem the judge faced was where to hold the trial, since all eleven hundred seventeen people who lived in Boomtown wanted to see it. No more than fifty could fit inside the regular courtroom at the Town Hall. Only three hundred could fit in the library at one time—and that's if we took out all the books! Maybe four hundred could fit inside the Great Room at the Boomtown Museum, but that still wasn't enough. Fortunately, the Hopontop circus had cancelled some of their end-of-July performances (they didn't want to miss the trial either). They donated their tent, and so it was settled.

News updates about the trial were on the radio day and night. It made the papers in Stickville and Ainogold and as far away as Spokane and Seattle. Soon we had eight newspaper reporters and even a film crew staying at Mitterand's Boarding House. Everywhere you turned, a reporter was pushing a microphone into someone's face. They were as common as cow pies in a cornfield—or maybe the annoying flies that were always buzzing around.

It wasn't so much fun for me. I was holed up like a prisoner in the house, watched day and night by my dad who couldn't go outside because of the reporters and on account of his bandaged head, broken arm, and twisted knee. He hadn't spoken more than ten words to me since the day of the cave-in. He had been back and forth to the hospital several times. He was going to make a full recovery. But I don't think his trust in me was ever going to recover. Not since the whole story had come out.

This is what Sheriff Ernie had been able to figure out once he arrested Xian and went down into the tunnels from the hole in the Town Square to investigate. He traced the tunnel all the way back to the fireworks factory where he found the secret entrance, Fred Cotton's truck, the conveyor belt system, Xian's underground hiding place, and all the things he had stolen. There were lanterns, clothing, shovels, pickaxes, wheelbarrows, lights, and all of the other things that had gone missing over the eleven months since he'd arrived. Worst of all, Sheriff Ernie found my flashlight with my name written right on the side—and a whole bunch of our clothes, Busy's extra boots, Bobby's hat, Rocky's jacket, the twins' old pants and shirts, and our footprints—all over the place. There was no question that we had been involved.

Xian was charged with a long list of crimes. Besides petty theft, he was charged with "corrupting children" (because he had involved my buddies and me in his illegal activity), the almost-death of my dad (caused by Xian's digging underneath Town Square), and finally, the most serious of the charges, attempted bank robbery. This last one was made up by the prosecuting attorney—a real baddy that one.

Horatio Hooke was a puffed-up blowhard from Stickville. He made no secret that the trial was a way for him to get away from prosecuting parking tickets. He wanted to step up to the big leagues. The trial would make a name for him, and after that he would run for governor of Washington. Or maybe senator. He didn't care. He just made sure the cameras were rolling and the reporters were listening every time he opened up his loud mouth.

Sarah told me all about it. The lawyer stood on the steps of the Town Hall, dressed in his black suit and white shirt, with his dark hair slicked back, waving his arms, punching the air with his fist, and crying about the latest crime wave. He blamed Sheriff Ernie. He blamed the mayor. He blamed the county government. He blamed the Congress. He blamed the Supreme Court.

Stomping his foot he shouted, "The only way to clean up our streets is to elect new representatives who can restore sanity to the towns and villages of Washington! You need *better* leaders—*stronger* leaders—*courageous* leaders! You need a man who will save our women and children from the rampant crime that threatens to destroy our way of life! You need someone like *Horatio Hooke*!"

the outcome of the trial

unpr
in th
few
thing
impr
we w
to be
eatin
and g
bed b
each n
well, th
always
year. U
then h

Horatio Hooke has been retained by Okanogan County as prosecuting atto in the case. He has been practic

He bowed and tried to look humble, but he wasn't fooling anybody. Especially the other lawyer they got to defend Xian. His name was George Rigdale. He came out to the house to ask me a bunch of questions, and I liked him right away. He was quiet and simple and didn't care about fame and fortune. All he wanted to do was find out the facts and get to the bottom of the story.

"Is it true they're calling him 'The Mysterious Mole'?" I asked Mr. Rigdale before he left.

Mr. Rigdale snorted. "The newspaper people are doing that.

Just the sort of trick they play to sell papers. It's more exciting that way."

"I suppose. We call him by his name, Xian. Did you know that he was the great-grandson of Chang?"

"Yes, he told us that. Not surprising when you look at him. Like two peas in a pod." Then the lawyer changed the subject. "Do you know what he was looking for?"

I shook my head. "None of us guys did. Xian wouldn't say. I know it was really important to him. It *must* be very valuable. He came all the way from China to find it. Xian left his family and everything—just like Chang did all those years ago."

"The prosecuting attorney has accused Xian of trying to rob the Bank of Boomtown. The tunnel underneath Town Square, if he kept on going, would have gone right underneath the vault inside the bank. What do you think about that?" He shifted forward on his chair and looked straight into my eyes, waiting for an answer.

"It's ridiculous! Xian wasn't going to rob the bank! He's not like that. He's a nice man. He felt terrible about all the things he was taking—but he was afraid."

"Afraid of what?"

"I don't know. Afraid of everything! Wouldn't *you* be? Leaving his home and coming to a strange place. I guess he thought he couldn't trust anybody—even though the letter said he should."

"Ahh," the lawyer sighed. "The letter. What more do you know about that?"

"Not much, only what Sheriff Ernie figured out. There are some missing pages—but Xian wouldn't show them to us or tell us what they said. So, no, I don't know why he came or what he was looking for—only that we decided to help him. I was wrong about that. I know that now. It was stupid. It almost got my dad killed—again."

My dad shuffled around the corner leaning on his cane. He had been in the kitchen listening in to our conversation. His eyes were tired, and he had a sad look on his face.

"Jon, I'm glad to hear that you are sorry about what you did—and that you realize how dangerous it was. But it's almost too late to be saying you're sorry. A lot of bad things have happened—things that could have been avoided if you'd just told the truth in the first place."

"Dad, I—"

He held up his hand and stopped me. "You're lucky that you've only just turned twelve. Too young to be thrown in jail as an adult. Even so, you're going to be put on the stand, and Mr. Hooke is going to ask you a lot of hard questions. Are you going to be able to answer them?"

I nodded my head.

"I hope so," Dad said and left the room, his cane scraping on the floor as he went down the hall.

I looked at Mr. Rigdale and sighed. "Maybe I need a lawyer too. How much do you charge? I got my life savings—about four dollars—and some baseball cards."

The attorney smiled and tried to sound confident. "Don't you worry. Somehow I think all this will come out right in the end. Keep your chin up. I'm working on it."

I watched him go out the door and climb into his big black car and drive away. It kind of looked like a hearse. It made me shiver. I wasn't feeling confident at all. Not one tiny bit. It was a huge mess, and I had no idea how to clean it up.

CHAPTER 29

Boomtown to the Rescue

In the end, Judge Rodriguez decided there couldn't be a jury trial. There was no way that she was ever going to find an unbiased panel in Boomtown. People were lining up to visit Xian since the day he was arrested and put into Sheriff Ernie's jail cell. Grandma Edna and her lady friends brought pies and cookies and casseroles. The Welcome Wagon served him breakfast every day. Chinese men and women from the fireworks factory showed up one after another to meet the direct descendent of Chang and to catch up on news from their homeland. Xian was more like a local folk hero than a criminal. It was making the prosecutor very angry. It was the first thing he complained about on the first morning of the trial.

"Your Honor! I object to the way the defendant has been treated since arriving in Boomtown!"

She leaned forward and looked down from the raised podium that had been built especially for the trial. "You feel as though the defendant has been mistreated?"

"On the contrary!" Horatio stormed. "He's been treated like royalty! I only wish *I* could live as comfortably as he has over the last three weeks!"

"Did you want to join him in the jail? I'm sure the sheriff could find you some space."

"Don't be ridiculous!" he bellowed. "That's not the problem! It's these people who live here! They don't seem to understand the gravity of the situation! They've been *robbed*! Their children were duped into helping this so-called Mysterious Mole carry out his desperate scheme to rob their very own bank! Their life savings! He almost killed one of their pastors! And instead of demanding his head, they're ready to throw this criminal a parade! It's your job to make them see how serious this is!"

The judge frowned and waved Horatio back to his seat. "No, it isn't. That's *your* job. Are you ready to begin this trial or aren't you?"

The pompous lawyer marched back to his table, looking as much like a spoiled rooster as anybody could. "Of course, I'm ready. I just hope *they* are." Then he plopped down in his seat, crossed his arms, and stewed.

In fact, we were all stewing. It had to be more than ninety degrees in that tent with all the people, including the reporters and the camera crews and the lights. It was already hot outside, and it was only nine o'clock in the morning. By noon, it would be an oven in there.

The judge banged her gavel several times until the noisy chatter in the circus tent fell into dead silence. "Look," she pointed out, "it's going to get even hotter in here very soon. We don't have a lot of time for objections or any other shenanigans. I want you two lawyers to conduct your business efficiently, and I want this crowd to remain as quiet as possible. The faster we move through this, the faster we'll be done. Understand?"

Every head nodded, and every mouth closed. They couldn't wait for the show to begin.

"Then I call this courtroom to order. I am the honorable Maria Rodriguez presiding. Horatio Hooke for the prosecution. George Rigdale for the defense. Mr. Xian Chang on trial for petty theft, corruption of youth, attempted bank robbery, and assault for the bodily injury of Arthur Button, current minister of Boomtown Church. What say you?"

George Rigdale stood up on cue and faced the judge. "As far as all of the charges are concerned, the defense declares that our client, Mr. Chang, is *not guilty*!"

In spite of the judge's warning, the entire crowd jumped to their feet and started to cheer.

"You tell him, George!"

"That's the ticket!"

"Not guilty! You betcha!"

She banged her gavel over and over. It took almost five minutes to settle them down.

"I warned you!" She frowned, pointing with her wooden hammer. "One more outburst like that and I'll clear the courtroom! Just because we're in a circus tent doesn't mean this is a circus. It's far too hot in here for funny business. So that's your last warning!" She banged the gavel one final time.

"Mr. Hooke, call your first witness."

Fred Cotton was the first person to take the stand. He waved to his wife and saluted some of the farmers he knew out in the crowd. He'd come straight in from the field, dressed in his boots and overalls and a straw hat. He removed his hat as he took the oath to tell the truth, the whole truth, and nothing but the truth, so help him God.

Mr. Hooke approached and asked the first question of the trial, "Please state your full name for the court."

"Fredrick Lawrence Archibald Cotton, named after my granddad on my mother's side and my uncle on my father's side."

"Yes, thank you. Please refrain from any unnecessary elaboration. Just stick to straight answers."

"Yes, sir."

"As I understand it, your truck was stolen during a rain storm in mid-October of last year?"

"More like it came up missing. Floated down West Chang Street to be precise."

"However it turned up missing, isn't it true that it ended up in the hands of the defendant, Mr. Chang, who used it to haul dirt from his secret digging site?"

"That's what I've been told."

"You're aware of the muffler system he installed so he could sneak around town without being detected?"

"I am. Very clever. Never would have thought of it myself."

"You must be furious knowing that your truck was being used in the commission of a crime."

"No, not really. Quite the opposite in fact."

"No? May I remind you that you are under oath? It doesn't bother you, not even in the slightest, that your precious truck, used in the daily conduct of your farming business, was stolen and secretly used by the defendant in a desperate plan to rob the bank, which, may I remind you, included the money *you* had on deposit?"

"Why should it? My truck is famous now. The Boomtown Museum wants to put it on permanent display. This is the most exciting thing that's ever happened to me!"

Everyone burst out laughing. Even the judge smiled before she tapped her gavel as a reminder. Horatio Hooke was stunned. This wasn't what he was expecting. He wanted outrage. He wanted indignation. He wanted demands for justice—not this.

"No further questions for this witness," he grumbled and sat down.

"Mr. Rigdale?"

"No questions, Your Honor."

Mr. Hooke's questioning of the witnesses went from bad to worse. Next on the list was Gramma Edna. She'd had three pies stolen by Xian. The prosecutor tried the same approach as he had with Fred Cotton. It didn't work any better than it did the first time. Gramma Edna wasn't upset. Instead, she smiled sweetly at

Xian sitting at the defendant's table and said, "I hope they tasted okay. Sometimes I use too much nutmeg and cinnamon with the apples. And I overcooked one of the crusts. I'm sorry, dear."

Horatio Hooke paraded five more people through the witness box, according to him, witless "victims" of Xian's terrifying crime spree: Tom O'Grady, Captain Trudeau, Matthieu LaPierre, Ellis Brown, owner of the Red Bird, and Lazy Gunderson. None of them were angry. Instead they were curious as to when Xian had arrived, how he managed to move around town without being seen, and why he hadn't simply asked for help.

Lazy Gunderson said, "Xian did me a *favor*. My wife has been after me to fix the front fence for years. If he hadn't stolen the posts and wire, I would have been out there busting my back for a week!"

By then it was lunchtime and, as expected, almost a hundred degrees in the tent. The judge rapped her gavel and announced, "We're going to suspend the trial until tomorrow morning at eight o'clock. Any objections? No? Then court dismissed. Let's go have lunch."

My family and I watched as people quickly exited the tent, all except for Mr. Hooke, who stood at his table dripping in sweat and wiping his forehead in frustration.

Sheriff Ernie had Xian by the elbow and was leading him back to the jailhouse. Mr. Hooke stopped him and challenged the sheriff indignantly. "What's with the people in your town?" he demanded to know. "They're nothing but a bunch of ignorant hayseeds! Polyannas! Chuckleheads! Don't they know what's at stake here?"

"Do *you*?" Sheriff Ernie snapped back. I could tell he wasn't the least bit happy about the way the lawyer was talking about Boomtown.

"I'll tell you what. You put *me* on the stand tomorrow, and you can ask me all about it. Until then, I've got nothing to say."

My family and I followed Sheriff Ernie out of the tent. The last thing we heard was the lawyer mumbling angrily under his breath, "Oh, I will! You think this trial is over? You think I'm beat? You just wait! I haven't even gotten *started* yet!"

CHAPTER 30

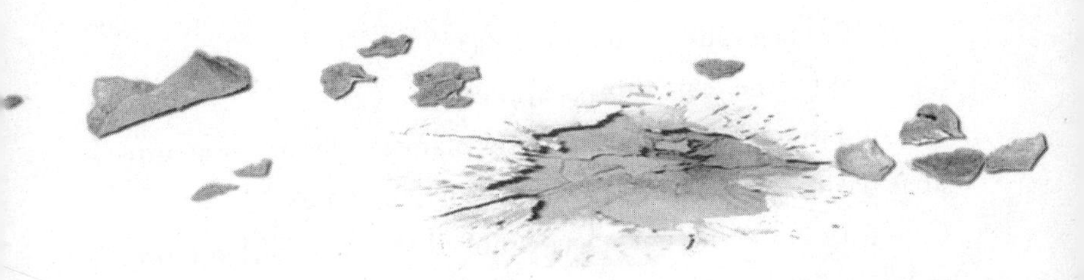

Out of the Frying Pan

A cool breeze had blown all that night, and by morning things were a lot more comfortable inside the tent. The reporters and camera crews had shown up early so they could interview the people on the witness list for that day. Sheriff Ernie was going to be on the stand first and then me and my friends. I was so nervous I felt like a cat tiptoeing across the hood of a black car at high noon. What was the lawyer going to ask me? What was I going to say?

The judge didn't waste any time. At exactly eight o'clock she called the courtroom to order and instructed Mr. Hooke to call his first witness for that day.

"I call Sheriff Burton Ernie to the stand."

The prosecutor had no idea what he'd gotten himself into.

"Please state your full name for the court."

"Burton Albert Ernie."

"And what is your current position in Boomtown?"

"I'm the sheriff here."

"You've been sheriff for how long?"

"Twenty-one years this past June."

"And in that period of time, how many crimes of any significance have occurred here—crimes of a federal nature?"

"Just one. Frank Cavenaugh robbed the Bank of Boomtown back in 1929. Frankie the Banker. You can say hello to him. He's right there in the front row of the bleachers. Hey, Frank!"

"If you don't mind, please refrain from addressing anyone besides the officers of this court."

"Sorry. It's just that I didn't get to arrest Frank this week because of the trial and all. I'll let him rob the bank twice next week just to make it up to him."

"Exactly! That is precisely what I wanted to ask you about. As the sheriff of this town, you seem to have a complete disregard for law and order. You spend your days drinking coffee and wandering around town and wasting taxpayer money. If it weren't for the cave-in, your neglect and incompetence would have allowed the Bank of Boomtown to be robbed a *second* time! What do you have to say for yourself?"

Sheriff Ernie stared at the pompous lawyer. "I say you don't have to be so rude. What did I ever do to you?"

The crowd clapped and cheered. "You tell him, Burt!"

The judge rapped for order in the court.

Sheriff Ernie continued, "You come strutting into my town with your fancy suit and expensive shoes and big city swagger and talk to my friends like they're a bunch of daffy-headed donkeys. *You don't understand Boomtown at all!*

"I may not be the best investigator that ever was, but you forget that in more'n twenty years, we've only had *one* real crime. That crime was solved, and most of the money was returned. And you see Frank over there? We helped rehabilitate him. That's more'n most towns can say.

"And finally, when it comes to Mr. Chang, your theory is that he was heading for the bank—but you don't *know* that. All you know is that he's a piece of your political puzzle. You're just exploiting him to make a name for yourself. Well, I don't know how things are where you come from, but here in Boomtown, we don't have much patience for that sort of thing! You can just pack up your soapbox and hit the road!"

As soon as Sheriff Ernie was finished with his speech, the crowd let out another roar. This time the judge didn't stop them. You could tell by the look on her face that she was in agreement with Sheriff Ernie. She didn't like ambitious lawyers any more than he did.

Mr. Hooke threw up his hands and stomped back to his seat. Mr. Rigdale had no questions for the witness.

Then it was time for me and the guys to face the music.

The judge had decided earlier that because of our ages, she would have us take the stand as a group. We were supposed to elect a spokesman to speak for the gang, and the guys elected me. She could tell that we were terribly nervous.

She leaned over and said, "You understand that you are not on trial here? This lawyer is going to ask you some questions. You don't have to answer anything that will incriminate yourself. Do you know what that word means—*incriminate*?"

"It means I don't have to say anything that will prove that I'm guilty."

"That's right."

"But I *am* guilty," I admitted, hanging my head. I had discussed this with the guys. We decided that the only way out of this mess was to come clean. Admit everything. Throw ourselves on the mercy of the court—and hope that our parents didn't ship us off to Siberia.

"We helped Xian dig the tunnels. We brought him clothes and food. We kept what he was doing secret. It was wrong. I know that. I really should have told somebody. Especially my dad. I should have trusted him."

I looked over to where Dad was sitting in the front row next to my mom and sisters. The look in his bruised eyes was sad—and he was having trouble sitting up straight. I think he tried to give me a smile and nod of encouragement, but his face hurt so badly that all he could do was wince. Looking at him, it was really hard to know how he felt. I was sure he had to be angry—and disappointed. The rest of my story wasn't going to make him feel any better.

"When we first saw Xian on Halloween, we thought he was a ghost. After we caught him out at the fireworks factory, we thought it was a game. Busy said that we should help him. He said that Xian hadn't really *taken* anything from the town. It was all down in the tunnels. And he said that if anyone found out what Xian was trying to do, they'd all come and help him dig—and that would spoil the fun for us. Isn't that what you said, Busy?"

My buddy tried to sink into his shoes as he hid behind the other guys.

"Busy? Is that right?" the judge asked.

"Yes. I guess," he finally admitted. "But we didn't mean anything *bad* by it. We didn't think anybody would get hurt."

Horatio Hooke interrupted with a nasty sneer. "But people *did* get hurt, didn't they? Jonny's father was almost killed in the cave-in. You were helping a man to rob a bank. Not to mention what might have happened to you! You could have been buried alive if one of the tunnels collapsed. It was very, very dangerous—and not very smart."

I didn't like the lawyer, not one little bit, but he was right. "We know. We could have saved everyone a lot of trouble if we'da just told. But we didn't."

"And now your own father is sitting over there, lucky to be alive. What do you have to say about *that*?" the lawyer snapped.

"That's the worst part," I answered, my voice trembling with tears. "There's nothing I can do to make it up to him. Nothing I can do to fix it. He'll *never* trust me again—and I don't blame him."

I glanced over at Dad a second time—even though I was afraid to see him turn away in disappointment. But that's not what he did. Instead, I watched in amazement as he struggled to his feet. With help from Mom and Ruth, he was finally able to stand and lean crookedly on his cane. What I saw in his eyes took me by surprise. His face was beaming with forgiveness and pride.

The other fathers stood up and joined him. Mr. Gunderson, Mr. Mitterand, Mr. Odegaard, and Mr. Dougherty. All of them stood side by side with my father. At first the room was silent, but then the mothers began to clap. Once they started, it got everyone else going. The judge did nothing to stop it. Pretty soon everyone was on their feet, clapping their hands and stomping their feet. Sheriff Ernie and the mayor, the shop owners and neighbors, Pastor Platz and Reverend Tinker, even the newspaper reporters and the cameramen. All of them stood up and forgave us—right then and there.

I suppose it was because we were sorry. We had made mistakes, but we had admitted them. We were ready to pay for what we had done. That made them proud. My dad most of all.

When the noise finally died down, he spoke up for all of them. "We stand with you, boys! Whatever happens, *you can count on us!*"

Just like we should have counted on them from the very first.

CHAPTER 31

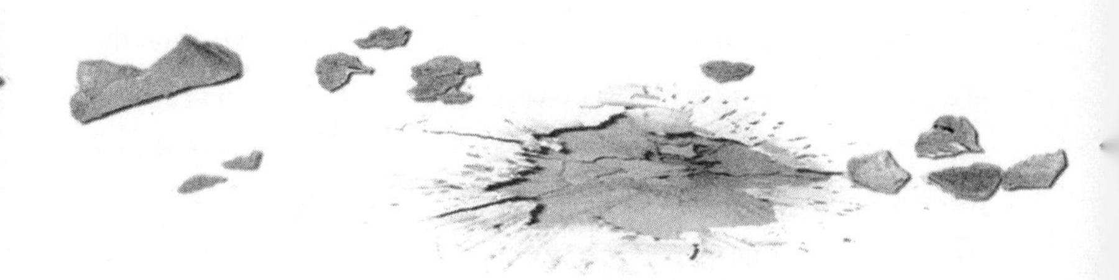

Into the Fire

After what my dad had done for me, I was feeling especially guilty. He had been so great. And it made it even worse when Mr. Rigdale told us that Xian insisted on testifying. He would be on the stand the next morning to confess everything.

Dad said, "That's noble, I suppose. But the judge won't have any choice after that. Xian will have to go to jail for a very long time."

"That's what I warned him," the lawyer agreed. "But he won't listen. He blames himself for everything. He got the boys into trouble. And he feels especially bad about what happened to you. He thinks the least he can do is get on the stand and tell the truth."

I had to figure out a way to help Xian. I waited until my parents tucked Sarah in for the night and stopped by my room to make sure I was okay. Then I got out of bed and slipped into my jeans and sneakers. I waited until I was sure everyone was asleep and then slowly and silently raised the window and climbed out onto a branch. I wedged a note in the window before I closed it, and then I carefully shimmied down the tree and hopped the fence.

If I could only find what he'd been searching for—that would fix everything, I was sure of it. The people of Boomtown had dropped the charges about the shovels and apple pies before the trial had even started—they didn't care about that—so Mr. Hooke was going to have a hard time convicting him of that one. Xian hadn't *tricked* us into helping him, so he wasn't responsible for our "corruption," no matter what the lawyer said about it. I think Dad had changed his mind about Xian too. That only left the stupid charges about bank robbery—I *knew* that couldn't be true! So all I had to do was find the missing treasure, or diamonds, or whatever else it was that Chang had hidden all those years before.

Find the treasure and Xian would be saved, that's what I was thinking as I ran through the empty streets.

There was only one place to look: down in the hole where the statue had fallen. Xian was convinced that's where it was. He had showed me the mark on the map during one of the breaks in the trial.

"What does it mean?" I whispered.

"It is the Chinese word for 'square,'" he answered.

"Square?"

"Yes. I didn't understand at first, because that's not how we use this word where I come from. But I think Chang must have meant *Town* Square."

"You think your treasure was buried under Chang's statue?" I looked around to make sure no one was listening.

"If I only had a chance . . . if . . . but no . . . it doesn't matter any more. It's too late. I'm sorry." And he wouldn't say any more.

But now I was going to take that chance. I ran through Farmer's Park and out into the main square. They had built wooden barriers around the sides of the hole and put up warning signs to keep people away from it. The ladder from the fire department was still there, so I climbed down and waited until I was at the bottom to turn on my flashlight.

As I swung it around, I could see that they had started to clean up some of the mess. There were ropes tied around the statue; I think they were planning to raise it back up, but it would take a herd of elephants to pull it out of there. It weighed more than a house, I thought. I shone my light on Chang's face. He seemed to be staring back at me over the distance with his unblinking eyes. *Find it*, his voice echoed. *Find it and save my great-grandson*.

"Don't worry, Mr. Chang. I'm on the job. You just stay right here."

I searched around the edge of the monument until I reached where the asphalt from the street had folded down all along the backside of the hole. Right at the bottom there was a space, not very big, but big enough for a boy to wiggle through—just big enough for me. I got on my hands and knees and pushed inside. As soon as I did, I was able to stand up and look around. Instead of a blank wall of dirt and rocks, I found an open tunnel, leading back into the darkness. The whistle of a night wind moaned in its throat. Now I was really scared.

"Can't stop now, Captain Marvel," I said out loud, trying to sound brave. "Get moving. The townsfolk are counting on you."

I moved along the passageway and noticed that it was different from anything else we had seen. The ground was smoother, and in a few minutes I saw that the walls had cement on them. It was more like a train tunnel than anything else. Overhead, there was a string of old tin-covered lights that must have worked at one time. Spiderwebs hung from them like gray nets, and I could hear the steady drip of water echoing down the corridor. The tunnel tilted down and narrowed. I almost smashed my head on some low-hanging pipes. I turned a corner and then . . . there it was . . . right in front of me. This *had* to be it!

It was a metal door, strapped in steel, rusty with age and studded with bolts. There wasn't a lock, not that I could see, or even a door handle, but there were hinges on the left. It was supposed to open, but how? I pounded on it, and it sounded hollow. I tried to get my fingers into the crack and pull. *Ouch*. That hurt.

I found an old greasy rag on the ground and used it to brush a hundred years of dust off the surface. When I did, it uncovered a mark. A square box painted in red. Chang's signature. I remembered it from his letter.

"*Whoohooo!*" I shouted, dancing up and down and listening to my echo that bounced up and down the tunnel. It wasn't very hero-like; I'll admit that. But I was awful excited—and there wasn't anybody down there to see or hear me. I just wished Xian had been there to see it or my dad. *Somebody* who could help me figure out how to open the door. Where was Busy when I needed him?

I sat down on the ground to think. *Chang was smart, that's for sure. He wouldn't use a key, not like a normal person. What would he do?*

I played the flashlight along the walls and ceiling and kept coming back to the locked door. I stood up and searched the cracks along the ceiling, around the edge of the small cement room, and stopped when I came to where I'd found the greasy rag.

Why didn't I notice that before?

On my hands and knees I pushed away the dirt until I could see five metals disks buried in the cement. Each of them had a Chinese character etched into the middle. I couldn't read them, but they reminded me of the buttons in the Boomtown Museum. Suddenly I understood.

"Chang and Mfana were friends! Mfana must have known about Chang's secret hiding place. He probably helped him *build* it! But how are these supposed to work?" I said out loud again. I wondered what Busy would say if he knew I'd started talking to myself.

I pushed the first one. The button clicked down and popped back up again. Nothing. I tried all five, one after the other. Nothing. This had to be the way in, but I didn't know the combination. I could be there all night pushing buttons and never guess the right order. I was stuck.

Stop, Jon, and think! It *had* to have something to do with

Chang. I had a combination lock on my bicycle. It was 7-22-12. My shoe size, my baseball number, and my age. Simple, right? It had to be something like that. Something that would matter especially to Chang. Something that only he . . .

And that's when I got it! Of course! How obvious was that? I leaned down and punched the numbers, barely able to breath. Five, four, three, two, one. Blast off!

The door creaked and then cracked and then swung open with a hiss and a sigh.

"Eureka!" I shouted, not stopping to look where I was going. I ran into the room and shone my flashlight all around. What was I going to find? What had Chang hidden for all this time? What treasure? What fortune? What amazing discovery? But before I could find out, I heard the sound of the door swinging shut. *Creak. Swoosh. Bang!*

Oh great. *That* was stupid. One-way door. No knob. No buttons. No nothing. *Now* what was I going to do? Captain Marvel was trapped.

CHAPTER 32

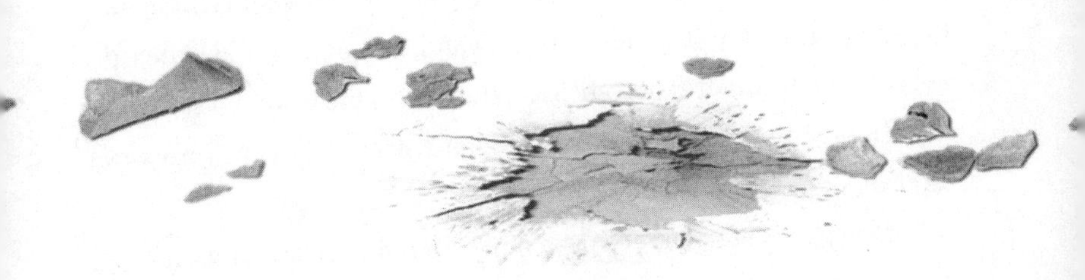

A Busy Chapter

I want to thank Jonny for asking me to do this. I've never written in a book before—with sentences and everything!

Of course, if he hadn't gotten himself trapped in a cave, he could have written this chapter himself. That's what he gets for running off without telling me! Serves him right, that's what I say.

Anyway, he had to ask his best buddy Busy—that's me—to write this chapter for him. Personally, I think it's the best chapter in the whole book since *I* was the hero! *I* was the one who figured out where he was. *I* was the one who had to rescue him, the big dope.

This is what happened, just the way I remember it. Don't let him tell you any different.

We got up early to make it out to the trial. We wanted front row seats because Xian was going to testify. We were pretty excited to find out what he was going to say, but we never got to hear it—not right then, anyway. Instead, Pastor Button came stumbling into the tent on his cane. He was all upset and waving a note. He went right up to the judge and gave it to her. She banged her hammer and ordered everyone to be quiet. Then she read the note. This is what it said:

"Dad, I'm going to look for Chang's treasure. It's the only way to save Xian. Don't worry. Jonny."

Everybody started talking at once. That dumb lawyer man kept shouting for a "mistrial," whatever that is. Sheriff Ernie started organizing search parties. Mr. Button came over to talk to me and the other guys.

"Do you know where he is? Did he tell you about this?"

"No, Pastor Button. Honest. But he *shoulda*! I can't believe he went off looking without us! What a rat—stealing all the fun for himself."

"This isn't *fun*," Pastor Button told us. "It's dangerous to go off alone like that. Any idea where he would have gone?"

I looked at the other guys, and they shook their heads. "Nobody knows those tunnels as well as Xian over there. But I don't think the lawyer guy will let him help."

"Oh yes he will!" Jonny's dad insisted. He left us standing there while he hobbled over to where the lawyers were arguing with the judge.

This was my only chance. I pulled the guys into a huddle and whispered, "Let's not wait for any of them. I think I know where he is! Are you guys in?"

"You betcha!" the twins agreed. Rocky and Bobby said the same.

"It's super heroes to the rescue! Where we goin'?"

"Follow me!"

The trial was being held in the Hopontop's circus tent—that was all the way out on the far side of the river. But that was lucky for us because we knew the shortcut. We slipped out underneath the bleachers and under the edge of the tent. We ran through the cornfield and out near the river by the woods. I got there first, of course, because I'm the fastest runner. We went through the cave and into the tunnel. There was a kerosene lamp lying right where Rocky had forgotten it. That was lucky too. He had left some matches next to it so we lit the lamp and ran into the darkness.

"So where do you think he is?" Rocky huffed and puffed.

It was a long run, and even I was getting out of breath. We stopped for a minute to rest, and I told them, "Yesterday before we went home, Jonny told me something that Xian told him."

"That's not fair! Why just you? Why didn't he tell us?"

"'Cause you guys were already gone by then. Besides, it was a secret. So he told me—I'm the boss of the gang, anyway."

"So what did he tell you?" Rocky was getting mad at me.

"I don't think I'm gonna say. Instead, I'll just *show* you. C'mon. Let's get going. We got to get there before the grown-ups do."

We kept running until we got to the Boomtown Cemetery. That was another one of our discoveries. Way back in March when we were searching the tunnels we found this spot where there were a lot of big trees roots hanging down. We squeezed through the roots and found these stairs. They went up inside this cement room with a skinny window way at the top. Rocky said it was a sarcophagus, like in ancient Egyptian times. But there wasn't a casket or anything. Just a door where you could go out. It was creepy, coming out in the middle of the cemetery at night sometimes. But it was another one of our secret exits.

This is our secret exit (don't tell nobody). – *Busy*

Now all we had to do was run down Bang Street. It was weird seeing all the stores closed and the shades pulled down. Even old Walt the Butcher was out at the trial. The streets were completely empty except for us.

"It's like that movie we saw—the one where everyone in the whole town disappears," Frankie said. "What was the name of that movie?"

"I don't remember—but it was just like this. Weird, isn't it?"

By then we were passing Top's Soda Shop and Guenther's Gun Coral. Nobody was there either. We went across Cave-In Road and then Crumble Street. Finally! There was Town Square out in front us and then the hole. By the time we got there we were all out of breath and about to pass out.

"Do you see him?" Tony gasped. He fell on his knees and looked over the edge.

"Don't be a dope," Frankie answered. "He's not going to be right there! If he was, he'd just climb up the ladder. He's got to be trapped or something."

"Then let's go get him," I said, grabbing the ladder. "This is where Xian wanted to look, behind the statue. That's what he told Jon."

I went down the ladder first and held it for the other guys. It didn't take long to find Jon's footprints.

"He was here," I said. "The shoes are too small to be a grown-up's. And these steps look fresh. Watch where you're going."

The trail led behind the statue and underneath the asphalt. I went first and then the twins and Bobby, but Rocky got kind of stuck. He was the biggest in our gang.

"Pull!" he shouted. We all got a grip on his wrists and yanked. He finally popped through the hole with a grunt.

"Thanks, guys. That was a tight fit!"

Now we could stand up and see down the tunnel. More footprints. I raised the kerosene lamp and led the way.

"He went down here. See? There's a fresh track in that little puddle right there."

It didn't take long for us to find the steel door. We started pounding on it right away. We could hear Jonny yelling at us from the other side.

"Over by the wall!" he shouted. "Find the buttons!"

"Got it!"

He told us how to push the buttons, even though I could have figured it out all by myself. All of a sudden the door swung open with a hiss. It sounded like a snake blowing out a candle.

"Block the door!" Jonny yelled. "Hurry up! Put this in there."

He was dragging a heavy rock across the ground. Me and Rocky helped and got it wedged in the opening.

"Wow! I'm glad we did that!" Jonny said, slapping me on the back. "Don't want to get stuck in here again. That stupid door shuts by itself, and there's no way to open it from the inside. I almost froze to death—you guys got anything to eat?"

"You wouldn't have gotten trapped in here if you had told us you were coming out here! That was really dumb."

Jonny kind of hung his head and kicked the dirt. "Yeah, I know. I'm sorry. I forgot all about our oath—are you going to kick me out of the gang?"

I punched his shoulder—hard. "That's for being a dope. But you're still in the gang. Don't do it again."

Then Jon was happy again. "But it worked out in the end, didn't it? You're here now. And just *look* at this! Look at what I found!"

I almost couldn't believe it when he pulled back the canvas covering and showed me what was hidden underneath. I never seen anything like that—it was more than anything I ever could of imagined! More than what was in Fort Knox! More than what the king of England had! More than all the kings in the whole world put together!

"Have you counted it yet?" I asked.

That's when we heard Jon's name—and the rest of our names—being called, echoing down the tunnel.

"Jonny? Are you down there? Are you boys all right?"

"They found us!" I said. "C'mon. We got to show them."

We took Jonny back down the passageway and out through the crack. One by one we crawled back out into the bright sunshine. It was almost impossible to see, but there had to be five hundred people up there! My dad was standing next to the statue waiting for me with a big grin on his face. All the dads—even Pastor Button—had climbed down the ladder. Sheriff Ernie and the fire chief were standing by with shovels. The mayor and the judge and the lawyers were up on the edge. Horatio Hooke looked like he was going to explode; he was all red in the face, and his eyes were bulging out.

Best of all, I saw none other than Xian himself, with his wrists in handcuffs and guarded by the bailiff. He also had a big ol' toothy grin on his face—the first time I think I ever saw him smile. He was probably just happy to see that we were alive, but then he didn't know the rest of it, not by half!

"Xian! You're here! You ain't gonna *believe* what we just found!"

CHAPTER 33

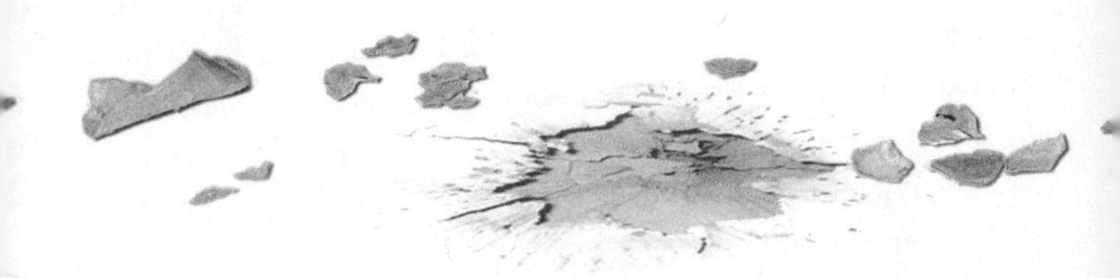

Xian Takes the Stand

I suppose I should thank Busy for coming to rescue me. Actually, I do appreciate it—and for writing the last chapter. I'd be more grateful if he hadn't called me a dope so many times. Also, I think he may have exaggerated some about how great he was during the rescue. But still, I appreciate him doing that for me.

By the time everyone had looked at the treasure and gotten back out of the hole, it was late in the day, so Judge Rodriguez decided the trial would start again the next day. Burton Ernie took Xian back to the jail as soon as he saw that we were all right so I never got a chance to tell him much about what we'd found. There was something else I had to show him too, but that had to wait until the next morning.

A little storm blew in during the night and dropped a ton of rain. We joined the caravans of cars and cows and horses and tractors as all of us tromped through the puddles and out to the circus tent for the final verdict.

The wet weather didn't stop anybody from showing up. If anything, there were more people than before. News had spread like a grass fire from town to town, in the newspapers and over the radio. There was a huge new headline in the *Stickville Times*, and people were saying that there was a man down in Hollywood that might want to make a movie about the Mysterious Mole and his adventure in Boomtown.

Busy said he wouldn't be in the movie unless they gave him his own trailer with a star on the door. And he wanted his name on the poster in big letters. I think maybe *he's* the dope.

When Xian took the stand and was sworn in, you could have heard a pin drop. He sat there very dignified and calm with his hands neatly folded in his lap. He was wearing a simple pair of black linen pants and a black jacket, with slippers on his feet and a black hat that looked like a small basket turned upside down. He had his hair pulled back in a ponytail (he called it a *queue*). On the front of his jacket was a golden design with a dragon in the middle of it.

He wasn't much taller than I was, but he was as strong as an ox. I know. I'd watched him haul rocks for almost nine months. It was weird seeing him all cleaned up and wearing a suit. When we first met him, he was covered in mud from head to toe. From then on, it was usually the same. But now his hands were washed and his face was clean. His eyes didn't look tired anymore. He seemed happy.

He didn't even flinch when Horatio Hooke came charging up to the witness box. The lawyer looked like a fat old cat that had cornered a bird and was about to eat him—like Sylvester and Tweety Bird. He grinned with his sharp teeth and tapped his claws on the railing. It even looked like he was swishing his tail—if he had one. Maybe he did, hiding under his expensive suit.

"So the jig is up, isn't it, Mr. Chang?"

"Excuse me, sir?"

"You've been caught red-handed. The petty thefts, stealing the food, dragging the boys into all this, nearly killing Pastor Button. You're not denying any of it?"

"No," he answered quietly.

"So you're changing your plea? Could you state that for the record? You're now saying that you're guilty of all charges?"

"Yes, I am guilty of everything for which I have been charged. Except for the bank robbery. I never planned to do that."

"No?!" bellowed the lawyer. "As we now know, you were planning something even *worse*! Can you explain for this courtroom exactly what it was that you were doing down in that tunnel? You realize, of course, that the secret room, the one supposedly constructed by Chang, is underneath the vault of the bank, just as we suspected? What are we supposed to think?"

Xian swallowed carefully and leaned back in his seat. For the next several minutes he told his story in short, simple words. I think everyone in the tent stopped breathing they were so amazed. Even I couldn't believe it—and I had been there! This is what he told us.

"My great-grandfather Chang was forced to escape from our village many years ago. From that time on, the government officials kept their eye on my family. They watched everything we did—and even seized our letters. That is why it took so long for us to discover what had happened to him.

"He came to America, as you know, and found his way to this place. He made a home here and had many friends. This is what I am most sorry about. He wrote to us in letters about how much you loved him. He told us that if we were ever able to make the journey to trust the people of Boomtown. But I did not. For this, I am very sorry."

The lawyer interrupted, "You stole from these people instead. Why?"

Xian hung his head. "It is hard for me to explain. Our family has been watched by spies and soldiers for three generations because Chang's father had not supported the corrupt emperor. Chang was considered a criminal. We could not go anywhere without being followed. We forgot how to trust anyone. I am no different. I did not know how to ask for help."

"So how did you know where Chang had gone?"

"There was a man who worked for the government. He was in charge of storing papers and letters. One day he found a box that contained all the letters my great-grandfather had written over the years. He was so amazed by what he read that he started to smuggle them out of the government building inside of his hat. One by one.

"Once he had taken them all, he found his way to our village. He gave them to my father and my father gave them to me."

"Letters, you say? Is this one of them?" Horatio asked, picking up the crinkled pile of paper from the evidence table.

"Yes," Xian answered. "Somehow Chang had learned that his wife back in China, my great-grandmother, had given birth to a son. *His* son. That man was my grandfather. He grew up knowing nothing of what had happened to Chang until the day the letters came to our village. It was too late by then, of course. It had been so many years since Chang had written the letters, we knew he must be dead. But in his letters he had sent for us, since it would have been impossible for him to return to China without being arrested and executed."

"He *sent* for you?"

"Yes. Some of the letters had been sent with money, but the government had taken that along with the letters. Still, my family decided to send me here to America since I was the only one in the family who had learned English. Chang had written that he had left something behind for us. They wanted me to search for what he had hidden."

The lawyer frowned and lifted the golden object off the table. He grunted when he picked it up because it weighed so much. I know because I had tried to lift one when I was trapped inside the vault. They each weighed fifty pounds apiece—and there were *hundreds* of them.

"These?" he demanded, shoving the glowing bar of gold under Xian's nose. "Is this what you're talking about? The sheriff sitting over there has just finished counting them this morning. There are a total of five hundred bricks down in that vault. Five *hundred!* That is a total of twenty-five thousand POUNDS of gold! Do you have any idea how much that is worth? Forty dollars an *ounce*. Six hundred and forty dollars a *pound*. Times *five hundred* pounds? *That's sixteen MILLION dollars!*"

Jeepers! I had spent a whole night sitting on top of that pile! I had even fallen asleep, dreaming of all the riches I'd found. I was sleeping on a *bed* of gold—a king's fortune in gold! I had no idea it was that much.

And neither did anyone else who was there. It was pandemonium. The judge kept banging her gavel and shouting, but nobody would listen. The reporters were jumping up and down, and they kept flashing their cameras. The film guys were rolling and recording the stampede. Sheriff Ernie kept blowing his whistle, but even then it took almost ten minutes to get everyone back to their seats.

Once order was restored, Horatio Hooke got this nasty smile on his face. He figured he had Xian trapped. And here's why.

"You sit here expecting us to believe that Chang your great-grandfather amassed this vast fortune without anyone knowing about it? That all of it was for you and your family? And we're supposed to let you walk away with it, no questions asked?"

"My great-grandfather was a great and honorable man. He found this gold while digging for sulfur—it was an accident. He never wanted it. He was already rich—as rich as a man could be. He had a home—he had friends. He didn't need anything else."

"You can't be serious."

"He wrote about it in his letters. He knew that if anyone outside of Boomtown ever found out about the gold, men would come here and dig up your streets. They would tear this town apart looking for more gold. He didn't want that to happen to the place he loved so much. He knew that greed would destroy it. It's true! I can see it in your eyes. You are just the sort of man that would have come to take it if you knew. He would not allow that to happen."

Everyone in the tent had been stunned to silence. They knew what Xian was saying was fact. Their beloved Chang had saved them from something terrible. Imagine! No Boomtown! Nothing but holes in the ground and crazy, greedy monsters creeping around searching for gold. It would have happened. Chang was right.

But Horatio Hooke wasn't listening. He held up the brick of gold and pointed his pasty white finger at the emblem stamped in the top of it.

"A nice story." He laughed triumphantly. "But nothing more than a story. Because you can see it right here, stamped on the very top. It's the city's name. This gold belongs to the people of Change, Washington. *Not* to Chang. *Not* to you. It belonged to Boomtown before it was even *called* Boomtown!

"So you weren't here to find *your* gold—you came to steal *their* gold! Can you deny it? Can you prove otherwise? I don't think so!"

He slammed the gold back down on the evidence table and nearly broke a hole in it. Then he strutted back over to his chair and plopped down in it like a man who had just eaten an entire cake all by himself, including the candles.

"Judge," he said grinning. "The prosecution has presented its case. Mr. Xian Chang, the great-grandson of Yi Chang, is guilty as charged. Guilty, I say. And there is nothing that his lawyer can say to prove different. I win!"

And with that, he folded his arms and dared anyone to argue.

CHAPTER 34

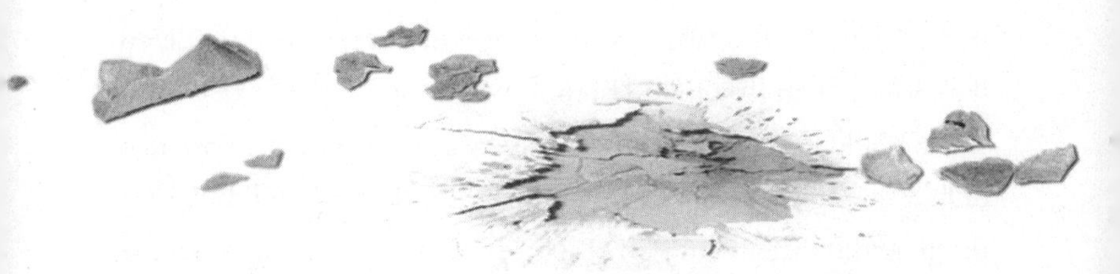

One Last Surprise

"Mr. Rigdale, Sir?"

I tugged on the lawyer's sleeve while he rattled his notes and tried to think of how he could save his client. He was pretty upset, like everyone else in the tent. They were excited about the gold, of course, but what they really wanted was for Xian to go free. There didn't seem any way that was going to happen. Not with the gold having that Change, Washington, stamp. The judge really didn't have any choice. But I had suddenly remembered what was in my pocket. I'd been so distracted by the gold and the locked door and all the excitement when they found me that I'd completely forgotten about it.

"Yes, what is it, son?"

"I found something. In the vault. When I was trapped in there."

"What?" he asked, suddenly sitting up straight to see what I was holding.

"These," I answered, handing him the two scraps of paper that I had tucked in my pocket. They were even more wrinkled than when I had first found them.

He held them up and studied the two small squares. Both had only a few Chinese characters written on them. I couldn't read them, and neither could Mr. Rigdale. But we both recognized the chop mark in the corner. It was Chang's, just like on the door of the vault and the ones on his letters.

"Tell me everything you know."

I whispered in his ear, and as soon as I was finished he jumped up from his chair and ran up to the judge.

"Your Honor! New information has just been handed to me. I wish to enter these two scraps of paper into evidence—and bring Jonny Button to the front so I can ask him a few questions."

"I object!" screamed Horatio Hooke as he barreled up to the judge's podium waving his arms like a scarecrow in a windstorm.

"You object to what?" the judge asked.

"I object to this so-called new evidence so late in the trial. I've never seen it! It's probably a trick by the defense because they are so desperate to win. His client is guilty—he knows it—so they've manufactured fake evidence to try and confuse the judge, Your Honor."

She leaned forward in her chair and gave the puffy lawyer a cold stare.

"Do I look *confused*, counselor?"

"Um . . . no, Your Honor," he stammered. He looked like a puppy that had missed the newspaper. "I didn't mean it like that."

"Then go and sit down, Mr. Hooke, and be quiet. Your objection is denied. The evidence is accepted. Mr. Rigdale, ask your questions."

He waved for me to come forward. I could hear Horatio Hooke mumbling underneath his breath as he went by. He didn't want anything to upset his master plan. Win the trial. Become famous. Run for governor. Get rich. Too bad for him.

I stood in front of the witness stand and gave Xian a little smile while he continued to sit there and wait. Mr. Rigdale held the two pieces of paper up so everyone in the tent could see them. Mom and Dad were in the front row, craning their eyes to catch a glimpse. I could see that Mom was worried—what was this all about and why was I in the middle of it—again? Dad and Ruth were curious. Sarah couldn't sit still. And my buddies were watching too. I was a nervous wreck.

"Jonny, you were telling me that you found these in the vault—is that correct?"

"Yes."

"And exactly *where* did you find them?"

"On top of the piles of gold."

"Piles, you say? Not pile? Not one stack?"

"No," I answered. "There were two. A big one and a small one."

"*Two* piles? And *two* notes?"

"That's right."

"And which one of these two notes was on the small pile?"

"That one. The one in your left hand."

"And the big pile?"

"The other one. That one in your right hand."

"You're sure about that?"

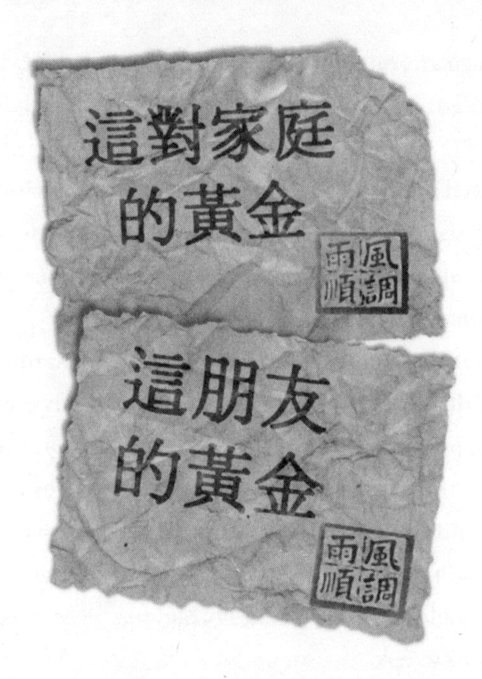

"Sure I'm sure. I remember because the small one had a tear in the corner. You can see it, right there."

He held it up so everyone could see. It was easy to tell. Both notes were old and yellow. They were dirty from the dust in the vault. There was a lighter spot on each of them where a rock had held them down in place for all those years, just waiting for someone to come along and find them. And the note from the small pile was torn in the corner. I was sure of that.

"As you can see, Your Honor, these notes are written in Chinese. I am unable to translate, but if there is no objection, I would like Mr. Chang to read them for us. They do, after all, have his great-grandfather's signature on them. So I assume they were meant for him to read."

Horatio Hooke had had enough by then. He leapt to his feet and charged up to the front. "I object, Your Honor! I strenuously, repeatedly, and emphatically *object*! You can't let the defendant read these notes! He could say anything! Anything at all!"

The judge was not amused. "I told you to sit down and be quiet, Mr. Hooke. Do you think I can't run my own courtroom? You think I can't make up my own mind? Sit down, or I'll have the bailiff *make* you sit down. I'll have him tie a rag around your mouth if you say one more word."

Everyone in the tent cheered as the lawyer sputtered and spat, but he couldn't stop the judge. He marched back to his chair and steamed. Mr. Rigdale handed the notes to Xian while addressing the court.

"Your Honor, if you please. We can have Mr. Chang read the two notes, and if there is any question, we will find a translator to confirm whatever he says. Will that satisfy my worthy opponent?"

"It satisfies *me*," she snapped, glaring at the other lawyer and daring him to speak. Just then Sheriff Ernie stood up and said, "Your Honor."

"Yes, Burton." Judge Rodriguez sounded a little exasperated.

"I can read a little bit of Chinese. I can check Xian's translation."

"Very well. Mr. Rigdale, please proceed."

Mr. Hooke looked liked he was about to argue with the judge one more time, but he closed his mouth slowly and slumped back into his chair.

I held my breath as Xian studied the two ancient pieces of paper. At first, he scrunched his brow. Then he tilted his head. Then he began to smile. Then he began to chuckle. And then all of a sudden, he burst out into laughter.

"Oh my," he gasped, hardly able to contain his happiness.

"What do they say?" I shouted.

"This one," he answered, holding up the one with the torn corner, "the one that was on the *small* pile—is that what you said?"

"Yep."

"It says, 'This gold is for my family.'"

"And the other one? The one on the *big* pile?"

"It says, 'This gold is for my friends.'"

I blinked. And then I got it. Xian kept laughing while he handed the notes to Sheriff Ernie, who'd come up to the front. He studied the notes for a few seconds and then looked up with a big smile on his face.

"Yep, Your Honor, that's exactly what they say."

Everyone in the tent seemed to be holding their breath and leaning forward, toward Xian.

I turned to Xian and asked, "Are you going to do what it says? Are you really?"

"Yes, I am!"

As soon as he said the words, the entire room exploded in laughter and shouting and whooping and cheering. Mr. Hooke collapsed even further down into his chair. The judge banged her hammer, over and over again, and shouted as loud as she could over the explosion that was taking place in the circus tent.

"Case dismissed!" she yelled.

And then the party really started.

CHAPTER 35

So What Happens Next?

I found my dad standing in the window, watching the leaves fall off our tree. He stood there a lot these days, staring out the window, counting the buttons on his favorite sweater. I could hear him repeating the poem he had come up with, one line for each one of his buttons, whispering under his breath.

"One. This isn't any fun.

"Two. What am I going to do?

"Three. Why is this happening to me?

"Four. I can't take it any more.

"Five. I'm lucky to be alive.

"Six. I'm in a tight fix.

"Seven . . ."

He paused as he looked down at his hand. The last button had popped off and was lying there staring up at him, like a black eye that never blinked.

"Seven . . . time to go to heaven."

He dropped the button, and it rolled across the floor until it bumped into my shoe. I picked it up and looked at my dad. He was looking back at me.

"Jon," he sighed. "I think it's time we moved away from Boomtown."

"What? *No!*"

He reached up and rubbed his face. I could tell he was exhausted. He wasn't sleeping. He was barely eating. Nothing had happened since the trial. He hadn't gotten hurt again. He was walking fine now; the cane was sitting in the corner. But he was scared all the time. And now the button. Button number seven. It had come unraveled, just like his nerves.

"It'll be okay, Dad. Everything is fine now. It's been almost two months, and nothing else has happened."

"No?" he mumbled. "Maybe not. But I can't help worrying. I'm jumpy all the time. I think it would be best if we went somewhere else."

"Where?"

"It doesn't really matter. We've got all that money now. We could go anywhere. And our family is famous—*you're* famous. I've gotten all kinds of offers from other churches to come and be their pastor. We just have to pick someplace safe. Maybe Kansas. Or the moon. Who knows?"

Dad was right about the money. Our portion of the gold came to almost seventy thousand dollars. That was enough to buy a couple of houses and ten cars back in 1950. We didn't ever have to worry about money anymore. But that wasn't the point.

Boomtown was our *home*. All my friends were there. Burton Ernie, my buddies, my school, the Hopontops, even mean old Walter the Butcher. Xian was staying; he was bringing his whole family over from China. It was going to be great. *Leave*? We couldn't leave!

"Dad, do you remember that story about King Saul and Prince Jonathan?"

Dad walked over to his easy chair, sat down, and buried his face in his hands. "Sure, Jon, I remember. What about it?"

"You remember how the king was afraid all the time? He was so afraid that he taught all of his people to be afraid. And he wanted his son to be afraid too."

He raised his head and stared at me with his sad, red eyes. He didn't answer, but he was listening.

"But Jonathan *wasn't* afraid. Instead, he marched right down the middle of the road and took on the whole Philistine army single-handedly. As soon as the people saw that he was winning, they joined the fight and chased their enemies all the way out of the country. Remember that?"

Dad nodded and said, "Instead of being grateful, the king got angry with his son. Even after all that, the king was still afraid."

"That's right, Dad. But it didn't have to be like that, did it?"

This time he smiled, with that crooked smile he gave me when I knew he was proud. He stood up and took me in his arms and hugged me tight. I think we stood there for almost five minutes. I could feel his shoulders shaking. I'd never seen him cry before.

"Jonathan, you *are* a prince. And we *will be* staying. All because of you."

"Honest?"

"Yep. I'll just have to learn to like fireworks, that's all. In fact, it's Friday today. Let's go down to the park. We'll shoot off some rockets—and celebrate. What do you say?"

What *can* I say? We stayed in Boomtown, of course, and I'm happy to report that my dad never got hurt, not ever again. That day in the living room when he decided to face his fears, that ended the curse, if there ever was one. His picture now hangs in the hallway of the church. He has a big smile on his face. The little plaque underneath says, "Pastor Arthur Button. 1949–Present."

And me? I'm a prince, just like my dad says. When visitors come to town, they ask me to show them the hidden vault and tell the story. Xian used some of his gold to fix the Town Square; he thought he should pay for that. The statue is back where it was, but now there's a door and some stairs to take you down underneath.

The lights were repaired, and you can walk all the way down the tunnel to the secret door that isn't secret anymore. Inside are pictures of Chang and Xian and their family. Some of the letters are inside glass cases—as well as the map and pictures of me and others from the trial, Mr. Rigdale, the judge, and Horatio Hooke pulling his hair out. There's even a case with the two notes in it. You can see the tear in one of the corners. And one of the bricks of gold just to prove it all happened just like I've told you.

Don't believe me? Then come and visit us in Boomtown, and I'll show you.

Of course, that's assuming I'm not off on another one of my adventures. And believe me, I've had a lot of them. There is always something crazy going on in Boomtown.

I'd like to tell you more, but I think I hear my dad calling.

He wants to try out the Rocket Shoes.

And I get to light the fuse.